Angel Unbound

by

Sharon Saracino

The Earthbound Series, Book 2

Angel Unbound

Cover Art by *Debbie Taylor*

The Wild Rose Press, Inc.
PO Box 708
Adams Basin, NY 14410-0708
Visit us at www.thewildrosepress.com

Publishing History
First Faery Rose Edition, 2014
Print ISBN 978-1-62830-648-4
Digital ISBN 978-1-62830-649-1

The Earthbound Series, Book 2
Published in the United States of America

"You're up early," Luca observed, once Piero was on his way to the hospital and he finally stepped inside and closed the door. He helped himself to an espresso from the pot still simmering on the stovetop. It was already half empty. Callista had obviously been up for a while.

"You're up late," she snapped back sinking into her chair and pushing the box of baked goods toward him.

Luca shrugged, flipped open the box, and snagged a *cornetto* before dropping into the chair opposite her and stretching his legs out in front of him. He took a sip of the strong, fragrant coffee and sneaked a glance at Callista from under his lashes. The threat of tears had passed, but it was impossible to miss the dark purple smudges beneath her thickly fringed blue eyes and the dampness spiking her lashes. Since they'd come to Rome, he'd heard her cry out in her sleep more than once. He also frequently heard her walking the floors well into the morning hours. Maybe he'd been a little hard on her earlier, but she needed to start using her head.

"Nightmares?"

Her eyes darted to his face in surprise then narrowed.

"Trollop?"

"What?"

"I assume you're asking if nightmares are the reason I'm up so early. I'm merely asking if a trollop is the reason you're up so late."

Dedications

To my editor Frances Sevilla, and my readers,
thank you for believing in angels...
especially those of the Earthbound persuasion.

~*~

Much gratitude to Jan Romes and Sharon Buchbinder,
who always cheer me on, set me straight,
and help me grow.

~*~

Endless love and appreciation
to my own personal angels, the Vinces.

~*~

And lastly, a special *Grazie Mille*
to the incomparable Asterio Pascolini,
who with his endless humor patiently corrected
my pitiful Italian in a valiant effort to prevent me
from inserting my foot in my mouth.
Any errors in translation are mine alone.
Buon riposo, dear friend.
I miss you more than I can say.

Chapter One

Hell, he might be an angel, but he never claimed to be perfect. Luca Fiorelli hadn't planned to visit Giovanna this trip. In fact, he'd made up his mind before leaving New York that he wouldn't be seeing her again. At all. When his uncharacteristic restlessness failed to dissipate once he was back on Italian soil, he'd convinced himself that maybe her familiarity would provide some clarity amidst the chaos that preoccupied him lately. It hadn't. He held a true affection for her, but it would never be anything more. The reality was he used her when it suited his convenience and she asked nothing in return. She deserved better. Of course, she also deserved better than to wake up in an empty bed to discover the man she loved was a selfish, cowardly bastard who'd skulked off without a word like a thief in the night.

Giovanna barely stirred as he quietly untangled his limbs from the twisted sheets and the warm, damp embrace of the sleeping woman and methodically donned the clothes he had so enthusiastically shed mere hours before. His icy detachment was legendary. Even those who knew him well were rarely privy to what lurked beneath the sardonically cocked brow and the nonchalant shrugs. His cold indifference was valued by his allies only slightly less than it was feared by his enemies. At the moment, however, he was in danger of actually breaking out in a nervous sweat as he struggled into his jeans. Ordinarily, Luca stayed until the first faint fingers of dawn crept into the third floor flat in the *Borgo*, but the last weeks had been anything but ordinary and he found even a night of exhausting lust with the warm and willing *pasticcera* had done little to assuage his unease. He'd just wrapped his fingers around the doorknob when a soft voice, thick with sleep and hoarse from passion, reached him. *Maledizione!* Well, he'd almost made it.

"Luca? *Si lascia?*"

"Uh, yeah, Gia...I'm leaving."

He heard her sigh of disappointment. Like Giovanna, he was an *Earthbound*, an order of angels descended from *Fallen* rebels. *Earthbounds* had been reconciled to the Heavens millennia ago in exchange for an agreement to battle the evil *Fallen*. Like others of his kind, he could easily read her thoughts when she forgot to block them. Thus, he knew exactly how she felt. He tried to feel worse about it, but he had always been clear. She understood he wasn't looking for a relationship. Though she usually hid it well, lately he sensed a certain desperation. She discounted opportunities for other, healthier, relationships as she continued to hope, one day, Luca would change his mind.

He hesitated as Gia threw her long, shapely legs over the side of the bed. She wrapped the sheet around herself against the early morning chill and hurried across the cold, marble floor to the door.

"Will you return later, *tesoro?*" Her long fingers cupped his cheek as her dark eyes searched his face for the answer he knew she hoped not to find. He covered her hand with his then gently pulled it away, lightly kissing her fingers before letting go.

"I...don't think so, *bellezza*."

"*Perche, amore*? Why?"

He saw her blink back the tears that sprang to her eyes. Yes, he had always been honest with her and never led her to believe there would be anything more. Still, he knew she had hoped...

"Gia, you are a beautiful and passionate woman. You deserve so much more."

"It is enough for me," she whispered softly, reaching for him again. He caught her hand before it touched him.

"It isn't," he replied quietly. "*Sono molto cura di te*, I care for you, but I can never give you what you want. It isn't fair to continue to accept what you offer."

"I offer it freely," she whispered in a tight, choked voice.

"*Mi dispiace*," he replied sadly. "I'm sorry, Gia." And he meant it. She was bright, and beautiful, and funny. He enjoyed the sex, but he also enjoyed her company. He would miss her. But it wasn't fair to monopolize her heart and rob her of the chance to find happiness with a man who could love her as she deserved.

Luca Fiorelli was not that man.

Giovanna swallowed hard and again blinked away tears, offering him a brave smile. He heaved a sigh of relief seeing she would not beg.

"I, too, am sorry, *bello*. But, I hope you will still come to the shop sometimes when you are in *Roma*? Beating you at chess is one of the few pleasures remaining to my uncle."

"I don't want to make this more difficult for you, *cara*. Your uncle will understand."

"Don't be silly, Luca. I am a big girl. We are friends. Besides, where else will you find *cornetti* as delicious as mine?" she teased with a forced lightness.

"I never shall," he smiled fondly. "They are the best in all of *Italia*."

"*Tutti il mondo*," she countered.

"Okay, have it your way...in the whole world," he laughed, then sobered quickly and leaned forward to kiss her tenderly on either cheek. He had hoped to avoid a tearful scene. He should have known Giovanna's pride precluded one. She made it easier for him than he deserved and would save her tears until he was gone. The relief he felt was entirely selfish, and he knew it.

"*Ciao, bella. Buona fortuna.*"

"*Anche a te*, Luca...good fortune to you, also. I hope you find whatever it is you seek."

The moment the door closed behind him Luca resolutely blocked her from his mind and faded to the deserted street below. As soon as he cleared her building, the faint prickles of energy running along his spine faded. It happened whenever he visited Gia. Someone or something unsavory resided nearby, but they had yet to reveal themselves.

The sound of his boots on the dew dampened cobblestones echoed eerily back from the ancient buildings rising up on either side as he quickly made his way along the narrow *Via del Falco* to *Borgo Sant'Angelo*. He kept to the shadows cast by the imposing *Passetto*, the elevated passage linking the Vatican City with the *Castel Sant'Angelo*, until he reached *Piazza Pia*, then he turned decisively toward the river.

He welcomed the long walk along the sluggish Tiber back to the villa owned by the mother of his best friend, Kassian McAllister. He and Mac had served side by side as members of the elite *Defensori,* the warrior branch of *Earthbounds,* for hundreds of years. He could have simply faded back to the villa, but Luca hoped the crisp night air would help to clear his head and alleviate some of the disquiet invading his every waking moment. A disquiet that exactly coincided with the moment he'd pulled a dagger from the chest of Callista McAllister and plunged it into the back of the evil *Fallen* Jacques Rapier, ending the century long reign of Jack the Ripper and the equally long term of Callista's captivity.

After more than a hundred years of frustration, Jacques Rapier was no longer a threat. Mac's sister Callista, whom Rapier had abducted after the Whitechapel murders, turned out to be alive not dead for over a century, as they'd all thought. Even more unbelievably, Luca had blood family again. A sister, Katrina, who had recently married his best friend, making him and Mac truly brothers. Any one of these things should have given him a measure of peace. Still, Luca could not shake the nagging discontent.

After Rapier's death, they discovered the Ring of Aandalena and with it, the startling revelation that not only was Luca's sister half *Earthbound*, she also descended from Archangels on her mother's side. Kat had unequivocally refused to have anything to do with the ring or its power. Her insistence on returning it to its creator, Michael the Archangel, had been the part of the reason for their journey to Rome. That and bringing Callista home to be reunited with her mother.

Mac and Kat were currently enjoying an extended honeymoon in the Tuscan hills near Fiesole. The sprawling farmhouse had been Luca's wedding gift to his sister. The place had been in the family for generations, but Luca hadn't used it since his father's death and thought Kat might appreciate having some tangible evidence of the father she'd never known.

Apparently, he thought correctly. In fact, according to Mac, his friend struggled with convincing her to leave. Luca might have conveniently forgotten to mention to Mac exactly how rundown he'd let the place become. Kat already had a laundry list of renovations and had spent the last week interviewing contractors. His little sister was giving her battle hardened *Defensori* a run for his money. It wasn't a situation Luca could ever envision for himself, but it did his heart good to see the positive changes love had wrought in his best friend.

Luca hunched deeper into the collar of his leather jacket as a rogue breeze whipped up from the river when he reached the *Ponte Garibaldi.* His acute olfactory senses detected the weak, metallic scent of blood. He tensed, then relaxed when he realized he stood almost directly above *Isola Tiberina,* the boat shaped island in the middle of the Tiber housing the *Ospedale Fatebenefratelli.*

Of course, he would detect the aroma of blood so near to a hospital. He turned onto *Viale di Trastevere* and the scent faded, but as he approached the corner, he once again felt the faint and unmistakable shocks of energy creeping along his spine heralding the presence of evil.

He quickened his pace, eyes scanning alertly for any threat on the nearly deserted streets. Almost dawn, lights already glowed faintly from isolated windows as the early risers in the *Trestevere* neighborhood shook off the remnants of sleep and prepared to greet a new day.

Though early, people milled about here and there, making it impossible for him to fade to the villa unobserved. By the time Luca started up the incline toward the house on *Via Dandolo*, the sensation of evil grew stronger, and he picked up his pace until he flat out ran.

He reached the Convent of the Ursulines and flattened himself against the wall, melting into the rapidly lightening shadows. There, parked at the curb, under the thick cover of the trees, between the convent and the McAllister villa, was a battered little delivery truck. Piero the baker delivered fresh *cornetti* and *pane* to both the convent and the villa every morning, but there were no parcels on the front stoop of the convent and no sign of the elderly Italian *panettiere* near the villa.

Luca inched carefully along the convent wall until he reached the spot where it joined the one surrounding the McAllister villa. Graffiti covered the walls again, though they were routinely scrubbed and painted. After making sure he remained unobserved, Luca faded into the garden running along the side of the house.

Again, he scented blood.

Alarms screaming now, he quietly unsnapped the sleeve of his jacket and slid a dagger from the intricate tattoo covering the inner aspect of his forearm. He nearly tripped over a body where it protruded from the bushes.

Piero. The gash on his head bled profusely, but the old man's chest still rose and fell.

Well, that explained the blood he'd scented, but not why a *Fallen* or one of their *animorti* servants would bother to attack a harmless old baker.

He heard the faint sound of a knock coming from the back of the villa and suddenly everything fell into place. He spared a thought for the good old days when the *Defensori* were the hunters, never the hunted.

He quickly faded again, materializing directly in front of the woman as she opened the door, forming a wall between her and the *animorti* carrying Piero's fragrant box of warm pastries and freshly baked bread. Luca plunged his dagger into the impostor's gut with his right hand and deftly caught the box of baked goods in his left as the creature disintegrated into a puddle of black slime at his feet. He nimbly spun on his heel and presented the box to the housekeeper with a flourish.

Except it wasn't the unflappable and rotund Maria regarding him with wide, shocked eyes.

It was Callista McAllister.

"What in the hell are you doing opening the door to a stranger?" he demanded hotly. "Setting *sigils* around the house doesn't do a damn bit of good if you blindly open the door to any Tom, Dick, or Harry!"

"I didn't realize…I thought…" she began.

"No, Callista, you didn't think. You never think. That's your whole problem. If I hadn't decided to come home, you'd be dead. Again. For real this time!" Something ugly and unwelcome twisted in Luca's gut at the thought.

Still pale and fragile after her years in captivity, Callista's slight frame was lost in the voluminous folds of a heavy fleece robe. Her long, dark hair hung in a thick braid over one shoulder, but stubborn tendrils escaped to curl charmingly around her small, heart-shaped face. Her wide, blue eyes fixed on Luca in astonished surprise and filled with tears. She snatched the box from his hand, and turned away to place it on the kitchen table.

Luca stepped outside and pulled the door closed behind him. Rubbing his hands together briskly, he turned the resultant blue energy emanating from his palms toward the foul remains of the *animorti*, vaporizing them instantly. Then he retrieved Piero's still form from beneath the bushes and dragged him around to the back, positioning him in such a way it would appear he'd fallen on the stairs and struck his head.

Satisfied that he had everything in order, he pulled out his cell phone. There would be a cursory investigation by necessity, but Gianluca, a fellow *Earthbound* and member of the police force, would ensure few questions were asked. He would also ensure the money Luca arranged provided for Piero's family while the baker recovered and that the injured man remembered nothing of the morning's events.

****

"You're up early," Luca observed, once Piero was on his way to the hospital and he finally stepped inside and closed the door. He helped himself to an espresso from the pot still simmering on the stovetop. It was already half empty. Callista had obviously been up for a while.

"You're up late," she snapped back sinking into her chair and pushing the box of baked goods toward him.

Luca shrugged, flipped open the box, and snagged a *cornetto* before dropping into the chair opposite her and stretching his legs out in front of him. He took a sip of the strong, fragrant coffee and sneaked a glance at Callista from under his lashes. The threat of tears had passed, but it was impossible to miss the dark purple smudges beneath her thickly fringed blue eyes and the dampness spiking her lashes. Since they'd come to Rome, he'd heard her cry out in her sleep more than once. He also frequently heard her walking the floors well into the morning hours. Maybe he'd been a little hard on her earlier, but she needed to start using her head.

"Nightmares?"

Her eyes darted to his face in surprise then narrowed.

"Trollop?"

"What?"

"I assume you're asking if nightmares are the reason I'm up so early. I'm merely asking if a trollop is the reason you're up so late."

She sounded sullen. Luca realized he seemed to have that effect on her. Callista kept her eyes glued to her empty cup. Lately, he'd been avoiding her more and more. For all intents and purposes, she'd lived in the nineteenth century one minute and the twenty first century the next. She'd been frozen in time with little exposure to the outside world for more than a hundred years. Everything was different. *Everyone* was different.

Every time he opened his mouth, he pissed her off,

embarrassed the hell out of her, or hurt her feelings. He'd always been able to speak his mind around Calli, and she'd never been shy. But that was another time. He simply didn't know how to talk to her anymore.

"They're not called trollops anymore, Calli," he offered in a tone a bit shorter than intended. "And no, she wasn't. Women are allowed to enjoy sex these days. It doesn't make them whores."

He couldn't miss the flush creeping up her neck and into her cheeks. He recognized her discomfiture immediately. Well, she'd asked, hadn't she?

Merda, he'd done it again.

"I'm a thoughtless bastard, *cara*," he sighed wearily. "I'm sorry I yelled at you. You really have to be more careful. Times have changed. The *Fallen* think nothing of coming after us right in our own homes now."

He shouldn't have bitten her head off. Yeah, he felt out of sorts, but it was nothing compared to what she must be going through. Insecure wasn't a word Luca would have ever associated with Callista McAllister in the past. Though stubborn and spoiled, her fierce independence and self-assurance had always appealed to him, when she wasn't busy frustrating and infuriating him. In the days immediately after her rescue, she'd seemed like her usual opinionated, outspoken self. In fact, she'd even gone so far as to tell him he'd taken long enough to find her. But in the days and weeks that followed, she became increasingly aware of how much the world had changed. She'd become more unsure, more withdrawn. She barely ate, hardly slept.

Earthbound typically lived for centuries and adapted to the changes in order to remain hidden in mortal society. Adapting to change while living through it was one thing, but Calli had been trapped in time while the world around her moved on. Except for books, she'd had very little exposure to the outside world. Luca thought she was doing pretty well, all things considered.

But she shielded her thoughts from him, making it impossible to guess what might be going on in her mind. Most days she drifted through the villa like a lost soul, a shadow of her former self.

He realized this was actually the first time they'd been completely alone together since her return. He heard her mother moving around upstairs. They wouldn't be alone for long. It was just as well. Sometimes it was best to leave the dead buried.

"No, I'm sorry. How you choose to spend your time is really none of my business," she whispered, crumbling the flaky *cornetto* between her fingers in lieu of eating it. "I think the lack of sleep must be making me shrewish."

Luca reached out and impatiently brushed the sad remnants of the pastry aside. He plucked another from the box, this one chocolate filled, and waved it enticingly under Calli's nose.

"Open."

"I'm not really very hungry, I—"

Luca shoved the *cornetto* in her mouth before she could get another word out.

"What's making you shrewish is spending every hour of every day cooped up in this house. Rome is a vibrant, exciting city. You've barely ventured any further than the garden," Magdalena McAllister interjected as she breezed into the kitchen. "Now chew that up and go get dressed. Luca is taking you out," she announced.

"I dom hab amyring oo air," Callista mumbled through the mouthful of flaky dough and gooey chocolate, her eyes darting to Luca. A pulse jumped in her throat and beat at a rapidly increasing pace that was clearly visible.

"You have an entire closet filled with clothes that Kat and Elle picked out for you," her mother argued. "Not that anyone's seen them. Now, go and put something on. Luca, go wash up. My hermit daughter will meet you right back here in thirty minutes."

Calli's eyes were as big as saucers.

"I...I can't, Mother. I'm not ready."

Luca saw the stark terror in her eyes and wondered if his looked similarly alarmed. He couldn't think of anything he'd like less than spending the day one on one in Callista's company. He narrowed his eyes at Madge.

"She can't go out alone, Luca. With Alec in Paris, and Kassian on his honeymoon, you're the only one I can count on to keep her safe. If she can't tolerate it, by all means bring her back, but even a walk to the corner would be an improvement. Think of your father. You of all people can understand the consequences of hiding from the world."

She sent the thought into his mind using a telepathic channel specific to the two of them rather than the common one all *Earthbound* used so Calli wouldn't hear.

Magdalena McAllister was no one's fool. Everyone else walked on eggshells around Calli, afraid of pushing too hard, afraid of upsetting her. Luca had years of

13

experience walking on eggshells. In the end, it hadn't done any good. It hadn't saved his father. Nicola's grief and seclusion had been more important to him than his own son.

But Magdalena had been there to pick up the pieces when Luca felt completely abandoned. He owed her. Yes, Madge understood him well. And she wasn't above using his feelings of guilt over his father to get her way. Luca wasn't thrilled about it, but if he had to be the one to play the bastard and force Callista McAllister out of her comfort zone to make her mother feel better, so be it. Even if it took him out of his.

"You're a scheming witch, Madge."

"But you love me."

Madge smiled and patted Luca's cheek as she passed by him to pour herself a cup of coffee.

He sighed inwardly, admitting defeat. Magdalena had been like a second mother to Luca for as long as he could remember. There weren't many things he would refuse her. It wasn't how he'd planned to spend the day, but he'd survive. He'd survived worse. Judging by the sick look on Calli's face, they'd be back in no time, anyway.

"Maybe you're right, *cara*...expecting you to be ready to leave the house in thirty minutes really is asking a lot, I guess," he goaded.

She nodded vigorously, still working to swallow the mouthful of pastry, a look of relief settling on her face.

"Make it forty-five."

****

An hour later, Luca cooled his heels in the kitchen after a quick shower. The ends of his hair were still damp and stuck to his neck, dripping onto his shirt. Deciding against his customary cashmere, he'd dressed in a pair of faded jeans and a simple black tee. Dropping into a chair, he stretched his legs out in front of him and crossed his arms over his chest. His lightweight leather jacket was neatly folded and waiting on the back of his chair.

Still no sign of Calli. His relaxed pose was at odds with his growing irritation. He simply wanted this over. The sooner they started, the sooner they could come back. He shoved his chair back and headed for the stairs.

Chapter Two

Callista was no closer to being ready than when she'd come upstairs over an hour ago. Everything Kat and Elle had purchased for her seemed so...well, indecent. Her breasts, which she'd always thought a bit too large for her small frame, seemed larger still when pushed up in the most brazen manner by the lacy black bra. The matching panties clung like a second skin and covered next to nothing. In fact, it seemed as though most everything she now owned covered next to nothing. Even the soft leather boots hugged her legs and showed the curves of her calves all the way to her knees, and it took a good deal of concentration to keep her balance on the high, thin heels.

If Katrina could be believed, and Calli couldn't imagine she had any reason to lie, the clothing chosen for Callista was relatively conservative. But in her opinion, everything she tried on seemed designed to emphasize everything she wanted to hide.

The contents of the now empty closet lay discarded around her on the floor. She stood in the middle of the pile, hands on hips, fighting back tears. Looking around at the jumbled heap of clothes, she wondered where to start. The mess around her felt as overwhelming as her life. She'd barely registered the rap on her bedroom door when it flew open and Luca's muscular frame filled the doorway. Long and lean, he exuded arbitrary elegance whether in silk and cashmere or denim and leather.

Denim was the flavor of the day, and it clung to his muscular thighs and high, tight butt in a way that left little to the imagination. He was six and a half feet of broad shoulders and hard muscle. He'd even taken the time to shave, leaving his chiseled jaw sharp and smooth and accentuating the cleft in his chin. She had to stifle the urge to catch her breath every time she saw him. But this time, her gasp was audible. He stood staring and she was just shy of naked.

Luca simply gaped, dumbstruck at the unexpected sight of Callista standing in a rumpled pile of discarded clothing, wearing some barely there black lingerie, and a pair of kick ass sexy boots.

Desire slammed into his gut like a physical blow. Something stirred. Something he'd buried deep as death, and something he would just as soon leave undisturbed.

Without a doubt, she was trying to kill him. She was thinner than he remembered, but no less painfully beautiful. High, full breasts, trim narrow waist, and to his surprise, even though she was a petite woman, she had exquisitely long legs.

She'd unbraided her hair, and it fell past her hips like dark, curling ribbons of silk. He found it impossible to look away, even more impossible to breathe. And then he felt suddenly, unreasonably angry at the clear and immediate response of his own treacherous body.

She stood there staring at him with wide, shocked eyes looking like a frightened virgin being led to slaughter. And that, of course, was impossible. He harbored no illusions.

The *Fallen* were depraved by nature, setting themselves up as demi-gods who answered to no one, and Rapier had been among the worst. Luca realized that on some level, he still harbored an incredible anger with her for having put herself in the situation that led to her capture and everything that had surely followed.

While Mac had spent over a hundred years blaming himself for Callista's abduction, Luca had spent almost as much time blaming her. He had no choice. Otherwise, he would have had to acknowledge his own guilt. He didn't stop to consider the rationality, he only knew when he believed her dead something inside him died too, and he'd feared if he examined it too closely, it would eat him alive.

When she tore her gaze from his and made a move to cover herself, his thin veneer of control nearly snapped.

"Don't bother, *cara*," he hissed through clenched teeth. He moved forward into the room and blindly pulled a pair of jeans and a sweater from the pile at her feet. "You don't have anything I haven't seen before." He dropped the clothes into her arms. "Now put these on and let's go."

He spun on his heel and made it as far as the door before he hesitated. He turned back to where Calli stood stock still, clutching the clothes to her chest. Beautiful, disoriented Calli, who struggled every day to fit in while watching him with quiet, troubled eyes that seemed to censure his every move. Every time she looked at him, she told him without words he wasn't the man she remembered.

Hell, *he* barely remembered who he was back then.

How could he live up to whatever expectations *she* harbored behind her sad, disapproving gaze? Well, at least he hadn't made her cry this time. Her big blue eyes were pained, but they were dry.

Maybe things were looking up.

"You can't hide in the house forever, Cal," he said in a kinder tone. "The best way to learn how to live in this world is to get out there and see what it's like. It doesn't matter what you wear. These days pretty much anything goes."

She offered no response.

"When did you become such a coward?"

Callista's eyes flashed with anger and more life than he'd seen in them in weeks. She opened her mouth then snapped it closed without a retort as color flooded her cheeks. The sound of a throat clearing behind him alerted him to the fact they were no longer alone.

He threw a look over his shoulder, feeling like the kid who got caught with his hand in the cookie jar. Madge McAllister stood in the doorway, manicured brows raised and arms crossed tightly over her silk robe and ample bosom.

"Is there a problem?" She looked past Luca and her eyes widened imperceptibly at Calli's state of undress. She glanced at the straining front of Luca's jeans and then raised her eyes to his.

His usual icy veneer was replaced by a hot flush creeping into his face.

She bit back a smile at his uncharacteristic disconcertment. "Well?"

"Uh, no…" Luca stammered. "Calli was having some trouble deciding what to wear." He heard the rasp of denim on leather and knew that behind his back Calli quickly pulled on the clothes he'd shoved at her.

"I see." She glanced around Luca once again. "Well, it looks like she's ready now. You two run along. I'll put the rest of these things away."

"Oh, but Mother, you don't have to..." Callista began.

"Nonsense. Get going. The city is beautiful at this time of day. Why don't you head over to the market at *Campo dei Fiori* and pick up some nice artichokes for dinner?"

She brushed past Luca and began to gather up the pile on the floor. She pulled a soft ivory cardigan from the heap and handed it to Callista. "Better take this. It's still a little chilly."

Callista stared at her mother, nonplussed. The woman wasn't the least bit disturbed that not only had Luca been in Callista's bedroom, but she'd been barely dressed at the time.

In the world Callista remembered, that alone would have resulted in a marriage proposal, certain disgrace, or both. Then again, it was a new world and as he said, it wasn't anything he hadn't seen before. In fact, if the gossip could be believed, he saw far more, and on a regular basis, too. Her appearance probably hadn't affected him at all. He would never see her as anything more than Kassian's little sister.

Her jaw was clenched so tightly she felt a headache coming on. She shook her head to clear it. There was so much to learn she feared she could never take it all in. She backed away from her mother to where Luca stood outside the door waiting.

"Well, I guess we'll be going, then," she offered in a shaky voice.

Her stomach churned at the thought of going out into the crowded streets, and her legs felt like rubber, making the boot heels feel even more unstable.

What if she did something foolish? What if she caused a scene?

Of course, Luca would be there, but that made it worse. If she made a fool of herself in front of him, he'd never let her live it down. Besides, Luca and Kassian had both been there over a hundred years ago, and it hadn't stopped her from getting into trouble. The minute their backs were turned, she'd allowed her heart to override her common sense and walked into a nightmare. But she would do it again. She'd had no choice.

"Please, Mother, I don't think I'm ready yet." She sent the plea to her mother mentally, not wanting to give Luca the satisfaction of knowing she was still afraid. But, her mother kept her back to her and pretended not to hear.

"Have a nice time, dear."

Have a nice time, dear? Surely she must be joking! Calli feared she might be embarrassingly sick at any moment and her lungs felt suddenly too small to take in enough air. Hands trembling, eyes wide, she handed Luca the sweater and pulled the heavy mass of her hair over one shoulder and quickly plaited it into her customary thick braid. When she finished, Luca held out the sweater and she slipped her arms into the sleeves. She stood passively as he buttoned it up as though she were a child.

Luca didn't need to be an empath like his sister, Kat to read the set of Madge's shoulders, or the faint tremor in her hands as she carefully folded the scattered clothes. Another few minutes and she would give in to Calli's pleas to remain in the house. She put on a brave front, but she was terrified for her daughter. He had to do whatever he could to alleviate her fears.

As soon as he finished with the buttons, he grasped Callista's hands in his own and faded. Surprised by the move, she stumbled against him as they materialized in the kitchen. He caught her shoulders to steady her, ignoring the way his muscles tightened at the unexpected contact, and stepped away.

"Ready?"

"I…" she began hesitantly. She kept her thoughts shielded, but Luca could almost see her mind working as she struggled to come up with yet another excuse.

"C'mon, *cara*, it's not the end of the world. There's no secret potion for this. No magic wand, no fairy dust. You just have to put one foot in front of the other. Once you take the first step, every one after will be easier. If it's too much, I'll bring you back. Don't be such a chicken-shit."

"A what?" Her brows drew together in puzzlement.

"Chicken-shit…'fraidy cat…coward."

Her brows lowered ominously and her lips tightened. Luca grinned inwardly while maintaining a look of calm disinterest. It worked every time. Raised with two older brothers during a period in history when women were considered decorative second class citizens, challenging her ability to do something was the surest way to ensure she'd at least make the attempt.

"Why are you doing this? You've made it plain you have no desire to be in my company any more than necessary, yet you've agreed to drag me around with you all day. Why?"

Surprised by the question, Luca hoped his façade hid his discomfort. He didn't realize he'd made it so obvious he was avoiding her. Instead of answering, he shrugged and propelled her out the door with a hand on the small of her back. He imagined he could feel the heat of her skin even through the layers of fabric and his jaw clenched.

He was a warrior. He was hundreds of years old. He'd fought, he'd killed, and he'd survived things most people couldn't dream of. So why did he feel like a horny teenager on his first date with the prom queen? Luca Fiorelli didn't do relationships. This was sexual attraction, pure and simple. If it was anyone else, Luca would simply take her to his bed and get it out of his system. But it wasn't anyone else. It was Callista McAllister and a couple nights of wham-bam-thank-you-ma'am weren't an option.

Damn, Mac and his brother Alec were so going to owe him for this! Of course, he couldn't tell them that, it would only lead to questions he wasn't sure he could answer.

He steeled his features and his emotions and set off with Callista click-clacking frantically behind him to keep pace with his long strides in the unfamiliar heels.

Though he'd been born further to the north, Luca enjoyed a familiarity with the city of Rome and her history that rivaled the most experienced native tour guide. He had, in fact, lived through much of it. And the fact that Michael the Archangel, commander of the *Defensori,* kept a residence in the city ensured most *Earthbound* at least visited from time to time.

Luca kept up a running commentary all the way to the *Piazza Farnese*, pausing there to regale her with the history of the imposing Renaissance *Palazzo* designed in the sixteenth century for the Farnese family and later expanded when Alessandro Farnese became Pope Paul III. While Luca waxed poetic about the central window revised by Michelangelo, and above it, the largest papal *stemma*, or papal coat-of-arms, Rome had ever seen, Callista's wide and interested gaze locked on something of more immediate interest.

Reclining against one of the two large granite basins from the Baths of *Caracalla* which had been adapted as fountains, a young couple shared an embrace so intense it was difficult to tell where one of them left off and the other began. The man's face was hidden by the girl's hair, but seemed to be buried somewhere in the region just below her throat and slightly above her breasts. Luca noticed Callista's fascination and waited with interest to see what her reaction would be to such a public display. She bit her lip in concentration and continued to watch them for several minutes. Finally, she took a deep breath and squared her shoulders.

"Hey, you two," she called out in a hesitant, but teasing voice. "Get a room!"

The dark head snapped up with brows lowered ominously. Catching sight of Calli's tentative smile and accompanying wave, the young man's expression cleared. He shot her a toothy grin and blew her a kiss before resuming his former position. Calli glanced up at Luca, a smile wreathing her face.

Luca's eyes widened with something hovering between horror and hilarity. Where in the hell had she learned *that*? Calli's bright smile dimmed as the seconds ticked by and it became obvious the praise she expected was not forthcoming.

"That's not right, is it?" she asked in a small voice. She blinked rapidly and her thin shoulders sagged, while she continued her struggle to balance on the spindly heels.

Luca noticed the subtle change in posture and realized she was bracing herself for his criticism. Well, why wouldn't she? It was pretty much the only thing he'd offered her in weeks. Her shields had been wavering all morning and he'd been able to sense the riot of thoughts swirling through her mind as she tried to take in everything around her, keep up with his long strides, and squelch the anxiety every time it rose to consume her. And she hadn't complained once.

Aw, *diavolo*, she really was trying and he expended so much energy trying to ignore his own reactions to her that he hadn't given her credit for any of it. He bit the inside of his mouth to keep from smiling lest she think he mocked her.

"It isn't exactly wrong, *cara*. But it's something you might say to tease someone more familiar to you if you saw them in that, uh, position. Like your brother and Kat. It isn't something you say so much to strangers," he tried to explain without making her feel badly. Callista's slim shoulders drooped even more with her heavy sigh.

"So I've offended them." Luca took hold of her shoulders and turned her to face the amorous couple who were right back in business and oblivious to everything around them.

"Do they look offended?"

Calli stared at the lip-locked pair and turned to regard Luca cautiously. He quirked a brow and the corners of his lips curled. He didn't look angry. He didn't even look resigned, the way he sometimes did when she said or did something inappropriate. There was a glint in his silver eyes. He looked amused, almost happy. She hadn't seen a look like that on his face since he'd carried her out of the tunnel to her brothers when they'd found her alive.

"Not especially," she grinned back. This was the Luca she'd missed. It seemed he only had two expressions these days, angry and indifferent. She wondered what had happened in the intervening years to change him so, but she was afraid if she asked him the shutters would slam down on the small spark of warmth she detected in his eyes and the distance between them would return.

"C'mon, we're almost there," he gripped her hand in his and shortened his long strides so she didn't have to struggle so hard to keep pace. As they emerged from the narrow alley into the market in *Campo dei Fiori*, Luca launched into yet another long winded history lesson.

Calli struggled to take in the sights, sounds, and smells of the busy market. Her head swiveled right and left in an attempt to absorb everything, and she listened with half an ear as Luca explained that the square originally sat on the unused space between Pompey's Theater and the Tiber River in Ancient Rome. She listened with slightly more interest as they approached the statue of Giordano Bruno peering down from a dark hood on his high perch in the middle of the square. Bruno was burned at the site for heresy in the seventeenth century, Luca told her, and Ferrari designed the statue with Bruno's back turned to the Vatican, a martyr to free speech, positioned in protest for all eternity.

The statue's ominous stare made her shiver. The melancholy atmosphere induced by the statue was mitigated by the two *Romani* musicians lounging at its feet, cranking out a lively tune on guitar and upright bass.

Luca started a long-winded discourse about *La Terrina*, the area of the piazza which used to serve as a watering place for cattle, when the endless mounds of fresh flowers occupying the spot captured Calli's delighted eye. She tugged her hand free and planted her fists on her hips.

"Luca," she pronounced with a grin. "You talk too much." She spun on her heel, her braid whipping around like a weapon, and made a beeline for the flower stalls.

Luca followed more slowly, all the while keeping her in sight. At six and a half feet, he towered over most of the crowd, so it wasn't difficult to monitor her progress.

Did she think he was boring? It shouldn't bother him. Okay, maybe he'd been rambling like a history teacher on crack, but he found concentrating on the distant past very effective in deflecting attention from the uncomfortable present. His irritation dissipated as he watched Calli move from one bouquet to the next like an enchanted butterfly, reaching out to gently stroke a petal or delicately sniff an exotic fragrance.

He realized he wasn't the only one watching when the old *signore* working the stall reached out to offer her a tissue wrapped bunch of blue Iris'. She buried her face in the soft fronds. Old men, pretty girls, and flowers. Some things defied the passage of time.

The flowers perfectly matched the wide, blue eyes she raised to Luca as he approached and he felt something shift in the region of his chest. She'd always loved fresh flowers. How had he forgotten?

Without taking his eyes from hers, he dug in the pocket of his jeans and tossed a handful of coins to the old man. It was far more than the price of the bouquet, and Luca absently waved off the vendor's smiling *'grazie mille'*.

Luca reached out and offered Callista his hand for balance as she picked her way out of the artfully arranged field of flowers, avoiding the bunches scattered on the ground. She tripped over a plastic bucket filled with sunflowers at the perimeter of the stall and fell into him. His arm came around her waist to steady her, and he felt her brief hesitation and swiftly indrawn breath before she stepped away, still clinging to his hand.

"Thank you for the flowers," she breathed, clutching them to her chest. Luca shrugged uncomfortably. He hoped she didn't misinterpret his brief lapse in coherent thought as some big romantic gesture. He sure as hell hadn't intended to buy her flowers, but, well, they'd matched her eyes. And oh man, if that didn't sound like something Mac would say about Katrina. *Merda!* His friend would have a field day with this.

"Artichokes," Calli announced suddenly, breaking into Luca's unsettled thoughts.

"What?"

"My mother wanted us to get artichokes, remember?" she chided looking around with a frown. "Where are they?"

"Callista, your mother detests artichokes."

"She does?" Callista snagged her full lower lip in her teeth and wrinkled her brow in thought. Luca briefly wondered what it would be like to run his tongue along that plump little lip before nibbling on it himself and quickly buried the wayward thought with a barely suppressed groan as Calli spoke again.

"It was an excuse to get me out of the house, wasn't it?"

"Yes, it was an excuse to get you out of the house." But Luca wondered if it was the only reason Madge had thrown them together. In fact, he worried Madge McAllister saw far more than he'd like.

The woman knew him better than anyone, except maybe Mac. He uneasily began to wonder if Callista's mother had an agenda of her own.

Chapter Three

Callista insisted on buying the artichokes anyway, and vowed to shame her mother into eating at least one all by herself. And she bought the biggest ones they could find. She also begged for a bottle of *Crema di Limoncello* from another stand for after dinner cordials, and though it would have been much easier to carry one of the more compact liter bottles, she insisted the decorative one with the long stretched glass neck was much prettier and looked at it so longingly that Luca finally gave in.

He couldn't help noticing that although she remained relatively quiet following her faux pas with the amorous couple, her anxiety appeared to be subsiding the longer they were out. When interaction with others was necessary, she turned to him for guidance, but smiled genuinely at the vendors and other shoppers, and when they smiled back, the hollow, haunted look began to fade a little from her eyes. Some of the recent tightness in his chest eased as he realized while there would be a learning curve and it might take some time, Calli had far too much innate strength to end up a broken recluse like his father. Of course, he'd always attributed a good deal of strength to his father, too. He'd tried to get through to him right up until the end. But Luca hadn't been enough.

The sun had passed its zenith and started its long

descent toward the opposite horizon. Luca was surprised to realize how many hours had passed. The vendors loaded crates and lowered awnings, packing up for the day as Callista finished her triple *gelato*. She'd been unable to decide on a flavor, so she'd tried several, and had ended up eating most of Luca's as well. He studiously avoided the sight of her delicate pink tongue licking and swirling the cold cream, and focused on the fact that at least she was eating something for a change.

They meandered slowly between the miniature trucks and half packed boxes, the smell of exhaust mingling incongruently with the perfume of ripe fruit, warm bread, and fresh espresso, as they wandered past the *trattorias* encircling the perimeter of the square. Calli took the lead. Luca followed slightly behind, consciously avoiding the sight of her gently swaying hips, accentuated by the high-heeled boots. He'd never seen her in jeans before, and all of those bustles and petticoats she'd worn years ago never even hinted at that phenomenal ass. He gripped the bag of artichokes and the bottle of *limoncello* more tightly than necessary in his left hand, leaving his right free in the event of trouble. They navigated the narrow alleys around the *Campo*, finally arriving at *Corso Vittorio Emanuelle*, the wide and busy thoroughfare connecting *Piazza Venezia* and the river.

"Where to?" He asked, squinting into Calli's upturned face and wishing he'd remembered his sunglasses. She imitated his shrug and grinned saucily.

"You're the expert, Professor. You tell me."

"Hungry?"

She laughed, genuinely laughed, and Luca felt his heart flip in his chest. It was the first natural, truly happy laugh he'd heard from her in all these weeks. Her blue eyes sparkled. Her cheeks were flushed, and for a moment he felt as though no time had passed. God, he'd missed her. He hadn't realized how much. He was old, tired, and cynical. Seeing the world through her eyes made everything seem fresh and amazing. It soothed him in ways he couldn't fathom.

"Have you not been paying attention? I must have eaten a gallon of *gelato*," she smiled. "I couldn't possibly eat another thing for hours."

"How about coffee or something? At least we could sit down and rest for a while," he offered. She had to be exhausted. She hadn't slept well, and they'd been walking around for hours. But she didn't look exhausted. She looked…almost energized.

"What's wrong, Luca? Has all the activity been too much for you? Oh, wait! I forgot how much *older* you are. Of course we can rest and have coffee. I wouldn't want to be responsible for you collapsing in the street," she teased.

"Don't worry about me, *cara*. You might think I'm old and decrepit, but I can outlast you on your best day. C'mon, *bambina*, there's a little place a couple of blocks away near *Chiesa Nuova*. Since someone ate my *gelato,* I could use something a little more substantial than coffee."

Callista suddenly sobered. "I'm not, you know."

"What?"

"A *bambina*. I'm not a little girl, Luca." She tilted back her head and regarded him steadily, challenging him with her eyes.

Luca's jaw tightened in direct proportion to the tightness suddenly erupting below his belt. He reached to cup her cheek, gratified when he heard her swift intake of breath at his touch. He stroked her jaw with his thumb and curled his fingers around her nape. He slid them into her hair and pulled her tightly against him, letting her feel the hard evidence of his desire. He brought his face down to within inches of hers and her eyes narrowed with a look that seemed part curiosity and part anticipation.

"Trust me, *dolcezza*," he whispered, his breath feathering against her lips. "I am well aware of the fact." He released her abruptly and strode away, taking for granted she would follow.

Callista stood in the middle of the sidewalk staring after him. Oh, she intended to follow him, as soon as her bones grew back. Well, that was…unexpected. She might be lacking practical experience, but a hundred years was a long time and Jacques had always possessed an excellent library. She knew all about the things that went on between men and women and then some…theoretically.

But no book could have prepared her for the breath stealing sensation being pressed so intimately against an aroused man could cause, especially if the man was Luca Fiorelli. Maybe there was something to be said for the fit of these modern clothes. They allowed such freedom of movement, yet eliminated the layers and layers of protection between two bodies. The thin, measly layers of silk and denim let her feel quite unmistakably that Luca Fiorelli had been aroused. She swallowed hard. In a *big* way, a *very* big way. A spark of excitement fluttered low in her body. Funny, he didn't seem at all happy about it.

"Callista!"

Her head snapped up. He stood in the middle of the sidewalk about twenty feet away, facing her, and simply waited while the crowds jostled around him. She hurried to where he waited and glanced at him nervously.

"You don't have to pretend to be shocked, Calli. Far be it from me to judge you for anything you did to stay alive."

"I...Luca, what are you talking about? You don't think Jacques...that I..."

But he did. His shields were firmly in place and she couldn't read him, but she saw it in his eyes. And why wouldn't he? Everyone accepted that Jacques Rapier was a monster, but fortunately for her, sex hadn't been Rapier's addiction of choice. She hadn't really thought about it before, but judging by the accusatory look in Luca's eyes, no one else would believe she'd never been touched, either.

She glanced pointedly at his bulging crotch and her laugh was tinged with bitterness as she stepped away from him and looked him straight in the eye. "What's that saying you have now? Be careful what you wish for? I worried you'd never see me as a woman. Well, I guess I was wrong on that point. It simply never occurred to me that you'd feel I was better off dead with my virtue intact than alive without it."

"*Diavolo*, Calli, I didn't say..." Luca began heatedly, wrapping his fingers around her arm to pull her back. She twisted out of his grasp and stepped away.

"Maybe not out loud. I may still have things to learn, Luca Fiorelli, but I've never been stupid. You aren't judging me? Oh, but you are. Maybe you're not judging me for what *you assume* I did to survive, but you're most certainly judging me for putting myself in the position in the first place, aren't you?"

His jaw clenched tightly enough to crack teeth as he looked away letting his silence serve as his answer. Mac had forgiven her the moment he laid eyes on her. She was his sister and he could forgive her anything to have her back. But she wasn't *Luca's* sister and his feelings were a little more complicated, though he hadn't actually acknowledged it until lately.

He knew what people said about him. His indifferent sagacity was legendary. His ability to remain emotionally detached and coolly logical in any situation was a valuable asset, and one it had taken over a hundred years to perfect. A century of pain and loss when he'd made a conscious decision to guard his heart. Now it all seemed to go to hell in a hand-basket when Calli was around.

The thought of her with Rapier ate at him day and night, leaving a raw, open wound that no amount of rationalization would heal. Some days it hurt just to look at her.

He steeled himself to look at her now. Her eyes were averted. Even so, he could see the earlier sparkle was gone, replaced by the sheen of tears. The haunted look returned and he'd put it there.

Her impulsiveness and spontaneity had always been her greatest charm...and her fatal flaw. He'd known that. He should have done more to convince her of the danger.

And when she disappeared? Given Rapier's track record, they'd all assumed she was dead. He'd mourned her along with the rest of her family, then locked his grief away in a place he never intended to visit again and got down to the business of vengeance. Even Mac never realized Luca's obsession with destroying Rapier exceeded his own.

Now it was done and still he struggled with the anger. Anger at Calli for allowing herself to be vulnerable. Anger at himself for not finding her sooner. It might be unreasonable, but he felt as though he should have known she was alive, should have felt it, somehow. He should have moved heaven and earth to find her. Because once she was gone, it left a hole in the very fabric of his soul he'd never been able to mend.

Over the years, he'd buried his feelings deeply. He never realized how much until he watched Jacques Rapier's dagger sink into the soft flesh of Callista's chest. In the dank tunnel beneath his sister's house, he thought he'd miraculously found her only to lose her again. *Merda!* What a time for an epiphany. He was having a freakin' Oprah moment right here in the middle of the *Corso*. Oh yeah, he was angry. But it wasn't Callista, or even his father, he was most angry with. Yet, she was the one who'd been bearing the brunt of it. And wasn't that a bitch?

"Do you know," Calli began, tugging at his conscience with her tear choked voice. "From the minute you carried me out of that tunnel, not a single person…not you, not my brothers or my mother or anyone…bothered to ask me why I went out that night. At first, I thought it was because no one wanted to upset me. Then I realized it was because I'd simply fulfilled everyone's expectations. Crazy Calli. Act first, think later. It never occurred to anyone for even a second that I might actually have had a valid reason for doing what

I did."

She swallowed hard, turned, and started walking away.

"Did you?"

"Did I what?" She stopped, but didn't turn around.

"Did you have a good reason?"

He saw her slim shoulders rise and fall as she took a deep breath. The seconds turned to minutes as he impatiently waited for an answer.

"It's rather a moot point, don't you think?" she said at last with a deep sigh. "Whether I did or didn't hardly matters now. It doesn't change anything."

He moved in front of her so quickly she gasped. Her gaze whipped to his, but he carefully schooled his face into its usual placid lines to ensure Calli had no hint of the turmoil raging inside him.

"You're right," he said, so softly he wasn't sure she would hear him over the chaos of the crowds and traffic. "I was judging you, and I had no right. I'm sorry."

"I'd like to go home now," Calli said, staring at her feet.

"You know what? You really did great today, *cara.* Why don't we—"

"I said I'd like to go home now," she interrupted firmly. "Everyone wanted me to get out of the house. I got out of the house. But right now, I'd really like to go home."

"Okay, *cara,* anything you want."

"Given my dubious distinction as a living anachronism, somehow, I doubt that, Luca," Calli said quietly. Then she fell into step beside him without further comment.

Luca judiciously reserved expounding on the variety of wonders displayed like an archaeological smorgasbord everywhere they looked. He'd hurt her, and that was something he'd never intended. He was a different man now than the one she remembered, and he wasn't the kind of man she could want. Not anymore.

Losing her once had damaged him. Losing her twice would destroy him. He wasn't about to open himself up to be abandoned again. It wasn't her fault the thought of Rapier laying one finger on her sweet little body twisted his gut into a knot the size of Texas and make him hunger to kill the *Fallen* all over again. This time with a little pre-death pain and torture thrown in. The bastard had died far too easily for all of the sins he owned.

But this roiling angst was his problem. Not hers. Callista was the victim. Whatever she'd had to do, she hadn't been a willing participant, and he needed to remember it and stop treating her as though she'd had a choice.

They hadn't gone far when they came upon the *trattoria* Luca had mentioned earlier. Set back from the busy street and fronted by a park-like courtyard surrounded with small tables protected from the afternoon sun by large green umbrellas, the enticing aromas of garlic and grilled meat emanated from the open doorway. Luca's stomach grumbled loudly and involuntarily as the scent hit him.

Callista slowed without looking up.

"I gather you're still hungry?"

"I'm fine. I'll grab something when we get back to the house."

Callista wanted nothing more than to get back to

the villa and lock herself in her room with her thoughts and perhaps a few tears. But that was childish. And the fact she wasn't a child was the very thing she was so eager to prove.

Luca was the size of a small country and hadn't eaten anything but a *cornetto* and a few bites of *gelato* since early this morning. She was sad, but she wasn't selfish. He had to be starving.

"Actually, I could use a rest anyway," Calli lied. Luca stopped and studied her intently. She carefully maintained an expression as placid and unruffled as his.

"Are you sure? Right about now I could cheerfully consume the Arch of Constantine, but I can wait if you've had enough for the day."

She shrugged. "I don't have the best sense of direction, but it's still a pretty long walk, isn't it? I guess I don't have as much stamina yet as I thought and these boots are starting to hurt. I wouldn't mind sitting down for a while."

"Well, I *could* use a bite to hold me over 'til dinner, if you're sure? When I'm done, we'll find a more isolated spot and fade back so you won't have to walk so far," he offered, quirking a brow.

Calli opened her mouth and then snapped it closed. She shrugged and followed him in. Luca pulled out a chair for her at an empty table near the entrance and dropped into the one next to it. As usual, he chose the seat giving him the best view of everyone and everything coming and going. Her brothers did the same whenever they were out.

The owner himself came out to greet them, and Callista realized Luca was well known at this establishment. The man spoke perfect English, and

Calli followed the conversation without difficulty. More than that, as an *Earthbound*, she was privy to his thoughts. Luca rarely came here alone. Judging by the man's quick appraisal and quicker dismissal, he obviously didn't consider her up to Luca's customary standards.

"Your usual, *signore*?"

"Uh, no, Luigi," Luca replied quickly with a furtive glance at Callista. "Actually, we'll just have something light." Luca then proceeded to order water, wine, three kinds of *bruschetta*, *Spaghetti alla Carbonara*, and *Veal Saltimbocca*. "*Cara,* are you sure you don't want something to eat?"

"I'm glad you only wanted a little something, otherwise I'd need a cart to get you home," she couldn't help but smile though she still smarted from their earlier exchange. "Just some water with a slice of lemon is fine."

"Oh, and Luigi? We're in a bit of a rush," Luca added as the man nodded politely and plunked a wicker basket filled with warm bread in the middle of the table.

"You don't have to rush through your meal on my account."

"In Italy, a meal is an event. Something to be experienced, savored, and never rushed," Luca laughed. "If I didn't tell him that, we'd be here until tomorrow."

"Oh," Callista offered a small smile in return. He was so familiar when he laughed. She wished he would forget to wear his façade of impassivity a bit more often. She missed the man behind the mask. The memory of that man had gotten her through some of the darkest hours she'd ever known.

Luigi must have taken the warning seriously.

Callista had barely taken a sip of her water when a large platter of *bruschetta* arrived. After offering her a piece, Luca consumed the thick slices of grilled bread topped with olive paste and tomatoes in a few bites and washed them down with generous mouthfuls of deep red wine. The pasta and veal were consumed equally quickly, and after asking her for the tenth time if she was hungry, he finally tossed a handful of bills on the table and pushed back his chair.

Calli did the same before he reached her side. "Feel better?" she smiled up at him.

"Much," he took her hand and pulled her toward the door and into the restaurant.

"Wait! Where are we going?"

"Out the back way. I told you we'd fade home. You've been a surprisingly good sport today, *cara*, but you have to be exhausted."

The restaurant wasn't crowded and few paid them any mind as they wove their way amongst the tables and through the controlled chaos in the kitchen at the back. Luca paused to frown at a young waiter whose gaze lingered a bit too long on Callista's chest before tugging her through another door and into a dark and narrow alley. It appeared quiet and empty, but they hadn't gone more than a few feet before Calli felt Luca stiffen beside her.

Two men stood at the entrance to the street and began to move slowly and deliberately in their direction. Luca shoved the bag of artichokes and the *limoncello* bottle into Calli's arms and pushed her into the space between two foul smelling and overflowing dumpsters before taking up a wide stance in front of her and unsnapping the sleeves of his jacket. He drew a dagger from each of the intricate tattoos he wore on his forearms and simply waited.

Calli could tell by the men's awkward ataxic gait that they were *animorti* and not *Fallen*. *Animorti* were little more than animated corpses recruited by the *Fallen* from the dredges of humanity, lowlifes easily persuaded by the promise of power. They were dangerous, but they were puppets nearly incapable of independent thought and much easier to kill than their *Fallen* masters.

"Get out of here, Calli," Luca ground out through tight lips. "Fade. Now. Go home. I'll be right behind you as soon as I take care of these two."

"But, I can't..." Calli began.

"Now!" Luca hissed before stepping forward to meet the approaching threat.

Calli clutched the neck of the liqueur bottle, barely noticing when her flowers and the artichokes fell to the ground. She huddled deeper into the space between the dumpsters so when Luca glanced briefly over his shoulder he couldn't see her. She didn't want worrying about her to distract him.

Precisely as she hoped, Luca must have assumed she'd finally learned to follow orders and he turned back to the *animorti* wearing a cold anticipatory smile. With Mac away and the evil ones generally avoiding Rome since it was Michael's unofficial headquarters, Luca hadn't been out hunting lately. He looked as though he was nearly itching for the fight.

Even two against one, she knew Luca had the advantage. As always, the *animorti* carried human weapons. They could hurt him, but they couldn't kill him. Only weapons forged in either Heaven or Hell could mortally wound an *Earthbound* or a *Fallen* and the dark ones weren't about to take a chance that their evil spawn could actually inflict damage should they decide to turn against their masters when they discovered how completely they'd been betrayed.

Calli peeked cautiously from her hiding place, still gripping the neck of the bottle, and watched in fascination as Luca lunged and dodged with a dagger in each hand. He appeared to be amusing himself with the creatures more than anything, and she couldn't help but admire the way his taut muscles flexed as he parried and thrust. She could have been quite content to hunker down and spend the rest of the afternoon appreciating his grace and strength while watching him enjoy himself if another creature hadn't used Luca's distraction with the *animorti* to sneak up behind him with his sword already drawn.

There was no time to call out a warning. Calli didn't hesitate. She didn't think. She simply acted.

She sprang from her hiding place brandishing the long necked *limoncello* bottle like a baseball bat as she'd seen Luca's beloved Yankees do and swung it with everything she had. The heavy glass connected with the side of the *Fallen's* head with a mighty crack and the dark one went down with a thud.

Home run, McAllister. Pieces of glass and the sweet, sticky liqueur splattered everything, infusing the alley with a pleasant lemon aroma that did little to mask the sulfur smell of the oily puddle that had been an *animorti* mere seconds before Luca's dagger found its mark.

Luca dispatched the other *animorti* with a casual flick of his wrist and spun, just in time to see Calli raise the *Fallen's* sword over her head with both hands and plunge it into the dark one's chest with so much force it nearly embedded in the cobblestones beneath him.

He faded to her in an instant and grasped her slight shoulders so hard she suspected she would be sporting bruises later. Calli made a move to step away only to find herself held fast. Trembling violently, she couldn't decide whether it was due to the close call, the realization she had just run a sword through a *Fallen's* heart, or the look on Luca's face. His cool indifference had fled completely and the fear and anger on his face was so impressive, he looked like a total stranger. She touched her tongue to lips suddenly gone dry, and Luca's control snapped completely.

"Do you have a death wish?" He emphasized each word with a shake. He shook her so hard her braid came undone and her hair fell about her face like a silken curtain. "I told you to go home."

Calli raised wide, angry eyes to his. It obviously hadn't dawned on him that she'd just saved his sorry ass. "You're welcome!" she shouted, wrenching free of his grasp. She stomped back to the dumpster and carefully gathered her flowers from the ground, leaving the artichokes where they'd fallen.

Merda! Luca didn't know whether to kick her ass or kiss her. The little minx thought she'd saved him, did she? He'd been perfectly aware the *Fallen* stalked him and he had the situation well in hand. He wasn't some rank amateur. Of course, she had no way of knowing that and had come out swinging with no thought for herself or her own safety. As usual. When he turned around and saw her standing over the *Fallen* clutching that sword, a fear unlike anything he'd ever felt gripped his heart so tightly he still found it almost painful to breathe. There was no way he could go back and tell Madge McAllister he'd allowed Calli to be taken again, or worse. That must be what had him so shaken. Yeah, that was it.

Calli stood a short distance away, mutinously clutching her bedraggled bouquet as Luca briskly rubbed his palms together and powered up his energy. He made quick work of vaporizing the telltale remains of the evil ones and slowly made his way to where Calli waited silently.

"All right," he sighed wearily. "Let's go. Straight home."

"But, Luca I…"

"Now, Calli." And he disappeared.

Luca materialized in the garden of the *Via Dandolo* house and waited impatiently for Calli to join him. He'd thought of several more points he wanted to drill into her thick skull, but she was taking her good natured time about following.

Several minutes passed before it dawned on him she wasn't coming. Punctuating the air with a string of curses in three different languages, he faded back to the alley primed for battle.

She wasn't there. Luca stood in the middle of the alley and looked around him in worried disbelief. She hadn't come home and she wasn't in the alley. He felt sure she really must have a death wish. She was trying to provoke him into throttling her.

His keen eye detected a hint of blue near the mouth of the alley and he recognized the petals of Calli's flowers. He came out of the alley and looked carefully around the piazza, but caught no glimpse of her long, dark hair or slight form. His stomach churned and his heart beat in a painfully rapid tattoo.

Where in the hell could she be? Luca forked an unsteady hand through his hair in frustration, ignoring the fact that the action left his perpetually perfect locks tangled in disarray for maybe the first time ever. She couldn't have gotten far on foot unless she'd decided to fade to someplace else, altogether.

He really was going to kill her! In desperation, he sent out a call, hoping she was within range. Now what?

Chapter Four

Alone in the gloomy alley, Callista sank to the ground as her legs gave out once her righteous indignation faded and the realization of what she'd done sank in. Maybe her actions had confirmed Luca's opinion of her as reckless and impulsive, but she wasn't about to lose him, even if he never offered her anything more than disdain and vague familial fondness. She climbed to her feet and made her way to the entrance of the alley. She had no idea where she was, but felt sure if she could make her way to the river, she could follow its course down to the *Trestevere* neighborhood and maybe ask directions to *Via Dandolo*. Since her only weapon now was a wilting fistful of blue flowers, she hoped she'd already seen her share of trouble for the day.

Calli kept walking until she came to an open piazza with roads veering off to the left and right. Navigating on instinct alone, she chose the right fork and walked a little further until, to her relief, she caught a glimpse of the Tiber flowing placidly between the high walls on either bank. Directly across the bridge stood the imposing *Castel Sant'Angelo,* the Castle of Angels, originally designed as a mausoleum by the emperor Hadrian, and these days serving as a museum for the masses. That it also served as the headquarters for the commander of the *Defensori* was something the streams of tourists wandering its ramparts day after day were blissfully unaware of. Calli had never actually seen the commanding edifice in person, but she'd heard enough about it that she would recognize it anywhere.

She swallowed her panic for at least the third time and started across the bridge, pausing briefly to admire the angelic statuary marching along the rails.

She reminded herself she'd survived over a century with a serial killer and had come out relatively unscathed. She could find her way home. She could do this. She wondered what the chances were that any of the mortals at the entrance of the *Castel* would know Michael's whereabouts.

Her brother and Luca had served under the Archangel for hundreds of years. Surely, he would see she got home safely. But she also realized she couldn't very well walk up to the gate and ask. Suddenly it occurred to her that if Michael was in residence, there might be other *Earthbound* nearby. She sent out her thoughts on the common pathway, held her breath, and hoped for the best.

"Callista!"

Her heart leapt in her chest. He'd come back for her. Her knees buckled in relief and she sagged against the stone railing of the bridge.

"Luca?"

"Where are you?"

"On the bridge."

Luca groaned. There were any number of bridges spanning the Tiber and Calli would have no way of knowing the name of any of them.

"What does the bridge look like, cara?"

"It has angels on it."

The *Ponte Sant'Angelo*. Thank the Saints! She was only a few hundred yards away. In addition, the pedestrian bridge was protected by *sigils* and led right to the front door of the *Castel*. No *Fallen* in his right mind would venture that close to Michael's lair. She would be safe until he reached her.

"Callista, don't move. I'm on my way."

"All right. The sculptures are lovely, aren't they?"

She sounded as though she hadn't a care in the world. But then, he thought, why should she? She had no concept of danger. She'd proven it often enough. Luca would bail her reckless ass out again, right? He fought to keep the anger from his voice lest he frighten her into bolting as he strode quickly in the direction of the river.

"Bernini."

"What?"

"The angels....they were designed by Bernini. Each angel holds an instrument of the Passion. Do you see? The cross, the whip, the crown of thorns?"

He could hear the hint of laughter in her voice when she replied.

"Yes, Professor...I see them."

He finally caught sight of her as he stepped onto the bridge. She stood about halfway across near the center of the roadway with her head tipped back and her eyes shaded against the sun as she studied the master's work. Luca's heart finally resumed a normal rhythm once his eyes locked on her and he knew she was safe. He discovered he was even able to take in enough air to expand his lungs fully instead of the short gasps which were all he'd been able to manage after he faded into the empty alley and found her gone.

"If you wanted to continue the tour, you should have said something, *cara mia.*"

His expression remained impassive, and the controlled timber of his voice belied the simmering rage and worry he'd been feeling. Instead of being nervous about his anger, as any reasonable woman would, he saw Calli's shoulders relax at the sound of his voice and wondered if she was losing her mind when she turned to him with a smile.

The urge to shake her senseless again faded as soon as he saw that her lashes were spiked with moisture. She'd been crying. He pulled her into his arms and simply held her, unable to ignore the way she fit against him as though she'd been made for him.

"You didn't give me much of a chance to say anything, Luca. You simply disappeared and assumed I would follow," she mumbled against his chest.

"Of course I assumed you would follow, Callista. I really thought you had more brains than to wander off on your own after everything you've been through," he hissed quietly.

"I do have more brains than to wander off on my own, Luca, and if you'd have let me get a word in, I would have told you that I. Cannot. Fade."

Luca set her slightly away from him and stared down at her blankly. He could have sworn she said she couldn't fade. He didn't know what excuse he'd been expecting for her blatant disregard of his orders, but this one was far more creative than he would have given her credit for. It was ridiculous. Calli was *Earthbound.* All *Earthbound* could fade.

"And I may as well confess I didn't deliberately open the door to that *animorti* this morning, either. I also don't think I can sense evil anymore," Calli continued when Luca failed to respond and continued to stare. "I guess I probably should have mentioned those two little handicaps sooner, but it wasn't as though you'd given me the chance. And I hadn't even been aware of my inability to sense evil until today. I *had* briefly wondered why I hadn't detected the *animorti* at the door, but in the alley before, I didn't even feel a whisper of sensation."

She narrowed her eyes against the glare of the late afternoon sun and stepped away from him resuming her inspection of the massive stone angel perched on the railing of the bridge. "I'm always amazed at the lifelike details a talented sculptor can coax out of a block of stone, aren't you? The drapery is incredible."

"Callista, what in the hell are you talking about?" Luca finally ground out. "That's impossible."

Calli shrugged, clasped her hands behind her back and slowly strolled to the next angel. Luca followed so closely he nearly knocked her over.

"Luca, who knows better than we do that nothing is impossible? My inability to fade is the result of a spell. Jacques knew a witch, a sorceress. Call her what you will. He wasn't taking any chances I might escape, so he had her bind my ability soon after he took me," Calli said. "The inability to sense evil…well, that I can't explain. For the first several years with Jacques, I felt it nearly constantly, uncomfortably so. After a while, I didn't notice it so much. I don't remember feeling anything at all since you found me."

Luca's anger dissipated completely in light of her revelation. At least his anger toward Callista did. His anger toward himself for leaving her unprotected was only beginning to surface. She must have been terrified. Alone and defenseless in a strange city with no idea of how to get home.

Luca grasped her upper arm and pulled her against him at the rail as a tour group comprised mainly of high school students jostled by them and gathered at the foot of the nearest angel, laughing and snapping pictures of it and of one another while a disheveled chaperone flitted among them and endeavored to keep track of everyone. He turned Calli around to face him and wrapped his arms around her, pulling her close. He didn't stop to examine his reasons. He simply felt an overwhelming compulsion to hold her and know she was safe.

Calli didn't protest and instead wrapped her arms around his waist and laid her cheek against his chest, curling into him and pressing her entire body along his. He could feel the way she used his body to support hers. He felt her exhaustion. His tension ebbed. Holding her felt...right. In the place inside he always kept hidden, Luca had been afraid he would discover that very thing.

"Fiorelli?" Luca looked over the top of Calli's head and became aware of a large *Defensori* regarding him with an amused expression. He was built like a bull and dressed in black leather from head to toe. Coupled with his long black hair and the wicked scar on the side of his face, Dimitri Radchenko would stand out anywhere, even a city as diverse and multicultural as Rome.

"Dimitri? What are you doing here, brother? I thought you were still in the States," Luca stuck out a hand in greeting while keeping the other arm firmly around Calli.

"Had some business to discuss with the boss," the huge man flashed a set of even white teeth, taking the proffered hand in a bone crushing grip. His gaze flicked to Calli. "I see you beat me to the punch. Shouldn't surprise me, I guess. You're always johnny-on-the-spot when a woman is involved."

Luca felt Calli stiffen slightly before she pushed away from him and turned to face the newcomer. One good look at Dimitri had her shrinking back against Luca's chest, but after a moment's hesitation, she offered her hand as well.

"Thank you, sir. I appreciate your offer of assistance. But, as you can see, everything is fine now."

"Your offer of assist—" Luca began in a puzzled tone.

"Apparently the little lady was lost, so she sent out a distress call on the common pathway asking for assistance from any *Earthbound* in the vicinity," Dimitri cut in. "Considering our location," he jerked his head in the direction of the *Castel*, "that was pretty quick thinking. I just happened to be getting out of a meeting with Michael. Isn't that how *you* found her?"

"Oh. No. I was looking for her, actually. We got separated in the crowd," Luca offered. "Callista, that was very… resourceful of you."

Though he kept his features typically deadpan, he realized his voice sounded as though he was having teeth pulled. Calli simply quirked a brow and shrugged in a passable imitation of Luca himself, for the benefit of their audience.

"Is it really so painful, Luca?"

"What?"

"Admitting you might have been wrong about me."

Before he could respond, Dimitri piped up.

"Callista? Hot damn, you're Mac's little sister, right? It's great to finally meet you! You're a legend, kid!" He pumped her arm so hard he nearly lifted her from the ground. "Hey, you're like that wizard kid...you're the girl who lived."

"Dimitri!" Luca barked sharply, pulling Calli back against him. He felt her entire body trembling, and he couldn't decide if it resulted from fatigue, Dimitri's appearance, or the knowledge that her ordeal was apparently the topic of *Earthbound* dinner conversation around the globe.

"Oh, uh...sorry." The hulking giant actually blushed. It was an odd look on such a menacing countenance. His obvious discomfiture made him seem somehow less intimidating. "I didn't mean...well, anyway, I'm glad everything turned out okay and uh, welcome home."

"Thank you," Calli smiled. "And thank you for responding to my call. I appreciate it."

"No problem, kid." Dimitri flashed the perfect smile so at odds with the rest of his appearance. "Hey, why didn't you just fade back home?"

"Well, I..." Callista began, but Luca gave her a discreet squeeze. "Luca and I had a bet, and I hate to lose," she finished smoothly.

"Ah, well I can get on board with that kind of thinking," Dimitri laughed. "You're a McAllister, all right!"

"Thank you, again," Calli smiled back.

"Well, my brother, it's always good to see you, but I've got a plane to catch. When will you be back stateside?" Dimitri punctuated his statement with a hearty whack on the shoulder.

"Mac and Katrina should be heading back soon, but I'm not sure what my plans are yet. I'll keep you posted."

"Fair enough. Callista, nice to meet you. I'm sure we'll meet again soon." And with a wave of his hand, he headed off at a brisk trot across the bridge, away from the *Castel* in the direction of the *centro storico*, the city center, his long hair streaming behind him like a dark curtain. More than one woman on the bridge followed his progress with interest.

Luca still had an arm around Calli and she made no move to step away. Instead, she turned her head to the side and craned her neck to look up at his face.

"You didn't want him to know I can't fade. Why? He's one of us, a *Defensori*, no less."

"I think for the time being, the less people who know about your temporary…disabilities, the better."

"But what if they aren't? Temporary, I mean."

"They are," Luca retorted firmly, hauling her against his side and stalking straight for the entrance to the *Castel*. They had to be.

Chapter Five

After paying the eight euro entrance fee, Luca offered Calli his arm, and she latched onto him for balance on the uneven surface as they started up the long, winding ramp of Roman construction at the entrance to the *Castel.* At least balance was her excuse. The truth was that in addition to being physically exhausted and emotionally drained, her anxiety spiked to new heights at the prospect of meeting the legendary Archangel face to face and touching Luca calmed her. She didn't know what to make of Luca's reactions today. He was pulling her into his arms one minute and then berating her for something in the next. His shields never slipped, not for a second, and she couldn't read him at all. Her own head felt like it might explode from the whirling cyclone of thoughts she struggled to process all at once.

On the other hand, Luca didn't appear the least bit disturbed. He didn't bother with his usual historical commentary however, not even as they passed through the second floor storerooms that once contained oil and wheat, or the dark, eerie cells that were remnants of a time when the castle served as a prison. They didn't pause once to admire the antiquities and exhibits they passed along the way. Callista's legs quivered and her chest burned by the time they reached the military floor with its two large courtyards. Unbelievably, they continued to climb.

When at last they reached the level of the circular treasury room of Paul III with its walnut built-ins and large metal chests constructed to safeguard Vatican valuables, Luca paused and propped a shoulder casually against the ancient stone wall. A velvet rope, strung across the doorway of the room, allowed tourists to peek inside but proceed no further. A large sign also forbade photography in this area, the first such sign Calli had seen on their long and exhausting climb. She leaned against the wall at Luca's side and offered up a silent prayer that they'd reached their destination. She didn't care how amazing the purported views from the upper terrace were, she felt incapable of taking another step and, for the record, she was never wearing this particular pair of boots again.

Luca glanced over and grinned.

"You okay?" he asked, giving her heavy braid a playful tug.

"Fine," she panted. "What are we waiting for?"

"You'll see," Luca nodded absently at a final group of tourists passing through the area. The chattering assembly had no sooner stepped through to the next area when Luca spanned Calli's waist with both hands and swung her up and over the velvet rope, throwing his own long legs over as soon as her feet touched the ground. He grabbed her hand and pulled her across the room to the far cabinet looming floor to ceiling behind the largest of the metal chests. He ran a hand lightly over the surface of the door in a complicated pattern and then pressed on a carved panel.

Calli heard a series of clicks and the door sprang open. Pushing her ahead of him, Luca stepped swiftly inside and pulled the door closed behind them. There was barely room for one person in the close, dark confines of the space, let alone two…especially when one of the two was an extremely large *Defensori*.

Calli had no sooner opened her mouth to ask why someone of Michael's stature couldn't afford headquarters with a bit more elbow room, when Luca chuckled and pulled her close as the cabinet launched into a dizzying spin.

"You could have warned me," Calli gasped, her nails biting into his biceps.

Light flooded the small space, and she realized they were now facing another room entirely, one suffused with a blinding, golden glow. When her eyes finally adjusted, Calli realized it wasn't the room glowing. The brilliance came from the nearly seven foot tall Archangel, with an equally impressive wingspan, approaching them from across the incredibly ornate room decorated in the Renaissance style.

She recognized Raphael's hand in the gloriously colorful frescoes decorating the plastered walls and coffered ceiling, and she stifled a nervous giggle at the incongruity of the seventy-inch flat screen television and oversized leather sectional occupying the space between two enormous paintings, one depicting the beheading of John the Baptist and the other, the martyrdom of San Sebastiano.

Thankfully, Luca kept a firm grip on her elbow as they stepped out of the cabinet and into the room. Otherwise, Calli feared her trembling limbs would have given out completely.

"I'm sure Callista is suitably impressed, Your Grace, so you can pack up the wings and tone down the light show," Luca remarked sardonically. He squeezed Calli's arm when she swallowed audibly at his audacity.

"Relax, cara. He doesn't bite."

"Well, not much, anyway," Michael's smile was mocking as he continued to approach, his massive wings bending and folding with dizzying speed until they disappeared completely, and his glow fading away as quickly. Calli knew her eyes must be as big as saucers, but she couldn't seem to help herself. "At least Miss McAllister seems more suitably impressed with me than your sister Katrina did."

"Kat is an empath, Michael. She had your number the minute she stepped through the door," Luca offered dryly.

His lips twitched at the memory of his less than five and a half foot sister standing toe to toe with the nearly seven foot Archangel, sticking the Ring of Aandalena under his nose, and basically telling him to take his ring and shove it. The Emperor Constantine himself was rumored to have been struck dumb in the presence of the powerful and intimidating Prince of the Heavens. But not Kat. By the time the visit ended, Kat's ancient ancestor looked decidedly thunderstruck.

"Yes, well if you had thought to mention that beforehand, I might have blocked a little better." Michael's lips twisted wryly. "Your sister is quite a woman. McAllister is a lucky man."

"We were all lucky to find her," Luca agreed quietly. Some days he still found it hard to believe he actually had a sister, let alone one who had accepted him and his world so completely and unconditionally. At least one good thing had come out of his father's relationship with Lilly Brookes. Luca offered his trust rarely and his heart with even more caution, but his sister Katrina had managed to gain a full measure of both in a relatively short time.

"Well, come on in, you two. Have a seat and tell me what it is you want." Michael waved them toward the enormous sectional. It had obviously been custom-made to accommodate the Archangel's massive size. Calli perched on the edge, her feet barely reaching the floor. She looked a bit like Alice must have after shrinking to mouse size.

"What makes you think I want something? Maybe we were simply in the neighborhood and stopped in to say hello," Luca offered.

"I've known you a long time, Fiorelli. That in itself tells me this isn't a social visit, so let's get down to business. Why are you here?" Michael impatiently arched a golden brown that exactly matched the rich amber hue of his long, wavy locks. Massive physique aside, he exuded youth, appearing almost boyish in fact, until one looked deeply into his eyes. They were haunted by longevity and experiences few could guess at. There was nothing boyish or carefree in the shadows mirrored there.

"You don't waste time with pleasantries, do you?" Luca groused, stalling and flustered.

He detested asking his powerful commander for a favor. He'd asked just once before in his long life, and had been refused outright. His gut twisted at the prospect of being refused yet again, but Callista's safety was far more important to him than his own comfort.

"Fine, we have a problem I have no idea how to solve, and I figured you were my best bet."

"Always such a flatterer, Luca."

"It's a gift," Luca flashed his teeth. "So here's the deal. Calli can't fade. Rapier had a sorceress put a spell on her years ago so she couldn't escape. In addition, she apparently can't detect evil anymore, either. She opened the door to an *animorti* this morning and would be dead now if I didn't happen to arrive at exactly the right moment. I need you to tell me how we fix this."

Michael let out a deep breath in a long, low whistle. He rose to his feet, clasped his hands behind his back, and paced slowly behind the long sofa.

"Well," he said thoughtfully. "I suspect the reason she can't sense evil is because she was exposed to so much of it for such a long period of time. Her powers…basically shorted themselves out so she could protect herself. My best guess is it will come back gradually now that she is away from the constant stimulation."

"Your best guess? And the spell that keeps her from fading?"

"That might be a little more complicated."

"Why should it be complicated? You're a freakin' Archangel! Just fix it, Michael. You must realize how vulnerable she is without her powers. I didn't…I mean, *we* didn't just get her back in order to have her at risk again."

Luca would have jumped to his feet, but Calli laid a soft hand on his arm and shook her head. He satisfied his agitation by combing his fingers through his hair.

Michael's brows rose a notch. Luca realized he'd allowed more emotion and animation in his expression in the last ten minutes than he had in the last half century. He also knew that Michael valued his cool logic and icy calm in battle, but mourned the fact that Luca applied the same cold detachment to love out of fear he'd somehow inherited his father's weakness.

He appeared entirely too interested in the fact that Luca didn't seem able to maintain his usual composure where Callista McAllister was concerned. Luca carefully resumed his patent look of disinterest. Michael's lip curled and Luca knew he hadn't fooled his commander for a moment.

"I'm sure there's a solution, Luca," Michael ignored the disrespectful outburst. "But it may take a little time to find it. I'll need to consult someone with expertise in Dark Magick to determine how to break the spell. We'll figure it out."

Luca stood and pulled Calli to her feet. Her gaze darted between him and Michael.

"Well, thanks for nothing, *Your Grace.* I guess I shouldn't be surprised," Luca snapped. "C'mon, *cara.* Let's get you home."

"Do you think I don't know you've never forgiven my refusal to intervene with your father?" Michael asked in a deep, trembling voice. "I lost him, too, you know. I told you then and I'll tell you now, it wasn't an arbitrary decision on my part. It was your father's decision to mourn himself into an early grave. I would have helped you if I could have, but even *I* am forbidden from interfering with free will."

Luca couldn't believe Michael brought up the root of the tension between them in front of Calli.

"What if it wasn't?" Calli interjected quietly, her eyes fixed on Luca's face.

"What?" Michael's gaze swung back in her direction, with a look of surprise.

"What if Nicola's actions weren't a result of free will?" She turned her head to look steadily at Michael.

"*Cara*, what are you talking about?" Luca sighed wearily. "You weren't even here."

"Thank you for enlightening me, Sherlock Holmes," Calli shot back in a mocking tone complete with eye-roll. "Maybe I wasn't *here*, but I *was* with Jacques and Miranda and I know she hated Nicola. She believed he was the one who convinced Lilly to keep the ring from her."

"Calli, we aren't here to revisit ancient history. We have more pressing problems at the moment," Luca admonished.

"Right before Kat escaped, Miranda said something to her. Something about Nicola," Calli went on as though Luca hadn't spoken, narrowing her eyes. "She said she'd taken care of him. She said she may not have had the ring but she had something else."

"What did she say, *exactly*, *cara*?" Luca asked slowly, staring into her eyes as if hardly daring to believe what her words implied. Dark Magick might explain why no one, not even Luca, had been able to get through to Nicola. It would mean it wasn't some inherent weakness where love was concerned that destroyed him, after all.

Calli frowned. "At the time, I was more worried about helping Katrina escape and keeping you and Kassian away, so I don't remember exactly. Whatever it was, Kat was furious. She hit her over the head and the witch went down like a sack of grain. You could ask Kat about it, though. She might remember more."

"I'm sorry, Luca," Michael shook his head slowly. "Dark Magick. I should have suspected it. Nicola was an ancient warrior. Strong, fierce, unafraid. A fighter who had always been unashamedly proud of you. I never understood how the loss of one woman could destroy his love for everything else until he loved nothing except the prospect of death. It never made sense. But it does now."

Luca nodded shortly, acknowledging Michael's apology. He stared over Calli's head, his eyes fixed on some distant point. He swallowed hard over the lump suddenly lodged in his throat.

"No one knows how many times, how many ways I've replayed it, wondering if I could have done something to change the outcome. At least now, I know I was fighting an impossible enemy, one I hadn't known enough about to defeat. My father's actions weren't a conscious choice. Maybe there's some peace to be found in that."

Luca's shields were as solid as ever, and he felt confident that Calli couldn't read a thing, but this woman knew him too well. At least she had at one time. No matter what had happened to change him, the man she'd known still existed in there somewhere. His soul remained the same. He wondered if she could still recognize it beyond the set of his jaw, the defensive stance he presented to the rest of the world. He realized she must when she didn't stop to consider the propriety or whether he would welcome it, but simply stepped into his arms and held him. And it stunned him to realize it was exactly what he needed. After a moment's hesitation, a shudder passed through him, his arms came around her, and he buried his face in her hair.

Michael cleared his throat loudly. Luca's head snapped up, but then he bent to press his lips to Calli's hair before letting her go.

"Actually, Luca, I'm glad you stopped by," Michael waved them back to their seats. "I wanted to ask if you've noticed anything strange lately."

"Strange in what way?"

"Well, you know the dark ones generally avoid my city. Recently, I've been receiving some concerning reports that there's been an unusual upswing in activity."

"An *animorti* came to our door this morning," Calli piped up. "And earlier today we were ambushed. That's when I realized I couldn't detect them anymore. They were right there in front of me and I felt nothing at all."

Michael's brows drew together in concern. "How many?"

"One *Fallen* and two puppets," Luca supplied.

"Three against one? You always were an impressive son-of-a-bitch, Luca," Michael barked out a laugh but it did little to dispel his apprehensive expression. "And you say one came right to your door?" The Archangel heaved a great sigh and appeared to consider his next words carefully.

"Someone has been making inquiries." Michael's gaze locked intently on Callista.

She sat up straighter, suppressed the urge to squirm, and managed to endure his scrutiny without flinching. As if sensing her unease, Luca reached for her hand and linked his fingers with hers. She gripped them tightly, suddenly overcome with a sense of dread.

"About me?" Relieved her voice sounded normal and strong, she felt more than saw Luca's curious glance.

"You tell me, Callista," Michael said gently.

"Someone is very curious about the night Mariana Ducati died."

"*Merda*, Michael! Mariana has been dead for over a century. It's ancient history," Luca exploded.

Callista felt the color drain from her face at the mention of the woman's name.

"In fact, if I remember correctly, Mariana's body was discovered right around the time Calli disappeared. She probably didn't even know about it until now."

"Mariana?" Calli whispered faintly.

"*Diavolo*, Michael. Why bring this up? Calli doesn't know anything about Mariana's death. She was busy sneaking off to the shelter that night. Mariana was found all the way across town. I'm so sorry about Mariana, *cara*," Luca turned to her and squeezed her fingers. "It was so long ago it never occurred to me to tell you. This isn't the way I would choose for you to find out."

"No, I knew. I just…" she trailed off, dropping her eyes to the floor. At that moment, she didn't even care that he confirmed her belief that he thought she was an impulsive half-wit who sneaked away without thought or care for the consequences.

From the moment she'd been freed, she expected the past would come back to haunt her, someday. She just hadn't anticipated it would be this soon. So acute was her grief, even after all this time, that she could no longer hold her shields, and they crumbled, allowing both men to share the agonizing scenes swirling through her mind.

"*Che Dio ti benedica*," Michael breathed and laid a consoling hand on Calli's shoulder, but she knew no blessing in Heaven or on Earth would erase the memories from that night. She barely noticed as the tears she'd held inside for so long tracked down her face.

"Do you realize the major part of Whitechapel was as orderly as any other part of London?" Calli began in a calm, flat voice. "The women who sought respite at the House of Angels were mostly good women who had simply fallen on hard times. But naturally, stories of good, moral people were of no use to journalists. No, the slums, the vice infested quarters, the criminal element, those were the things that garnered all of the attention. I never really believed the place was as dangerous as people said. Still, Reverend Barnett was concerned enough that he and his wife offered to take some of the women in temporarily at Saint Jude's if I would close the shelter until the Ripper was apprehended. They worried about me traveling back and forth from the place. The Barnetts were such lovely people."

"Wait a minute. You closed the shelter? Why didn't you ever say anything?" Luca interjected.

"And then, of course, both you and Kassian ordered me to stay in the house," Calli continued in the same level monotone, as though Luca hadn't spoken. "I realize I never exhibited the appropriate subservience expected of a lady, perhaps not in any of the centuries in which I've lived. I never excelled at taking orders either, but regardless of what you or anyone else believes, Luca, neither was I a contrary fool. I didn't leave the house to prove a point. I didn't leave the house on a whim. I didn't even leave the house to go to the shelter that night. I left the house to go to Mariana."

"Mariana?" Luca struggled to process all that he'd

just seen and heard. Of course, he'd assumed Callista had gone to the shelter, they all had. He hadn't ever thought she was a contrary fool, well not exactly. Well, okay, maybe the thought had crossed his mind once or twice, but it had always been tempered by the knowledge that her heart most often ruled her head. There were worse flaws.

"There was a man. He was a *Fallen*," Calli's voice cracked at last as her slight frame shook with mute sobs. "She begged me not to tell anyone. I think she truly believed her love could save him. I tried to tell her, I tried…" her voice broke and she cleared her throat several times before continuing. "When she discovered she was with child, she went into hiding. She was so ashamed. She wanted to spare her family the humiliation and disgrace. And she was frightened, so terribly frightened. You see, she'd realized by then that he was a monster. Even I didn't know where she was. But when the baby came, something went horribly wrong. She sent for me."

Callista's fingers tightened on Luca's in a death grip, and when she raised her wide, blue eyes to his, they were filled with an anguish he hoped he never saw in them again.

"I *know* you told me to stay inside. I *knew* I shouldn't leave the house, but how could I not go to her, Luca? How could I leave her to die terrified and alone? So much blood. There was so much blood."

"Don't cry anymore, *dolcezza,* your tears break my heart." Luca untangled his fingers from hers and pulled her into his arms. He pressed his lips to her temple. His gut clenched when he thought of the lonely years she'd endured, trapped with a mad man, while this horror played on an endless loop in her head. "Shhh, *cara*…it's okay. It's over."

Calli pulled back and swiveled her head to gaze at Michael. "No, it isn't over, is it? Because someone is asking questions and, other than me, the only ones who knew what happened that night are dead."

"What about the father?" Luca looked over her head at Michael with a troubled expression. "Could he be looking for the child? Now that Calli has been found alive, could he think she knows something about the child's whereabouts?"

Calli shook her head slowly from side to side. "The father is dead."

"How can you possibly know?"

Callista took a deep breath. "Because I watched you kill him, Luca. The child's father was Jacques Rapier, Jack the Ripper."

Chapter Six

Upon their return to the *Via Dandolo* house, Luca was both surprised and relieved to discover Mac and Kat had arrived back in Rome from Fiesole. He needed another perspective on the events of the day. Following a recounting of the meeting with Michael, along with a complete recap of the events of that November night so long ago, Magdalena had accompanied a pale and shaken Callista to her room. Luca fervently hoped she was finally, peacefully, asleep.

Mac stretched out in the corner of a massive leather sofa with Kat contentedly curled into his side. Luca reclined in an overstuffed armchair, propping his legs on the marble cocktail table centering the comfortable furniture grouping in front of the enormous stone fireplace. Mac tipped back the last mouthful of *Birra Moretti,* and Kat picked up her head as though she had radar.

"Another?" Kat began to untangle her limbs from his and push herself up against his solid chest. Mac sat up and dropped a kiss on her shining, blonde head.

"I'll get it. Luca?" Mac absently gathered the dozen or so empty amber beer bottles littering the room. Alcohol had little effect on *Earthbounds.* They both knew they'd have to drink a boatload more to achieve even a slight buzz that might take the edge off their current anxiety.

"Sure, why not?" Luca murmured, chugging down his remaining brew and handing Mac the empty. Luca wore his characteristic mask, but he was uneasily aware Kat's empath was more than capable of seeing beneath his applied veneer if he let his guard slip for an instant.

"So, how's the construction on the farmhouse going?" Luca threw out casually. It was the last thing on any of their minds at the moment, and as he expected, Kat saw his remark for exactly what it was, a lame attempt at diversion. He held his breath and risked a look into the gray eyes so like his own. They narrowed. His sister was pretty astute even without her empathic powers to guide her. Nope, she wasn't buying it. He sighed. He hadn't really expected she would, but hope springs eternal.

"Coming along," she tossed her hair over one shoulder and shrugged, again reminding Luca of himself. "Madge has offered to go up and oversee the contractors when we go back to the States."

"She did?" That was not welcome news. Given Calli's current *disabilities*, Michael had ordered her to stay in Rome for the time being. Though not absent, the number of *Fallen* and their cohorts was still lower here than most other places. In addition, he'd surprisingly and, to Luca, disturbingly, ordered Luca to serve as Callista's personal guard until her abilities returned or could be restored. Luca had counted on Madge as a buffer of sorts. With her in Fiesole, he and Calli would be alone, except for the daily help.

"You love her." Kat raised a brow and the corners of her generous mouth quirked up. It wasn't a question begging a response. It wasn't an accusation inviting argument. It was a statement of fact and Luca's wildly fluctuating emotions and his uncomfortable silence were his answer.

"Of course, I love her," he finally groused. "She's like a sister to me."

Kat burst out laughing.

"Oh, Luca! Keep right on telling yourself that if it makes you feel better, but don't try to convince *me*. I'm your sister. I can read *those* feelings loud and clear, and believe me, your feelings for Calli…are anything but fraternal, my brother."

"Love? The only thing I know about love is that it's destructive," Luca muttered.

"Really?" Kat's brows arched nearly to her hairline. "Yet you were quite happy to shove your sister and your best friend down one another's throats, weren't you?"

"That was different."

"How so? Because love is fine for everyone except you? Because of Nicola? You've clung to that excuse for years, Luca, but now we know there were other forces at work. He wasn't responsible for his actions. That excuse doesn't hold water anymore."

"*Diavolo*, Katrina! Mind your own business." Luca jumped to his feet and stuffed his hands in the pockets of his jeans. He strode to the window, throwing off waves and waves of irritation.

"If you really wanted me to mind my own business, my brother, you would have blocked me better. We both know you can," Kat returned. "So talk to me. What are you afraid of?"

Luca barely remembered his mother. He'd cared for Calli once, and then suddenly she was gone. Then there was his father. Nicola withered away, leaving

Luca alone in the world and feeling as though he wasn't important enough for his father to have made an effort. Maybe Kat was right and that excuse didn't wash anymore, but knowing the truth and learning to un-feel the emotions he'd lived with for so long were two different things. Now Calli was back, living in a century and a society that had moved beyond everything she ever knew. She was still struggling to fit in. Luca was familiar, she felt comfortable with him. It was easy for her to cling to him, maybe even imagine she had feelings for him. But what about later? What happened when she regained her confidence and her abilities and realized there was a whole world waiting for her away from this house, away from this city, away from him? What was he afraid of? He feared trusting in love and then finding himself alone. Again. Maybe he'd become too cynical to fall without proof of forever. In his experience, when the going got tough, the ones you loved got going.

Luca knew Kat easily read and felt everything he couldn't say. Sometimes it was a royal pain, but at the moment he welcomed her support and the fact that she could feel what was in his heart without his having to say the words. She crossed to the window and slid her arms around his waist from behind, silently laying her cheek against his back as though giving him a moment to get his erratic thoughts and emotions under control. He took his hands from his pockets and folded his arms over hers where they wrapped around his waist.

"Do you really believe Callista is so shallow?" She said at last.

"Shallow?" A shadow of a smile flitted over his face. "Once upon a time Calli was the most spoiled, impulsive, and self-centered little chit you could imagine. Still, even then there was something about her."

"And now?"

"She risked her life to help a friend. She even came back to offer what comfort she could after getting the child to safety with no thought for herself, even knowing Mariana was likely already dead. *Merda!* What that cost her! What it cost all of us."

Luca could still clearly envision the scene Calli had shared with them earlier. She'd arrived to find a squalling newborn and Mariana bleeding to death faster than even *Earthbound* healing could reverse. The human midwife distraught and verging on hysteria, unable to save the girl. Mariana had already made arrangements for a mortal couple with knowledge of the *Earthbound's* existence to take and raise the child, hoping to keep her far from the influence of her *Fallen* sire. She'd begged Calli to take the child to them. Mariana feared Rapier had discovered her location and would arrive to claim the child at any moment.

With great reluctance, Calli did as her friend asked, but could not bear the thought of Mariana dying frightened and alone. And so she went back. Mariana was already dead, and Jacques had massacred the midwife when she refused to reveal the child's whereabouts. Calli had enough presence of mind to deny any knowledge of the child, pretending to have just arrived in answer to Mariana's desperate summons. The moment Rapier realized that she was Callista McAllister, the treasured sister of the *Earthbound* who had slain his beloved brother short hours earlier, her fate was sealed. He could have slaughtered her on the spot, but he thought it would be far more satisfying to keep her alive and let McAllister suffer in contemplation of what evil might befall her at any given moment.

"Then today, she could have, should have stayed in hiding, but she thought I was in danger and she barreled into the middle of a fight, swinging that damn liquor bottle with no thought for herself," Luca continued. "You should have seen her standing over that bastard with the sword raised over her head. I think it took a century off my life. No, Kat, she's anything but shallow. Still, her heart rules her head. Exactly why, under the circumstances, I think she could easily fool herself into thinking she feels something she doesn't because I'm safe and familiar."

Kat sighed dramatically. "Like most men, you are an idiot and you underestimate women completely. I understand you can't help it. It's an inherent flaw of the Y chromosome. Look, I understand what it's like to lose everyone you love, Luca, and frankly, it sucks. Big time. But no matter what happens, you won't ever be alone. You'll always have me. You're my family, my blood, and no power in Heaven or on Earth will ever change it."

"Not even, Mac?" His smile colored his voice.

"That's not fair," she squeezed and then released him. "I love you both more than life, but in different ways, so no, not even Kassian could keep me from you if you needed me."

"Good to know, *cara*," Luca turned and wrapped his sister in an embrace, acknowledging to a higher power for the thousandth time how grateful he was to have found her. "And ditto. Not that I would ever make you choose. Mac has been like a brother for more years than I can count. In fact, before you came into my life, the McAllisters were my only family for a long time. Maybe that's just one more reason to let sleeping dogs lie."

"So you think if you acknowledge your feelings for Callista and things go wrong, you'll lose the McAllisters, too? Oh, Luca," Kat sighed. "You really don't give people enough credit. You don't give yourself enough credit. And you most definitely don't give love enough credit."

"Okay, since you seem to know so much, how about some sisterly advice?" Luca challenged his sister, once again firmly in control of his thoughts and emotions.

"I seem to recall being on the other side of this conversation, dear brother, and you telling me you weren't getting in the middle," Kat laughed. "I think I'll claim that same right."

"That was completely different."

"Was it?" Kat retorted, her silver eyes sparkling with amusement. "I'll say this... there's nothing I can tell you that you don't already know in your heart. You simply have to accept it and decide what you're willing to do about it. I can't imagine how I would survive losing Kassian, but I wouldn't trade a moment of what we have together in exchange for the certainty of never losing it. If someone told me I could have his love for a year and then I would lose him, I wouldn't sacrifice that year for anything, not even to avoid the inevitable pain. Maybe instead of worrying about what you have to lose, you should concentrate on what you have to gain. Some things are worth the risk."

"You know, *Katrina,* I was perfectly content being an only child."

"Oh bite my ass, Luca! You were so *NOT.*" Kat's peals of laughter produced an answering smile in her warrior husband as he came back from the kitchen juggling four bottles of *Moretti* for Luca and himself and a glass of cranberry juice for Kat.

"What's so funny?" Callista's quiet voice asked from the entrance to the hall. Had Kat really told Luca to bite her bottom? That couldn't be right, could it? It must be another of those confusing slang terms she struggled to comprehend.

"Callista, you should be asleep," Kassian scolded fondly.

"And you should remember I'm not a child," Calli retorted peevishly, shuffling into the room and plopping down in the chair Luca had vacated earlier. She tucked her bare feet beneath her and settled the voluminous folds of her robe around her. "I can't turn my mind off simply because you think I should be tired."

"Your brother knows that, Callista, he's just worried about you," Kat said gently, sinking back onto the couch beside her husband and reaching for her glass.

"I know," Callista sighed with a fleeting smile. "I'm sorry, Kass. I didn't mean to snap at you."

"It's okay, kiddo. I get it. Want something drink?" He leaned forward as if he would get up, but Calli waved him back into his seat.

"No, thanks. I'm fine. So what were you all talking about?" If she hadn't walked in on Kat laughing, she would have assumed it was her. Since she doubted anyone could find one iota of amusement in anything she'd told them earlier, she deduced they must have been talking about something else entirely.

"Luca was just wishing he was still an only child," Kat smirked. "And Kassian was about to announce we were taking your mother back to Fiesole tomorrow."

"I was?" Kassian stared at his beautiful wife with a blank look.

"You weren't?" Kat smiled back sweetly snuggling even closer into his big body.

"I, uh, thought you were staying here, Kat," Callista said, looking from one to the other. It was obvious to her that her brother and his wife were communicating on a private level and she uneasily suspected it had something to do with her. "I hoped we could spend some time together, maybe go shopping or something." She glanced at Luca. "Some of those clothes…well, I don't think they're really my style."

"No doubt those would be the ones Elle picked out," Kat laughed.

Elle Gates was Katrina's best friend. She was a bit flashy and had a certain affinity for drama. Elle had a real flair for fashion, too, but her fashion sense suited her own dramatic and eclectic style far better than Kat or Calli's simpler, more classic one. Callista wondered how she and Kat had ever become friends. They seemed so opposite. Still, Kat loved her, so Kassian made the effort to consider her a member of his extended family.

"No doubt," Kassian responded in a dry tone.

"Tell you what, we'll go shopping before your brother and I return to New York. There are some wonderful shops here. In the meantime, I'm going to make a few calls tomorrow morning before we go and see if I can get you set up for a day of beauty and pampering. There's a great salon in *Piazza del Popolo*. All of the ex-pats swear by it," Kat smiled delightedly at her own brilliant plan. "Won't that be fun, Luca? Content with being an only child, indeed!"

Calli glanced over at Luca who had drifted back toward the window after grabbing another beer. He still wore the jeans and tight, black tee he'd donned that morning. Without the jacket, Calli could clearly see the ornate ink of the daggers on his forearms and the way the dark cotton of the shirt strained and molded the tight, heavy muscles of his arms and chest. His expression was as cool and placid as if Kat hadn't spoken at all. Something warm and nervous uncurled in the pit of her stomach and moved lower the longer she watched him. They would be completely alone here until Kassian and Kat returned. She wished she had some inkling of how Luca felt about that, but his usual unreadable expression was firmly in place.

"You can do that?" Calli turned her attention back to her sister-in-law with difficulty.

Kat hooked her thumb in her husband's general direction. "Billionaire," she chuckled.

Kassian rolled his eyes and hauled her against him with a mock frown. "I thought you didn't care about my money?" he growled against her lips.

"I don't," she agreed after pausing to return his affection. "But you have to admit, it comes in handy when you want to get something done in a hurry. So what do you think, Calli?"

Calli glanced nervously at Luca again. He had to be less than thrilled at the prospect of spending hours in a salon.

"I don't know, Katrina. I appreciate the thought, but…" Calli trailed off uncertainly.

"Make the arrangements, Kat," Luca said decisively. "It sounds like a great idea."

Three pairs of shocked eyes swiveled to Luca where he lounged against the window frame, as unreadable as ever.

"It does?" chimed three astounded voices simultaneously. It was difficult to say who was more taken aback.

Callista tamped down her excitement, trying hard to maintain a blasé demeanor on a par with Luca's. She'd never been to a salon. Kat had offered to take her before the wedding, but she hadn't yet felt comfortable enough to go. Her excursion into the city today had shown her that though times had changed, people were basically the same with the same virtues and vices.

She felt far more comfortable now at the prospect of going out, especially with Luca nearby. She'd noticed many women, including Kat, still wore their hair long, but she hadn't seen any that wore it hanging well past their buttocks as she did. In the nineteenth century, Callista's long, thick hair had been a source of pride. Today she'd felt as though it made her stick out like a sore thumb. How could she expect Luca to see her as a modern woman when she looked as though she should still be wearing bustles and corsets? It was time to move into the twenty-first century and what better place to start than a make-over that would hopefully give her at least the veneer of style and sophistication sported by the women Luca chose to spend time with.

Luca shrugged and levered himself away from the

window.

"Sure, why not? I admit I don't exactly relish the thought of spending the day in a den of artificial beauty being asphyxiated by the scent of perm solution and hairspray, but it should be easy enough to protect Calli in such a public place."

"Maybe it would be better if I went with Kat and Kassian to Fiesole?" Calli offered hesitantly.

Luca shook his silvery head as he crossed the room to perch on the arm of Calli's chair.

"No way. Michael's orders are to stay in Rome and it's easier to protect you here. It's also far more likely that whoever is asking questions about Mariana is still hanging around and I want to get to the bottom of it."

"Luca's right, Calli," Kassian agreed. "Though I still think the most likely explanation is Mariana's child has discovered Calli is alive and wants information about her mother. The upswing in *Fallen* activity in the city could be completely unrelated."

"Probably," Luca granted with a shrug. Calli didn't believe it for a minute, and she doubted anyone else did either. A girl looking for information about her mother could simply knock on the front door and ask. A girl looking for information about her mother didn't send *animorti* to the kitchen door, nor set up an ambush in an alley. But someone had. The question was, who? And why?

Chapter Seven

After checking every dressing suite, lounge, and treatment room in the salon for security purposes, while suffering the offended gaze of the owner, Luca relinquished Callista to the stylist. That had been well over three hours ago. He shifted awkwardly for the hundredth time on the small, upholstered Queen Anne style vanity bench. The dainty furniture, chosen for its elegant appearance, had never been intended for function or comfort, especially for someone of his size. He froze as the wood creaked ominously. The last thing he needed to do was to land on his ass on a pile of splintered wood in a room filled with gawking women. He released a sigh of relief when the delicate piece held together. He was gaining a new appreciation for the trouble women went through to appear attractive, but Calli had always looked fine to him without any artifice whatsoever. Still, he wasn't completely blind. Women enjoyed this kind of thing, though the why of it defied his understanding. Calli had been excited about the appointment, though she tried to appear blasé.

The faint pin prick shocks traveling up and down his spine heralding the presence of evil interrupted Luca's boredom. Mindful of the delicate furniture, he rose slowly as the sensation increased in intensity, and eased toward the archway leading to the area of the salon into which Calli had disappeared. Distracted by his surveillance, he nearly jumped out of his skin when Calli gave him a tentative tap on the shoulder. He spun on his heel to face her.

"What do you think?" Calli asked, her large, blue eyes sparkling like twin sapphires.

"I…" Luca worked to draw in sufficient air to speak. Freed from the weight of a good twelve inches, her dark hair tumbled and curled over her shoulders in a thick, shiny mass that ended slightly above her waist. The make-up was subtle and enhanced her natural beauty and coloring rather than detracting from it. Her cheeks were slightly flushed and he wasn't sure if it resulted from an artist's brush or her excitement. If Luca had thought her pretty before, now she literally took his breath away. He was powerless to stop the tightening in his groin and wished he'd left his jacket on despite the warmth of the salon. He was so screwed.

Before he had time to reflect on exactly how screwed, a wave of evil diverted his attention, slamming into him and crawling up his spine with a vengeance. There were too many witnesses to draw his daggers, but whoever the bastard was, he would have to go through Luca to get to Calli. Even with Luca unarmed, that was no easy task. He shoved Calli behind him without answering and turned to the door to face the threat.

Giovanna stood frozen in the doorway, eyes wide with astonishment as they locked on Luca standing tensely across from the entrance. A car was parked in the piazza behind her, and over the roof Luca's eyes met the dark, inscrutable gaze of Ignazio Monte, a *Fallen*. Luca relaxed only slightly. Monte was a wealthy businessman well known to the *Earthbound*.

He maintained a high profile and respectable façade both in business and in his private life and never actually got his hands dirty. He could well afford to hire the less savory elements of his race for that. His high visibility and carefully cultivated reputation as a philanthropist made him nearly untouchable. The *Fallen* nodded at Luca and ducked back into his car. No confrontation today. After a brief hesitation, Giovanna allowed the door to drift closed behind her and strode confidently forward toward Luca. Okay, maybe there *would* be a confrontation today.

"Luca! *Tesoro!*" Gia smiled too brightly. "What are you doing here?" She kept walking until she was close enough to brush her generous breasts against his chest, then placed her hands familiarly on his shoulders, and kissed him on either cheek. A few days ago, that would have been adequate contact to jump start his libido. Luca found it now had no effect on him at all. Gia apparently realized it too and her expression tightened imperceptibly.

"Interesting company you're keeping, Gia," Luca offered, stepping back slightly and nearly trampling Calli who still stood behind him. He reached back and pulled her to his side, his attention never straying from Giovanna.

"Oh, you know," Gia waved a hand dispassionately, her eyes widening and then narrowing as Calli came into view. "I was thinking of expanding the shop. Igna has plenty of money at his disposal."

"You could have gone to a bank. Or you could have come to me. I don't think you'll like his interest rates," Luca said shortly.

"That is no longer your concern, is it?" Giovanna

ground out between clenched teeth frozen in a smile.

"As you said the last time we spoke, we're still friends, Gia. You know I would help you. Don't do something stupid. You're in over your head."

"Ah, but it's my head, is it not? *Mi scusi*, I'm running late for my appointment. But first, you must introduce me to your little friend."

Before Luca could respond, Calli stepped forward and stuck out her right hand while resting her left possessively on Luca's forearm. "Hello, I'm Callista McAllister." Her small chin rose a fraction of an inch. Luca bit back a grin as he realized Calli was looking down her nose at Gia though Calli stood nearly a head shorter. "And you are?"

"Ah, *piacere*! I am Giovanna Moscato. So you are the infamous Callista McAllister back from the dead." Giovanna smiled without warmth and failed to offer her own hand in return, simply staring at Calli's as though it was something soiled and tainted. Calli dropped her hand to her side and curled the freshly lacquered nails into her palm. "And people say there are no more miracles. Yet here you are."

"Here I am." Calli confirmed with an equally cold smile. "And here is exactly where I intend to stay." Luca's heart swelled. This was the Callista he'd missed. She'd suffered experiences she might never feel comfortable enough to share with anyone, but she'd survived. More than that, she picked herself up and dedicated herself to adapting and moving on. Gia was an intimidating bitch when she wanted to be, and Calli wasn't backing down an inch. There was something incredibly beautiful about watching her rediscover her confidence. *Welcome back, baby.*

"I would wish you *buona fortuna*, for you will need it, but we both know it would not be sincere," Gia sneered.

"I doubt I'll need it at all, but by all means, tell yourself that if it will make you feel better," Calli smiled serenely. "And now, as pleasant as this hasn't been, you must excuse us. Luca and I have an engagement elsewhere, and we're also running late."

"We do?" Luca's eyes widened as he looked down at Calli. "I mean, oh yeah, we *do*. Think about what I said, Gia. Don't let anger or disappointment blind you to the obvious danger you're putting yourself in."

"You flatter yourself, *Signore* Fiorelli. I have nothing to be angry or disappointed about. My association with Igna is strictly business. *My* business."

"Suit yourself." Luca nodded and strode from the salon, grabbing Calli's hand and pulling her along behind him. He'd planned to take her to the church of *Santa Maria del Popolo* after the salon to see the paintings by Caravaggio, but he hadn't planned on an uncomfortable confrontation with Giovanna in the interim. What was she thinking? If spending time with Monte was a ploy to garner Luca's attention, she'd certainly succeeded, but not in the way she'd hoped. He would gladly help her financially. Heaven knew he could afford it, but the relationship was over and she needed to accept it. His placid expression betrayed none of the emotion seething beneath the surface as he headed out of the square, between the *chiese gemelle*, the twin churches of *Santa Maria dei Miracoli* and *Santa Maria in Montesanto*, and out onto the *Corso*. A few meters along, he ducked into the doorway of a shop, stopping so quickly that Calli plowed into him from behind. He pulled her around to face him, and then casually cocked a hip against an archway in the stone façade.

"Exactly what in the hell was *that*?" He enquired mildly.

"What was what?" Calli replied with deliberate casualness. She blinked up at him, once, twice. She looked as innocent as a lamb, but her nails gouged into the back of his hand as she spoke.

"Cal?"

"Hmm?"

"Ouch," Luca grinned as he pried her pink tipped talons away from his skin one at a time. Callista winced as the bloodied crescents were revealed. He started to release her hand then decided he liked the way it felt in his and kept hold of her fingers as he leaned back against the building again. "Now talk to me."

"What would you like to talk about?" She pretended to be totally captivated by the window display.

"The tension in there was thick enough to cut with a knife. How can that be possible when you and Gia have never even met?"

Calli continued to stare up at him. She knew how stubborn he could be and he wouldn't let it go. He must be angry with her for being not only rude, but terribly presumptuous. Maybe he actually cared for the bitch?

"I hadn't expected to meet your lover," Calli said in a quiet voice while looking somewhere over Luca's right shoulder as though fascinated by the afternoon shoppers hurrying up and down the street. Her heart skipped painfully as she uttered the words. She'd known there was someone, more than one someone actually. It had been over a hundred years and Luca wasn't a monk. Had she really expected he would be sitting on his thumbs mourning a dead woman? Still, the way he looked at her sometimes. She'd begun to hope it was the look a man gives a woman he wants, a woman he cares for. It was wishful thinking. Giovanna was a straight up man eater, one who was capable of molding herself into whatever a man needed her to be in order to get what she wanted. And what she wanted was very clear. Gia wasn't ready to relinquish Luca without a fight. For all of her bravado in the salon, Calli knew she lacked the experience and killer instinct to go head to head with someone like Giovanna for any length of time. Calli didn't know how to compete. She only knew how to be herself.

"She *was* my lover," Luca shrugged, watching her closely. "Not anymore. How did you know?"

"Women's intuition," Calli returned the shrug, unable to meet his eyes. Women's intuition and the kaleidoscope of intimate scenes Giovanna had been only too happy to open her mind and share. Calli didn't know how Luca felt, but she knew with certainty this Giovanna was in love with him. She'd given Calli fair warning she didn't intend to disappear quietly.

"Women's intuition, huh? Look, Calli, I never claimed to be some knight in shining armor. I may be an angel, but I'm no saint. So what? Now you know and you can't even look me in the eye? *Diavolo!"*

"She's very beautiful," Calli began in a hoarse voice. She cleared her throat, then threw her head back and met his gaze head on. "She obviously still cares for you."

88

"The feeling isn't mutual. She's a friend, nothing more."

"But you were…sleeping with her," Calli persisted. "Surely you must feel something?"

"Lust, Callista. What I feel…*felt* for Giovanna was lust. A certain fondness, but never anything more. I was honest with her from the beginning so don't look at me like I'm some big, bad wolf who ravaged an innocent maiden," Luca grumbled. "I'm not a wolf and she sure as hell wasn't innocent."

As much as Luca enjoyed a woman's body, only one woman had ever touched his heart. In all the years he'd believed Callista dead, he'd never offered any woman more than transient affection before moving on to the next tidbit in an endless antipasti. Detached promiscuity provided a welcome amnesia that allowed him to concentrate his efforts on thwarting the *Fallen* and their schemes. He'd convinced himself it was enough. He'd been good at lying to himself. Now against all odds, Calli was back, and he felt like a beggar who'd opened a paper bag and discovered a trove of priceless jewels. He'd been wrong about Calli and he'd been wrong about his father. Conceivably, he could also be wrong about love. He could no longer trust words like "never" and "impossible." But neither had his comfort zone extended quite enough yet to trust words like "forever" and "always." Luca was used to his head being in control, but when it came to Calli his body didn't pay much attention to his head. Worse, his heart ignored it completely. She was the one woman he was afraid he couldn't walk away from, but that didn't mean she couldn't walk away from him. Though he'd buried it deeply, after dozens of years and dozens of women he'd never really gotten Callista McAllister out of his system. Could that mean she was supposed to be there?

Using the hand he still held, Luca tugged Calli forward but she resisted. Her proximity afforded him a whiff of mint and flowers from her freshly coiffed hair, but underneath he could still detect the scent of vanilla and sunlight that was pure Calli. His groin twitched in direct opposition to his brain's orders. Maybe Kat was right. He'd spent so many years protecting himself from what he might lose he'd lost sight of what he might gain. Maybe some things really were worth the risk.

"Have you ever been in love with *anyone*?"

"I didn't used to think so, but now I'm not so sure," he replied, wondering at the hard edge in her voice.

Calli let herself be pulled into Luca's arms on his second attempt and buried her face in his shirt. She knew he felt lust for her just as he did for…how many others? In fact, the hard evidence of it currently pressed against her where their bodies met. She wanted him to desire her, of course. For over a hundred years, with her nose buried in books describing every conceivable erotic fantasy, it had been his face, his body she'd envisioned. Beyond all hope of rescue, she was convinced it was all she would ever have of him. Yet, now she stood in his arms, and with the slightest bit of encouragement she suspected she could find herself in his bed. Lust. How empty the word sounded to Calli now. Because now she understood it wasn't enough.

"I thought we were going to see the Caravaggio paintings," Calli mumbled against his chest.

"You still want to go?"

She nodded without looking up. She didn't want to

talk about his lovers anymore, didn't want to contemplate his feelings for other women. She detested and resented every curvaceous, faceless one of them. Still, she was the one in his arms at the moment. If he didn't love her, she knew at least he wanted her. They had a shared history, a certain closeness the other women in his life could not claim. Maybe she could use it to her advantage. The problem was, she had no idea how to do that. She had no idea how to be a seductress. And she wanted more than his hunger. She wanted his heart.

Chapter Eight

Situated next to a gate in the Aurelian Wall, Calli saw nothing notable about the long side of *Santa Maria del Popolo* facing the piazza. The façade, which sat perpendicular to the *Porta del Popolo*, was in a simple Baroque style. Compared to the prominent façades and conspicuous domes of the twin churches on the opposite side of the square, Calli thought it would be easy to overlook the unassuming church altogether.

After climbing a short set of stairs, they stepped through the tall marble door-case and into the hushed and reverent shadows of the interior. Calli's nose stung with the scent of incense and lemon wax. She gasped with delight as she saw the church's unremarkable exterior hid incredible artistic and architectural treasures. Except for a few small groups of tourists, guidebooks in hand, who whispered in respectful awe at the chapels around the perimeter designed as mortuaries for prominent Italian families, Calli and Luca nearly had the church to themselves. Calli smiled inwardly when Luca reverted to professor mode, understanding now that he used it as a way to distance himself and remain emotionally detached. He guided her to the first chapel on the right of the entrance, pointing out the must see features, though the details were clearly identified in both English and Italian on printed cards along the altar rails.

Their footsteps echoed on the uneven stone and marble floor as they slowly worked their way toward the front of the church with Calli picking her way around the interesting slab tombs set directly into the main floor. Luca pointed out other tombs worth looking at on the arcade pillars in the aisles and on the walls in between the chapels. When they finally reached the front of the church, Calli paused to admire the huge altarpiece painted by Carlo Maratta.

"Tradition says the emperor Nero was buried here," Luca whispered. "After the burial, the people living nearby complained of being constantly disturbed by a horrible noise coming every night from a walnut tree growing on the site. They were convinced it was the ghost of the mad emperor and that a flock of crows living in the tree were demons waiting for the re-incarnation of Nero as the Antichrist. Pope Paschal the Second wanted to suppress veneration of the dead emperor by the fearful locals who were leaving flowers in his tomb, so he had Nero's ashes thrown into the Tiber, and the tree cut down. Then he had the chapel built right here where the grave had been."

"Really? Do you think the *pope* believed the crows heralded Nero's reincarnation?"

"No," chuckled Luca quietly. "I think it's far more likely he wanted to pacify the peasants by chopping down the tree. He actually built the chapel to celebrate the capture of Jerusalem by the First Crusade."

"Still, demon crows and the ghost of a mad emperor make for a great story," Calli smiled back and wandered off to the left of the altar where they finally reached the *Cappella Cerasi,* The Chapel of the Assumption. The Caravaggios were on the side walls, facing each other with Carracci's Assumption serving as the main altarpiece in between. Calli had always loved art, and in Italy, it seemed a work of genius waited to capture her attention around every corner. She'd been eager to see this chapel as soon as Luca told her it was one of the few places in Rome where masterpieces of such importance could be viewed in their original setting. Even after the difficult scene with the brazen woman earlier that day, she was glad she'd decided to stick to the original plan and have Luca bring her to see the works. They were incredible.

Calli stepped away from Luca and craned her neck to study the artwork. Luca moved to follow, then stiffened and glanced around the church. The faint shocks racing along his spine warning of evil were faint, but he sensed them nonetheless. He stood near the entrance to the chapel and moved slightly to the side peering around the marble pillars running the length of the building on both sides of the center aisle. His jaw tightened as he spotted Giovanna cautiously making her way along the left side of the nave. She looked decidedly uncomfortable and he guessed the sensations he felt were from someone who waited for her outside. A *Fallen* did not willingly enter a consecrated building without a damn good reason.

Gia looked up and flinched at the unmistakable anger on Luca's face.

"Luca, to the sacristy, quickly."

He crossed his arms over his chest and planted his feet, unmoving as she sent the mental message.

"Please. I'm being followed and I need your help. There isn't much time."

The fear in her voice was evident. He fought the

urge to walk away, but maybe he owed her this, at least. He turned to grab Calli's arm as Gia headed toward the sacristy to the left of the chapel.

"What's wrong?"

"Giovanna is here. She says she's in trouble. I'm sorry, *cara,* but I…feel obligated to help her. We'll come back another time, I promise." He stroked a finger across her cheek feeling genuine regret at tearing her away from the paintings she'd so longed to see.

"Of course, we must help her if she's in trouble, Luca. We're *Earthbound.* It's what we do."

Luca felt humbled by her generosity of spirit. She had no reason on earth to feel compassion for Gia, especially after the woman's earlier stunt. He'd also seen the images Calli had been privy to, even if she wasn't willing to discuss it. Yet she didn't hesitate to offer her assistance. With a hand at the small of her back, Luca propelled her in the direction of the sacristy, hidden from the main body of the church.

"In case I forgot to tell you today, *cara*, you are beautiful."

"So you *do* like my hair?" Calli tossed over her shoulder as they hurried along the dim corridor past even more Renaissance tombs.

"What? Oh, yeah, your hair looks great, too."

They made a quick right and entered the sacristy. Giovanna already waited near the door, wearing a path in the tile floor and anxiously wringing her hands. A wizened priest of indeterminate age watched her from the corner of his eye as he made a great show of arranging a rack of ornate vestments in a walnut cabinet on the far side of the room.

Luca strode to the wary man, who, after a few

abrupt words from the *Defensori*, bowed his way from the room. Luca returned to the women, surprised to see that Calli, drawn no doubt to the look of fear and distress on Gia's face, had taken the other woman's shaking hands in her own.

"I know I have no right to ask anything of either of you, especially after…but I did not know where else to turn," Gia began.

"Just tell me what's going on." After her little escapade earlier, Luca didn't trust Gia as far as he could throw her.

"Not here. We need to leave. They're watching all of the entrances, and it's only a matter of time before they come looking. Consecrated ground will not stop these fiends." Wild-eyed, Giovanna looked around as if expecting her pursuers to appear in the sacristy at any moment.

"Fine. Do you know the McAllister villa on *Via Dandolo*? We fade there." He pulled Calli into his arms and reached for Gia's hand. The *sigils* protecting the house were woven with the molecular signatures of only those allowed to enter and leave. Unless Gia was touching him, she couldn't pass the barrier. Calli clung to Luca as the world spun away. In a heartbeat, the three *Earthbounds* materialized in the kitchen of the McAllister home. Poor Maria, standing at the sink and peeling vegetables for the evening meal, nearly jumped out of her skin.

"*Mi dispiace, signore*," she fanned herself laughing breathlessly. "I never get used to that no matter how many years I have served this family."

"Maria, could you excuse us please? In fact, take the rest of the day off. *Signorina* Callista and I will eat out tonight."

"Well, if you are certain, *signore.*" Maria's full face crinkled in delight. "My daughter is visiting from Milano with my grandson and I would not mind spending the rest of the day at home."

"*Certo*! *Vai, vai.* Go, go…we'll clean this up later." Luca made a shooing motion, and Maria wasted no time gathering her handbag and heading out the door with a wave, not even pausing to remove her apron.

"Okay," Luca pulled out a chair for Calli and remained standing behind it. He motioned Gia into another. "What's going on? Who is threatening you and why?"

Giovanna appeared calmer now that she was in a safe place, though she still looked paler than when they'd seen her earlier at the salon. Her eyes darted back and forth between him and Calli as she seemed to struggle with what to say. Her gaze settled on Luca for a few moments before the color rushed into her face and then drained away just as quickly.

Luca's hand settled on Calli's shoulder, and his thumb absently stroked the side of her neck beneath her hair. Gia continued to regard him cautiously, and then bit her lip. Finally, she took a deep breath and reached for Calli's hand.

"Before I begin, I owe you an apology, Callista. *Mi dispiace*, I truly am sorry. What I did this morning…it was petty and hurtful. My only excuse is that I was angry and afraid. I hope you can forgive me, though I understand if you cannot."

"I used to be a bit impulsive, myself, Giovanna, so I can understand an error in judgment. I'm willing to overlook it. Once." Calli did not deliver her response unkindly, but her tone made it clear she would not tolerate a repeat performance.

Gia nodded. "*Grazie.* It is more than I deserve after the way I behaved."

"Let's forget about it for now. You said you were afraid…what are you afraid of?"

"Of losing Luca," she blurted. "But not for the reasons you think," Gia hastened to add. The woman's shoulders slumped. "Maybe I should start at the beginning."

"Perhaps that would be best," Calli agreed.

"Do you have anything to drink, perhaps? This story requires a little something."

"There should be some wine in that cabinet over there," Calli directed Luca before turning her attention back to the other woman. "I'm afraid Luca and my brother finished all of the *Moretti* last night."

"*Grazie.*" Gia sighed as Luca plunked a glass and the bottle on the table in front of her.

"We could have offered you some lovely *limoncello* if Calli hadn't wasted the bottle by breaking it over a *Fallen's* head," Luca said in a mock mournful voice.

Calli wrinkled her nose at him. "Lucky for you."

"If it pleases you to believe so," he winked.

Giovanna nearly choked on the wine.

Luca threw a glance in her direction. His eyes narrowed as he correctly interpreted the question on Gia's face. He nodded. Yes, this woman truly meant something to him. Giovanna took an even larger gulp of wine and swallowed hard, no doubt contemplating her earlier behavior at Calli's expense and thanking her lucky stars Luca hadn't decided to wring her neck.

He didn't return to his position behind Calli's chair, but he did pull his chair close to hers and rest a hand on her thigh.

Calli felt the heat of his palm like a brand through the denim of her jeans and decided the feeling was not unpleasant. At all. In fact, she found the heat seemed to be spreading from her thigh to an area just north of there and that new and strange sensation felt even more divine. It even made her feel a little naughty. She experimentally laid her hand on top of his larger one and was rewarded by a squeeze. Then he linked his fingers through hers and curled their hands together. They were home, they were protected by *sigils*, she was safe. He hardly *needed* to sit so close to her and hold her hand. She assumed he did it because he *wanted* to. She might still have a lot to learn, but Calli decided, then and there, that she liked the freedom of this new century. She liked it a lot.

"Luca and I had known each other for some time," Giovanna began at last. "He would come to visit me whenever he was in Rome. Our relationship was not a secret." Her eyes met Luca's briefly and quickly looked away. Calli's fingers tensed in Luca's, and he readjusted their hands so they were linked palm to palm, and ran his thumb soothingly across the racing pulse along her inner wrist. "Shortly after the news of Callista's rescue became common knowledge, two men came to see me. Two *animorti*. They didn't say who sent them. They said Jacques Rapier had an object of great power, and they demanded I use my relationship with Luca to get to Callista and discover where to find it."

"The Ring of Aandalena," Luca growled. "Well,

they're too late. It's been returned to Michael."

"It isn't a ring. They never mentioned a ring. It's a book."

Calli opened her mouth to speak, and Luca squeezed her hand. "Go on," he encouraged.

"I told them to go away. I told them if they hurt me, you would hunt them down and kill them," she looked at Luca who nodded.

Calli knew that whatever their differences, Gia assumed correctly. Luca would have taken it personally. An attack on someone close to him would have him turning Rome upside down.

"They told me they wouldn't hurt *me* if I refused to cooperate, but they couldn't guarantee the safety of *Zio* Enrico." Tears coursed down Gia's lovely face unheeded. "He isn't my blood, Luca, but he is the only family I have."

"Of course you would protect your family, Gia," Calli's free hand reached to cover the other woman's. "Whether by blood or by bond, family is family."

"You really are a kind woman, Callista McAllister," Gia offered a watery smile. "I can see why you are so beloved. And Luca, you are wondering why I didn't come to you sooner."

Calli glanced at Luca. An almost imperceptible clenching of his jaw was his answer.

"I thought I could handle them. What do I care about some book? I thought I could get the information they wanted, and they would go away and leave my uncle alone. I thought…it doesn't matter what I thought. I was a fool. After all of you returned to Rome, they watched me constantly. I never saw them, but I always felt them nearby."

"I felt them, too." Luca's voice echoed in Calli's mind. *"Every time I visited Gia. In fact, I swear I feel a faint sizzle right now."*

"But that makes no sense." Calli glanced at him with a frown. Luca merely shrugged.

"After you left the other night, they came to my door. I was…distraught. I told them our relationship was over, and I couldn't get them the information they wanted. They beat me…badly."

Calli gasped and Luca clenched his jaw so tightly it audibly cracked. He might not be in love with Giovanna, but *any* woman being brutalized would not sit well with him. She almost felt sorry for those men when he discovered their identity. Because he would, and then he and the *Defensori* would ensure the fools paid dearly.

Giovanna glanced up when Calli gasped, then returned her gaze to her lap. "Please don't worry on my account. I'm fine. It was…unpleasant, but *Earthbound* heal quickly, no?" Physically, at least, Calli thought. "Then, late this morning, Monte came into the shop. I was getting ready to close, as I really did have a salon appointment. He insisted rather…emphatically, on driving me there and, on the way, told me I must discover the whereabouts of this book. If not from you, then from Callista herself. You being at the salon was an unlucky coincidence, and I did the first thing that came to mind." She raised her head and her expression was anguished. "I'm not proud of it, but I…*Dio,* Luca, Monte has Enrico."

Luca rose and walked around the table to where Giovanna was pouring the last of the wine into her glass.

"Gia," Luca's voice was hesitant. "The men who beat you...did they...take other liberties, as well?"

A shudder wracked Giovanna's body and the curtain of her dark hair shielded her expression as she lowered her chin to her chest. She nodded. Once. Callista cried out in distress and jumped from her chair. She started moving around the table but Luca held up a hand to stop her.

"Gia, I-I'm so sorry, there's no easy way to say this, but I have to ask. I feel the presence of *Fallen*. It's very faint, but is it possible you carry the child of a dark one?"

The woman's shoulders began to shake. Luca laid a hand on her head and looked at Calli with a helpless expression. Callista clenched her fists and pressed one against her lips as tears streamed down her cheeks in the face of Gia's obvious despair. The woman finally raised her head and Calli was stunned to see Gia wasn't sobbing, but laughing, a harsh, humorless laughter bordering on hysteria.

"Oh, Luca, *caro mio,* if only that were the worst of it," she cackled bitterly. "No, I don't carry the child of a dark one. I *am* the child of a dark one. Jacques Rapier was my father."

Chapter Nine

Callista opened her eyes to Luca's face hovering inches from her own. He forced his tense features to relax into a relieved smile when she blinked and looked around. She struggled to sit up and he pressed her shoulders back onto the sofa.

"Easy, *carissima*. How do you feel?" He brushed a wayward tendril from her face and peered at her intently.

"Mortified,' she grimaced. "I can't believe I did that. I never faint. Well, sometimes when Giselle laced my corset too tightly, but thankfully, those torturous contraptions are a thing of the past. You can let me up now, I'm fine."

"Just take it easy for a minute, *cara*." Seeing her crumple into a still, silent heap on the cold tile floor took years off his life. At this rate, he would be an old man long before his time. He put his arm under her shoulders and assisted her into a sitting position, reassured by the soft, warm feel of her in his arms. Tipping her chin up with a forefinger, he searched her face.

"You're sure you're okay?"

"Perfectly, though I'm sure I'll be sore. Terracotta is quite unforgiving."

Luca regarded her for a minute more, then no longer able to resist, he dragged her across his lap and dropped a quick soft kiss on her slightly parted lips. She tasted even better than he dreamed, and when she melted into him like butter, what started as a brief peck, quickly became much more. When he finally lifted his head, they were both trembling. He was nearly undone by the slumberous passion darkening her brilliant blue eyes. Handing his heart into someone's keeping terrified him. In the past, it had always been a precursor to pain. Deep down, he knew it was too late. His heart was already lost. Maybe it always had been. He held his breath and waited for the fear to hit. But it never came. Instead, he discovered a feeling that had been so long absent from his emotional repertoire he barely recognized it. Peace.

"Took you long enough," she whispered, echoing the sentiment she'd voiced the day he rescued her from Rapier. He guessed she referred to the kiss, but it felt as though she'd read his mind. Of course, that was impossible. His shields were stronger than the vaults in St. Peter's grotto.

"Yeah, I guess it did. Callista McAllister, are you trying to seduce me?" Not that she had to try. The feel of her soft, warm mouth left him so painfully hard he feared he'd explode if she twitched her heart-shaped little bottom in his lap just one more time.

Her cheeks burned and sudden tears pricked the back of her lids. Seduction. He had all of the practical experience in that department, didn't he? She had nothing but book smarts. She'd worked hard to convince herself she was a modern woman, ready to share his bed if that was all he had to offer. Now she doubted she could survive the loss if they made love and he walked away from her as he had all the others.

She sat up straighter and pushed against his chest to climb out of his lap and get to her feet.

"I must have a concussion after all."

He tried to tug her back, but she stepped away out of reach.

Luca rose to his full height and looked down at her with concern. "A concussion? Are you dizzy? Nauseated? How many fingers am I holding up?" He buried his hands in the thick mass of her hair, his long fingers massaging her scalp as he felt for injury. She grabbed his wrists and tugged his hands away, struggling to assume a matter-of-fact demeanor.

"I was being facetious, Luca," she sighed. "I'm fine. Now where is Giovanna? Can you believe she's Mariana's daughter? She must have been the one asking questions."

When she wasn't otherwise occupied in Luca's bed. Calli swallowed hard as the afterthought immediately leapt into her mind. She pressed a hand to the sharp and unwelcome pain searing her chest. *So this was jealousy.* There was a phrase in twenty-first century vernacular she'd come to understand, and it perfectly fit the bill in this case. *This totally sucked.*

"I sent her up to the guest room to lie down for a while," Luca dropped his hands to his sides. "You're right, she was the one asking questions. It appears the people Mariana relied on to raise her baby weren't exactly the good Samaritans they portrayed themselves to be. They raised Gia as little more than an unpaid servant, told her that her father murdered her mother, and the friend who'd been entrusted to raise her, namely you, dumped her on their doorstep at the first opportunity."

"What kind of people would do that to a child?" Calli's eyes sparked with rage. "If I had suspected for an instant, I would have kept that baby myself no matter what anyone said."

"I know you would have kept her, *cara*," He rubbed his big hands briskly up and down her arms. "I told her as much. Anyway, I guess it's a little more understandable why she wanted to hurt you today. She saw you as the woman who abandoned her, and then as the woman who took me away. I've explained to her what really happened that night. I think she believes me, but it takes time to trust and unlearn the thoughts and feelings of a lifetime. Believe me, I know."

The hint of regret in his voice tugged at her. "You do?"

He nodded slowly, looking directly into her eyes.

"And what is it *you've* distrusted for so long?"

"My heart. It isn't easy to believe in something you've learned to be so suspicious of."

"But not impossible?" Calli watched him carefully, trying to read his face. He hesitated and for a moment, she thought he wouldn't respond. Then he stroked a finger along her jaw and turned her toward the stairs pushing her along with a hand at her back.

"No, not impossible," He dropped a kiss on the top of her head. "But, maybe that's a conversation we should have later. We have other things to worry about at the moment. Like what we're going to do with Gia. She can't go home, and she can't stay here. Then we have to figure out where Enrico is and get him back. Somewhere in there, I'll have to take care of the bastards who hurt Gia, too. Then we have to figure out what they're looking for and make sure they don't get it."

"Quite an ambitious schedule." Callista stopped on the first stair and turned back to him. He seemed different, lighter somehow. She would very much have liked to continue their conversation right here, right now, but he had a point. They had to consider other priorities. "Why can't she stay here? It's safe enough and there's plenty of room."

"I feel badly for what she's been through, *carissima,* and I promise someone will pay, but she deliberately hurt you and that's something I can't abide. Just because she knows the truth now doesn't mean she's been able to let go of all of the hurt and anger. I won't permit her to take it out on you."

"I can take care of myself, you know," Calli straightened to her full height, which fell far short of Luca's even though she now stood on the second step. But a small part of her thrilled at his words.

Luca chucked her under the chin with a crooked grin. "I know you can, *la mia tigre*. But you don't have to. You have me to do it for you."

Calli rolled her eyes, spun on her heel, and stomped up the stairs. His Tigress! She might not understand very much Italian, but he was making fun of her, she just knew it! Well, Luca Fiorelli had better watch his step. Tigers had very sharp claws and hers were freshly manicured.

All this tenderness and talk of trusting his heart. Was it possible he might actually care for her? She dared to feel a flicker of hope. Yes, she felt badly for what Gia had suffered. However, she wasn't sure she could cohabitate for any length of time with a woman who had known Luca so intimately, a woman who obviously wasn't ready for that intimacy to end. Luca was right. It was probably much better for everyone if they found her another place to stay.

Calli raced to the far end of the hall and rapped on the door of the guest suite. When she received no response, she cracked open the door and peered in. The bed remained neatly made and, at first glance, the room appeared empty. Then she saw her. Giovanna sat in a small, overstuffed chair gazing out of the long window overlooking the back garden. There wasn't much to see out there at this time of the year, but she appeared fascinated by the view all the same. Her chin rested on her pulled up knees. Her eyes were red, but at the moment, they were dry. With her hair scraped back and twisted into a clumsy knot and her face scrubbed free of makeup, Calli could clearly see the resemblance to Mariana. A sharp and familiar ache pierced her heart as it did whenever she thought of her lost friend. In repose, Giovanna exuded nothing of the assertive, manipulative woman who'd confronted them earlier today. Calli's heart went out to the frightened, vulnerable child she now saw before her.

"May we come in?" Calli asked quietly.

Giovanna's eyes remained fixed straight ahead. She shrugged. "It's your house."

Calli's step faltered at her hard, unwelcoming tone. Well, what had she expected? Gia needed their help earlier and was willing to play nice to get it, but apparently she hadn't really done an about face despite learning the truth. In *Earthbound* years, Giovanna was still quite young. She might be an experienced woman of the modern world compared to Callista, but for now, it seemed she'd chosen to revert to the sulky immaturity of a teenager. Calli guessed she would have to be the grown up. She straightened her spine and spoke to Luca without turning around.

"Could you excuse us for a few minutes, Luca? I think Giovanna and I need to have a little talk."

"*Cara*, I don't think that's such a good idea. Why don't we all go downstairs and decide what to do next?" Luca whispered close to her ear, his warm breath ruffling her hair and tickling her neck. "I think it might be a bad idea to leave you two alone. *A very bad idea.*"

Calli turned to face him and planted her hands on her hips. She compressed her lips into a tight, thin line and raised a brow. Luca took a step back. Clearly, he got the message. She was pissed. Totally and completely pissed. The corners of his mouth twitched, adding to her annoyance since she saw no humor in the situation whatsoever. Her foot beat an impatient tattoo on the marble floor until he turned toward the door and yanked it open.

"Maybe I'll just go make some coffee...or something." He stepped out into the hall and pulled the door closed behind him. Calli closed her eyes and counted to ten before turning back to the sullen woman huddled in the chair.

Callista closed the distance from the door to the chair in slow, measured strides until she stood between Giovanna and the window, blocking the other woman's view. Still Gia didn't look up. Calli took a few deep breaths to harness her anger and sighed inwardly. She'd so hoped they could resolve their differences in a civilized manner, but it seemed as though Gia was rethinking her earlier apology and had decided to act like a thwarted child. Calli truly felt compassion for the girl, but she wasn't about to be treated like a doormat in her own home, especially by someone she had done her best to help. More than once. Furthermore, she felt sure if she didn't take a stand now, Giovanna would interpret it as weakness and would simply continue to disrespect and torment her whenever she could.

In the weeks following her rescue, Calli had spent endless hours recovering from a deep chest wound that would have been fatal to a mortal. Much of the time, her eyes were glued to the wondrous modern device that was television. How many daytime talk shows had she watched touting the concept of tough love? Calli had listened to the theory, confounded. She'd never really comprehended circumstances that would warrant it. Until now.

"Nothing to say, Giovanna?" she began in a firm voice. "Well, that's fine. I'll begin. You can sit there and listen, and I'll tell you exactly how things are going to be. If you have questions about your mother, I'll be glad to answer them the best I can. I knew her well, and I loved her dearly. If you have questions about your father, I'll try to answer those as well, though I'd really rather not talk about him. I am truly sorry for what you've had to go through in your life, but we've all had our crosses to bear. As of this moment, I've reached the limit of what I will tolerate. Even after the hurtful stunt you pulled in the salon, I helped you today, Giovanna. I didn't have to do that."

"Luca would have…" Gia's head snapped up with a sneer.

"Luca would have walked away and left you to fend for yourself if I asked him to." Calli interrupted in a cold voice. She didn't know if that was true, but she counted on the fact Gia didn't either. "So, let's see…that makes two times now I've saved your life. Once when you were born and once today. And how do you repay that debt? You send *animorti* to my door, share intimate scenes of the man I love in your bed, and then subject me to your thankless, self-indulgent behavior in my own home, where, I might add, you are currently a guest."

"It wasn't me…the *animorti,* I swear," Gia interjected and looked away.

"Irrelevant. The bottom line is this, Giovanna. Right now, you need me and Luca a damn sight more than either of us needs you. Mariana's daughter or not, you are in *my* home and in *my* debt. You will stop your juvenile nonsense at once and treat me with courtesy and respect." Calli's voice rose with every syllable. She only realized she was shouting like a fishwife as the last word left her lips.

"Or what?" Giovanna taunted spitefully.

"Or…or you can bite my bottom and get the hell out!" Calli exploded so loudly she barely heard the muffled guffaw on the other side of the door that quickly turned into a strangled cough. She clapped a hand to her mouth. *Lord, had she really said that?* Then her lips curled against her palm. Yes, she had. And it felt *good*! She quickly rearranged her features into a stern expression.

Giovanna's head swiveled toward Calli, her eyes wide in alarm. "You're *Earthbound*. You help others. It's what you do. You wouldn't turn your back on me and let the *Fallen* win."

"Try me, Gia," Calli ground out through clenched teeth. "Yes, I'm *Earthbound*, but I'm not a masochist.

I've already helped you twice and suffered for it both times. You want *my* help? Then it will be *my* way and on *my* terms." Of course, the little bitch was right and Calli would never turn her back and let the *Fallen* have her, however tempting it might be. But Gia didn't need to know that.

"I hate you," Gia whispered and dropped her forehead to her knees.

"Duly noted," Calli responded evenly. She turned toward the door and gripped the knob. "Fortunately, I'm not interested in your affection, just your courtesy and cooperation. It's up to you to determine if your hatred of me is more important to you than your life and the life of your uncle. I'll be downstairs when you decide."

Calli stepped into the quiet dimness of the hallway and pulled the door closed with a click. She slumped back against it with shaking legs now that she'd cleared Giovanna's line of sight and let out a trembling breath she barely realized she'd been holding. She hoped Gia bought her show of false bravado, otherwise they would still be obliged to help her, and Calli's credibility with the woman would be destroyed. Concentrating intently on calming the uncomfortable thumping of her racing heart, she never noticed Luca leaning against the wall a few feet away.

She nearly jumped out of her skin as he stepped from the shadows and reached for her hand. She opened her mouth to speak, but he held a finger to his lips and tugged her toward the stairs. He pulled her into his arms the moment they reached the bottom and simply held her until her trembling subsided.

"Well played, *cara*," he laughed into her hair.

"Oprah?"

"Dr. Phil," she smiled into his chest. "Do you think she believed me?"

"Oh, she bought it, *dolcezza*. You were quite convincing. Now we wait to see if she's willing to accept your conditions." He leaned back slightly to smile into her face. It was a genuine smile, one that transformed his countenance completely. It was the smile she'd held close to her heart and relied on to get her through her darkest hours for over a hundred years. But this smile wasn't a dream to hold onto in the midst of a nightmare. This was real. This was Luca, and that smile was all for her. Her knees began to tremble all over again.

Keeping one arm around her, he brought the other hand up to cup her chin, and Calli offered no resistance when he raised her face to his.

"Did you mean it?" he asked in an odd, gruff tone.

"Of course I didn't mean it. You should know me better than that, Luca. You know we'll help her regardless."

"No, *carissima*. If Gia refuses to abide by your conditions, then someone will help her, yes, but it won't be us. But that isn't what I meant. You told Giovanna I was the man you love. Did you mean it?"

Calli's mouth went dry and she found it nearly impossible to formulate a single word as he continued to regard her with that odd intensity. She'd made decisions in the past that had hurt not only her, but the people she loved. If she admitted the truth, that she did love him, that he'd always been the one, and to him it meant nothing more than a casual affair in a long line of casual affairs, it might haunt her for the rest of her long life. And yet, she'd never seen a hint of anything other than complete confidence in his eyes. Now he looked…uncertain. Was it possible he was as nervous as she? Somehow the thought gave her comfort… and confidence. *In for a penny, in for a pound.* She stretched up on her toes and brushed her lips across the fascinating cleft in his chin.

"Yes, Luca. I meant it," she whispered. He closed his eyes and swallowed hard before opening them again with a dazzling smile. Then he swooped down to capture her mouth with his. She melted into him and her lips opened readily to his seeking tongue when he deepened the kiss. Her stomach muscles tightened as he pulled her closer, hitching her up by the waist to give him better access. A jolt of desire unlike anything she'd ever felt slammed through her. Books and fantasies were one thing…but this! His tongue stroked and plundered and Calli was thankful for the strength of his arms around her as her bones dissolved and her knees buckled. She felt the hard, pulsing heat of him against her belly and the force of his heart hammering against her palm and knew he was as affected as she. His hands skimmed along her back, down her spine, cupping her buttocks through her jeans and pulling her even more closely against him. She clung to him desperately as a low growl vibrated in his chest and he pulled away. Puzzled at first, Calli understood as Gia's irritated voice reached them.

"*Il mortacci tuoi.*"

Luca glared at Giovanna. "I know you're upset, Gia, but I don't think it's necessary to curse me and my dead." He looked back at Calli and leaned in for a final quick kiss that left her wanting more. Then he turned her in his arms so they were both facing Gia where she waited on the stairs. Calli was gratified to hear Luca's breathing sounded as ragged and unsteady as hers. She dug deep and pulled out her game face, stiffening her stance and raising her chin as she glared at the woman twisting her fingers nervously on the stairs.

"Well?" Calli asked.

Gia hung her head and sighed.

"I have been fighting someone or something my entire life. I grow tired. Luca, I wished you good fortune and hoped you would find what you were looking for. I hoped, in the end, it would be me. Now it becomes clear that your heart has always belonged to another. Truly, the ashes of loss are bitter on my tongue, but I accept there is no point in waging a battle I can never win. Therefore, I…accept your conditions," Gia finished in a resigned voice.

"Very well," Calli couldn't have been more surprised that her gamble had actually paid off. She acknowledged Gia's announcement with a regal nod. "Let's all go into the kitchen and figure out what our next step should be." With a sweep of her arm, she indicated Gia should precede them. After Gia passed, Luca leaned down and burrowed his lips into Calli's thick hair until they touched her ear.

"*Dio,* Calli, I love it when you go all domineering on me," he laughed softly. She wriggled out of his arms and headed for the kitchen. If she allowed it, he would have her senseless in seconds. She couldn't concentrate with him so close. It hadn't escaped her notice he hadn't said *he* loved *her*. The sudden realization caused her gut to clench. What if she really was simply another conquest?

"Like hell! I most certainly did!" Luca objected fiercely grabbing her arm and spinning her around to face him.

Calli grimaced. She really must try to remember she wasn't locked in a room with no one to hear her thoughts anymore. "No, you asked me if *I* loved *you*, and then you kissed me. That hardly constitutes a declaration, Luca," she argued. His expression softened.

"*Carissima*, you really can't tell?" He let out a long, shaky breath and smiled. "I guess I've struggled with it for so long that when I finally accepted it myself, I forgot to tell you. My bad." He smiled tenderly and took both of her hands in his, bringing them against his chest, right over his heart.

"Calli, right now my heart is so full, I wish I could tell you all of this in my own language, but you wouldn't understand, would you?"

Calli shook her head and stepped closer.

"It sounds a lot more romantic in Italian," he hedged.

"Maybe, but it's a lot more effective if I know what you're actually saying," she countered with a smile.

"Good point. Okay, here goes." He drew in a deep breath and blew it out slowly. Then he stared directly into her eyes. "I love you, Callista McAllister. I love you with every beat of my heart and every breath in my body. You are the missing piece of my soul, and my world was empty without you in it. I loved you yesterday, I love you today, and I will love you tomorrow. *Ti amo per sempre*."

Calli gazed back at him with happy tears pricking the back of her lids. Every word wrapped around her heart and crept deeply into her soul. Her Italian needed work, but she definitely understood *ti amo per sempre.* I love you for all time. She reached for him with a smile.

"*Dio*, Luca. I love it when you go all Italian on me."

Chapter Ten

Long moments later, Calli stopped, shocked into immobility, in the doorway to the kitchen. Luca plowed in to her from behind and pulled her back against him to steady her. Nearly every cabinet stood ajar. An assortment of bowls, spoons, and food items littered the table. Gia struggled to tie a kitchen towel around her waist like an apron. She looked up as they entered and froze. Then a deep flush suffused her olive skin, and she threw the towel onto the table.

"*Mi dispiace...*I don't know what came over me. I forgot myself for a moment," she stammered.

"What the..." Calli began. Luca bent forward and rested his chin on her shoulder.

"Gia bakes. She bakes when she's sad, she bakes when she's happy. She especially bakes when she's upset," Luca said as though it explained everything.

"Oh." Calli could understand that, although she did find it kind of odd that she would do it in someone else's kitchen. But then, it had been an odd sort of day.

"Cal?" Luca stage whispered. "She's really good at it, and I'm really hungry. We sent Maria home, remember?"

Calli sighed and raised a brow in Gia's direction. "Can you talk while you bake?"

Gia looked offended. "*Certo!*"

"Very well, carry on. My *cucina* is your *cucina* or

whatever the appropriate expression is. There should be an extra apron behind the door."

"*Grazie*, Calli." Maria's voluminous apron wrapped around Giovanna twice. She peered into the refrigerator and turned back with her arms loaded.

"*Un crostata di ricotta e spinaci*," she announced triumphantly.

"Ricotta and spinach pie," Luca translated. "Is there enough to make two?"

Gia looked around at the ingredients spread out before her. "*Si*, I think so."

"Excellent!" Luca grinned and Calli shook her head. The man really was a bottomless pit. He pulled out a chair for her and she dropped into it. He pulled up the one next to her and draped an arm across the back of hers cupping her nape in his large hand. His fingers drew tiny circles that concurrently relaxed and excited her. He loved her. She fought the urge to pinch herself, afraid he might notice and have an excuse to be even more arrogant than he already was. She tentatively rested a hand on his thigh. He scooted closer as though it was the most natural thing in the world.

Gia expertly measured flour and salt into a large pottery bowl. She cut a slab of butter into small chunks and began rubbing it into the flour with her fingertips, before adding a small amount of water and quickly working it into soft dough. Calli found herself amazed at the effortless grace with which the other woman worked. To Gia, baking seemed as natural as breathing.

"Gia, I need you to tell me everything you remember. What did the men who came to see you say about this book?" Luca asked.

"Not much," her mouth curled down as a frown

furrowed her brow. She set the dough aside to rest and continued chopping the spinach. "They said Jacques had acquired a book of great power. A very old book." She turned to the stove and dumped the chopped spinach into a pot of boiling water for a few seconds, then deftly drained it in the sink and set it aside as she grabbed another bowl and began cracking eggs. "I'm not certain they know much about it themselves, but it is enough that they believe it has power. The *Fallen* crave power."

"And Enrico?"

Gia's features twisted in grief as she feverishly beat the eggs and dumped the cheese into the bowl, adding the wilted spinach and some crushed garlic, salt, and pepper. Her lower lip trembled as she quickly divided the dough and rolled it into two large circles and a rectangle. She plopped each of the circles into round baking tins, divided the cheese mixture between them, and cut the rectangle into long strips, deftly weaving them into a lattice on the top of each pie before popping both in the oven. The entire process took less than ten minutes. It was obviously nervous energy. Nevertheless, Calli was impressed.

Gia slumped into the chair across from them and put her head in her hands, oblivious to the dough and flour smearing her face as a result.

"I went up to check on him this morning, taking his *cornetti* and *cappuccino* as I do each day. I heard the shower running, so I left everything on the table. I went back down to the shop and it was then I felt the evil. Monte was there. I thought he was alone…I never thought to warn *Zio*. As we pulled away from the shop, Monte made sure I saw his men forcing Enrico into a car...the same men who came to visit me after you left." She raised her head, her expression tortured, her tears streaking the flour on her face like clown makeup. "He didn't even have his leg, Luca. He'll be helpless."

"His leg?" Calli asked in confusion.

"Enrico was a *Defensori*. He lost a leg to a Hell-blade around the turn of the century. He wears a prosthesis," Luca explained.

"You said he isn't related by blood, Gia. How did you come to be with him?" Calli asked.

"After his injury, the couple who raised me came to work for him. They had always served *Earthbounds*...I suppose that's how my mother became acquainted with them," she added. "I was about thirteen, I think, and of course *Zio* realized at once what I was. A half-breed. He also saw the way I was being treated. He sent them away, and claimed me as his own. I've never told him who my father was. I was afraid he would disown me. He saved my life. And now I may have cost him his." Her face crumpled and she dissolved into tears.

"The last word I'd ever associate with Enrico Moscato is helpless, Gia, with or without his leg," Luca reassured her. "He's deadly. We just have to buy him some time. And you should know him well enough by now to realize he would never hold you accountable for the sins of your father."

"About this book," Calli began, turning to Luca and shaking her head. "I don't believe Jacques had it. He had an extensive library, and I read every book he possessed. Twice. A century is a long time to entertain oneself," she clarified when Luca's brows went up. "If he had some book of power, he would have told me."

"How can you be so sure, *dolcezza*?"

"How do you think I knew about the Ring of Aandalena?" Calli returned reasonably. "He liked to brag, he couldn't wait to tell me about his plan to get it. I suppose he was still trying to impress me." She laughed without humor. "Nothing else worked. Maybe he hoped I would find power attractive…wait a minute," Calli straightened. "The witch, Luca! You remember I told you Miranda said she took care of Nicola…she said she didn't have the ring but she had something else. She used Dark Magick. I know it! What if *she* had this book? Do you think Katrina might know something?"

Luca stroked his jaw. "I doubt it. Kat had no idea what she was before she met Mac, and she and her cousin were never close. But we can call her later and ask."

"The only person I've ever met with more thirst for power than a *Fallen* was that woman, Luca. I don't believe she ever intended to give Jacques the ring. I think she was using him to help her find it and planned to use it against him when she finally got her hands on it. And he was using her to get either the ring, or this book, or both. I can't think of any other reason he would have kept her around. She was an evil, malignant woman. If she had this book, she might have made promises, but she would never have handed it over," Callista stated emphatically. "That has to be it. Jacques never actually had it, though I wouldn't put it past him to brag to someone that he did."

Giovanna had stopped crying. Her eyes had taken on a speculative gleam as she listened avidly to the conversation between Luca and Calli. Her sudden interest did not go unnoticed by either of them.

"The witch is dead, *dolcezza,* so we may never know the truth," Luca redirected the conversation. "In the meantime, we have to find a safe place for Gia and discover where they are holding Enrico."

"But if we had the book, we could trade it for Enrico," Gia interjected. "If she knows where the book is, let her say so!"

"She doesn't and even if she did, we couldn't trade it for Enrico, Gia. Use your head," Luca admonished in a hard voice. "First, if you handed power on a platter over to the *Fallen*, even to save his life, Enrico would kick your ass into the second Tuesday of next week. Furthermore, if they get what they want, he's of no further use to them. They have nothing to lose by killing him."

Giovanna's shoulders slumped. Luca was right on both counts.

"What about Mariana's family?" Calli said suddenly. "Maybe we could take Giovanna there."

"I have a… family?" Gia whispered in a stunned voice.

"Of course you do. Grandparents, an uncle, and a couple of cousins at the very least."

Giovanna's expression twisted with bitterness. "I doubt they'll appreciate my showing up on their doorstep. They can't have wanted me anymore than my mother did, otherwise they would have raised me themselves."

"Is that what you think?" Calli cried in sudden understanding. "Oh, Giovanna you couldn't be more wrong. Your mother wanted you with every fiber of her being. When she realized she wasn't going to survive the birth, she sent you away because she was afraid her family was the first place Jacques would look for you."

Giovanna was quiet for several minutes. When at last she spoke, her voice was a harsh whisper. "All my life, I thought...I thought it was because she couldn't bear the sight of me...because I was the child of a dark one." She looked at Calli with stricken eyes. "I thought...she hated me."

"Mariana loved you, Gia," Calli shook her head. "Times were different then, and it would have caused quite a scandal, but she would have suffered it to keep you with her. It broke her heart that she would never see you smile, never hear you laugh. It broke her heart that you would never know her."

"I don't even know what she looked like," Gia whispered brokenly. "To have seen her, even once, to have some memory, some knowledge of where I came from."

"When we get this mess all sorted out, we'll take you to London to meet your grandmother," Calli offered gently. "She has a beautiful portrait of your mother hanging in the parlor. If they're still in London, that is. Regardless, we'll track them down. I can't imagine she wouldn't still have it wherever she may be living now. But until then, though I can't give you your mother back, Giovanna, I *can* give you this." Calli opened her mind and let Giovanna share her memories of Mariana. She slammed a thick mental door on every detail of that final, ugly night when Gia came into the world and allowed the girl to see only the good things. The fun she and Mariana had, the places they'd traveled, the pranks they'd pulled, usually on Luca and Kassian. But most of all, Calli showed her the love and laughter between two friends closer than sisters. By the time she closed the door on her memories, Calli's eyes burned and her heart ached with recollection and tears sketched a wet path through the traces of flour smearing Gia's enraptured face.

"You humble me with the capacity of your heart, cara." Luca's voice brushed her mind.

"Grazie, Calli. *Mille grazie,"* Gia murmured in an unsteady voice. "To see her as she was, to see her through your eyes…I never expected…I…it seems I am in your debt once again. This debt I can never repay." The profound moment shattered when Gia suddenly jumped from her chair. *"Merda,* I forgot the pies!"

Using the apron to protect her hands she yanked open the door and pulled the pans from the oven. They were a shade too brown, but they smelled divine and Calli laughed when Luca's belly rumbled in response. Gia cut a generous wedge for Calli and one for herself, and simply handed Luca a fork and set the rest of the pie in front of him with a knowing smirk. Calli wasn't sure what irked her more. The fact that Gia was obviously well acquainted with Luca's enormous appetite or the fact that the *crostada* was the best she'd ever eaten.

"You should taste her *cornetti,*" Luca rolled his eyes and mumbled over a mouthful of the savory pie. Calli gave him a look that required neither word nor telepathic communication to convey her thoughts. Luca blinked and continued eating, wisely keeping any further culinary opinions to himself.

Calli and Giovanna finished first and began to clear the table and rinse the soiled dishes in the large farmhouse style sink before loading them into the modern dishwasher. Luca had no sooner put the last bite into his mouth when his cell phone jangled in his back pocket. He fished it out and checked the display. A calculating look came into his eyes.

"*Dio*, it's a beautiful thing when a plan comes together, especially since I didn't really have one in the first place." He tapped the screen and lifted the phone to his ear.

"*Pronto?*" Luca listened for a moment, looked at Calli, and winked. "Yeah, Michael, we know who's been asking questions about Mariana, too. I'm glad you called." His brows drew together. "Yes, *really.*"

Luca waved the phone in the air and stepped out the back door into the garden for privacy, snicking the door closed quietly behind him. Calli watched him go, mesmerized by his high, firm backside encased in tight denim and the play of muscles rippling across his broad back under his snug, black cashmere sweater. *She'd become completely shameless.* She favored Giovanna with a dark, threatening look when she realized the other woman was admiring the same view. Gia quickly averted her eyes, gathered up the remaining dishes, and carried them to the sink. They worked together in uneasy silence to clear and wipe down the counters and table. When everything was back in order, Luca still hadn't come in.

"Well, I guess we may as well sit down..." Calli offered, waving Giovanna into a chair and taking one herself. "So, how long have you and Enrico lived in Rome?"

"We first moved here in, let's see, I think about nineteen hundred and five. We moved around for a few decades until anyone who might recognize the fact that we weren't growing older as we should was gone. We came back about eight years ago."

"Is that when you met Luca?" Calli struggled between wanting to know every detail and wanting to ignore the affair altogether.

"No, I met him just three years ago. He was in the city and came to visit Enrico. *Zio* and Luca's father had been great friends." Giovanna opened and closed her mouth as if unsure whether to continue. "Luca spends most of his time in the States. I did not see him often and he never led me to believe there would be anything more. I hoped of course…but, well, I would not want you to think badly of him. He was always honest with me." She finished in a rush.

"Well, er, thank you for that, I think. But, there is nothing you could say that would make me think badly of Luca Fiorelli. I know what kind of man he is, and I've loved him for longer than you've been alive, Giovanna." Calli hated that her words would cut, but in the end, she was really doing Gia a kindness. It would be crueler to let the woman cling to the hope of any kind of future with Luca. Callista McAllister had waited well over a hundred years to capture his heart. Any woman who wanted to challenge her for it would have to pry it out of her cold, dead fingers.

"Good to know, *dolcezza*," Luca grinned from the doorway. A guilty flush colored Calli's cheeks. She hadn't heard him come in. He crossed to stand behind Calli's chair and began to knead her shoulders. Now that he felt the freedom to do so, it seemed he couldn't stop touching her. And she didn't mind in the least, rubbing her cheek against his forearm like a contented kitten.

"Well, the good news is I've found a place where Gia will be completely untouchable," Luca began, but anything further he had been about to say was interrupted by a loud pop that coincided with the appearance of Michael the Archangel in the McAllister kitchen. Both Calli and Gia jumped, but Luca didn't react at all.

"Fiorelli," Michael growled with a curt nod.

"Your Grace," Luca mocked inclining his head slightly. He wore the odd expression of a man attempting to look grave while biting back a smile. Michael, on the other hand, offered an impressive imitation of a thundercloud personified. Luca seemed to be enjoying every minute of it.

Michael started toward Luca, hands clenched, jaw rigid. Then he seemed to remember they weren't alone and pulled up short. He uncurled his fists slowly.

"Hello, Callista. How are you, child?" He offered Calli a benevolent smile.

"I'm very well, thank you. And you?" Calli replied.

Michael blinked. "Me? No one ever asks me how I am. I just…am. I mean, I'm uh, fine. Thank you for asking." He shook his head slightly and turned to Gia who sat ramrod straight and saucer eyed. "And you must be Giovanna." He bowed slightly in her direction. She remained frozen.

"Michael," Luca hissed quietly. "Wings."

"Oh! Damn, I forgot," the Archangel muttered before folding his massive wings out of sight with the same effortless efficiency Calli had witnessed at their previous meeting.

"Gia, this is Michael. Who likes to preen and then pretend it was an accident. You're going to be staying with him for a while," Luca smirked.

"I am?" Giovanna looked absolutely terrified.

"It's really the best solution, *signorina*," Michael began while glaring at Luca. "The *Castel* is impenetrable. Besides, your uncle is most anxious about you." He concluded, turning back to Gia with a dazzling smile.

"Enrico? But how…"

"After the attempts on Calli and me, and with the increased *Fallen* activity in the city, Michael augmented the *Defensori* presence in the neighborhoods around the *Castel*. You weren't the only one who saw Enrico being forced into a car," Luca grinned.

"Do you mean...he's safe? He's okay?" Gia breathed as though hardly daring to believe it could be true.

"If by okay you mean cranky, critical, and worried sick about you, then yes, Giovanna, he's perfectly fine," Michael confirmed with a sigh. "He's back at the *Castel* waiting for us. I would have brought him along, but he's having a little difficulty getting around without his prosthesis. I'll send men to retrieve it once I'm sure your place isn't being watched. Monte and his cohorts will have no idea where either of you are. I imagine that will aggravate the hell out of them." The thought seemed to cheer him considerably.

Gia unexpectedly leapt from her chair and threw herself at the imposing figure of the Archangel. Though she was a tall woman, with Michael standing at his full height, she could barely reach his neck, so she settled for wrapping her arms around his waist and sobbing her thanks and relief in a torrent of rapid fire Italian into his midsection. Michael's expression hovered between incredulous and pained. He looked first to Luca and then to Calli for direction on how to deal with the nearly hysterical woman. Luca raised a brow and shrugged, but his usual bland expression held a hint of mischief. Calli simply bit her lip and tried not to grin. Michael glared at both of them, then rolled his eyes, and patted Gia awkwardly on the back with his big hand, looking decidedly uncomfortable.

"Hey, try flashing your wings again, big guy," Luca suggested. "That stunned her into silence before."

"One of these days, Fiorelli..." the Archangel growled.

"Promises, promises, Your Grace," Luca retorted with a cheeky grin.

Finally, Giovanna's sobs subsided to happy little hiccoughs and she seemed to belatedly become aware of her actions. With a gasp she stepped back and craned her neck to assess Michael's reaction to her unanticipated outburst. He schooled his features into a pleasant expression and Gia visibly relaxed. She turned to Luca and Calli.

"*Grazie*, for... everything. It is more than I deserve after the way I behaved. And Calli, after this has all been settled, I-I would like to meet my grandmother...if you really think she would welcome me, I mean."

"I have no doubt she will welcome you with open arms and great joy, Giovanna," Calli took the few steps needed to embrace Gia. She was Mariana's daughter, after all, and Calli could not fault her for resorting to desperate measures to keep Luca. Calli herself would do whatever it took if anyone threatened to take him from her now. She wouldn't hold Gia's behavior against her. This time. As she wrapped her arms around the young woman, she was surprised to feel a faint frisson of sensation along her spine. It was so mild that she almost thought she'd imagined it, but no, it was definitely there. Maybe Michael had been right and her ability to sense evil was coming back on its own now that she wasn't constantly exposed to it.

"I'll call Mac and update him on the situation. Not sure what he'll make of it. I know you wanted us to stay in Rome, but it may be necessary to head back to the States. Can you spare some men to keep an eye on Madge in Fiesole if we need to travel?" Luca asked Michael.

Michael nodded. "Don't worry about Madge. I'll get someone up there and if necessary, I'll bring her back to the *Castel*. Monte will be nearly impossible to touch. He isn't your average *Fallen* who can be taken out with no questions asked. His high profile guarantees an investigation if he suddenly disappears. You'll need to tread carefully, Luca." He hesitated, glancing worriedly at Callista. "If, as I suspect, this book really is the Key of Azakriel, Monte will stop at nothing to have it. We've effectively removed Giovanna and Enrico from his reach. You understand what this means?"

A chill moved through Calli and she shivered as understanding dawned.

"He'll come for the person he believes knows its location," she whispered. "He'll come for me."

Luca pulled her into his arms and nodded shortly, his expression glacial. "He can try, *dolcezza*. He can try."

Chapter Eleven

Kassian McAllister disconnected the call and shoved his cell phone roughly into the back pocket of his jeans. He raked a hand through his long, dark hair. He sure as hell hadn't gotten his sister back to lose her to some overachieving *Fallen* with an agenda and delusions of grandeur. Michael was right. They couldn't simply eliminate Ignazio Monte without provoking a lot of questions and unwanted attention, but there had to be a way to get rid of the bastard. Or at least neutralize his threat. Anyway, if Kassian couldn't be in Rome himself at the moment, he could rest easy knowing Calli was with Luca. Luca hadn't said a word that gave anything away during the tense call, but Kassian knew him long enough and well enough to recognize that something had changed back in Rome between his sister and his best friend. Added to Kat's uncanny intuition, by the time the call ended, his wife grinned from ear to ear.

"I guess you called that one, baby," he sighed.

Kat grinned. "Well, I *would* say I told you so if we didn't have more important things to worry about at the moment. Oh, who am I kidding? I told you so, McAllister. I'll let you reward me for my shrewdness later. Luca sounds happy, doesn't he?"

"Yeah."

His wife frowned. "They're perfect for each other,

Kassian. Why don't you look happier about it?"

"It's not that I'm not happy about it," Kassian began. "It's just…"

"What?"

"Kat, I've know your brother a lot longer than you have and I know you love him, but let's face facts, he's been kind of a man-whore for years. Don't get me wrong, Luca is the best man I know, *Earthbound* or human. I just don't want Callista to get hurt."

Kat rolled her eyes. "Okay, we've already established the fact that Luca hasn't exactly been noted for long term, committed relationships, but can you please stop calling him a man-whore? And honestly, has he ever actually treated a woman badly?"

Kassian thought about that for a minute. "No, but that's not the point. This isn't any woman. This is my baby sister we're talking about."

"Callista isn't a baby. She's a three hundred year old woman who knows her own mind and her own heart. She managed to survive over a century with a psychotic serial killer and come out on the other side with her sanity and disposition intact. Luca loves her, McAllister. Truly, deeply, completely, to the exclusion of everyone and everything else. Luca loves your sister the way I love you. So maybe it took him a little while to figure it out and work up the courage to have faith in it. He doesn't trust his heart easily, you know that, but he's learning." Kat stretched up on her toes to plant a kiss on her husband's jaw. "You know Luca as well as anyone. If he's finally worked up the nerve to acknowledge his feelings, and she feels the same way about him, which I am absolutely positive she does, he won't let anything or anyone come between them.

Certainly not Monte and his goons. Not even a big, cocky *Defensori* like you, my love, even if you are her adored older brother. Get over yourself."

"Yeah." Kassian sighed. She made a valid point, but…well, it felt strange. He couldn't think of anyone he would rather have at Callista's side. Luca would always treat her well and keep her safe. And Kat was right. Luca didn't trust his heart or give it away easily. If it truly belonged to Callista, McAllister knew it was forever. What more could a brother want for his sister? He would get used to the idea. Eventually. He just had difficulty picturing Luca as—relationship material. Then again, he guessed there were those who'd thought the same thing about him once and yet he'd never been happier. His wife was the best thing that had ever happened to him in his hundreds of years of existence. In any event, the first order of business was to figure out what their next move should be.

"Luca said Calli thinks the book may have belonged to Miranda. She seemed pretty convinced Jacques never had possession of it. What do you think?" he asked his wife.

"McAllister, you're well aware I didn't even know my mother was a witch until I met you and Luca, so I have no idea what Miranda may or may not have had," Kat frowned. "And she wasn't exactly my favorite person so we didn't do a lot of warm and fuzzy."

"Did she say anything when she had you in the cave?" Kassian asked.

"I do remember something about a grimoiré." A worried crease appeared between Kat's eyes as she looked up at him. "She said something about using it to get rid of my father. I'm sorry I don't remember if there was anything else. I was a little preoccupied at the time, what with trying to escape from a serial killer, keeping you and Luca from barging in and getting yourselves killed, and discovering your sister was alive."

Kassian folded her into his arms and stroked her back. He would never tire of feeling this woman against him, and never cease to wonder how he had been lucky enough to find her. If Luca felt for Calli even half of what Kassian felt for Kat, he supposed he had no choice but to be happy for them.

"Grimoiré is a nonspecific term for any book of magic, Kat. If Miranda did have the key and was calling it a grimoiré, chances are she either had no idea what it really was, or was unsure how to unlock its secrets. If that's the case, it might still be there packed in a box," Kassian replied thoughtfully. "I'll call Dimitri to have him go out to your place and start going through Miranda's things. He can make arrangements to ship anything that looks promising or suspicious back to New York. We'll go through it all when we get home. I just hope to hell Michael is wrong."

Kat had been Miranda's only living relative. Upon the evil bitch's death, Kassian had done little more than have his people pack up and padlock her home and business, call the local animal shelter to retrieve the cats, and hire a local estate agent to keep an eye on things. He'd then had all of the boxes shipped to his wife's family home in the Pennsylvania mountains until the McAllisters returned from Italy.

"You'd better warn him that Elle might be there," Kat laughed, referring to her best friend. "She asked if she could camp out at the house for some down time to finish her edits. She's on deadline and though she adores her editor, she claims the CEO is an unforgiving slave driver. At least that's what she tells me. Personally, I've found him to be *exceptionally* accommodating."

Kassian rolled his eyes and nodded. "Thanks for reminding me. I'll let him know. Elle Gates shouldn't be sprung on any unsuspecting person without notice."

Kat laughed and thumped a fist into her husband's chest. "McAllister! C'mon, you know you love her!"

"No, I know *you* love her, therefore I'm willing to tolerate her. Frankly, she is a little too hyper for my taste. Translation? She makes my teeth ache. Then again, she does make me boatloads of money," he grinned. Elle wasn't just Kat's best friend she was a prolific best-selling romance author under contract with McAllister Publishing.

"Well, thank goodness for that since we're in such dire financial straits," Kat mocked. Then she sobered. "Is this book really so much of a threat, Kassian? I mean, if it *is* this Key of Azakriel, Miranda must have had it lying around somewhere for years. How dangerous could it be?"

"Short version? Azakriel is the demon of the abyss, synonymous with death and destruction." He swore under his breath. "Damn Michael anyway."

"McAllister!" Kat gasped. "He's an Archangel, your boss, and my...I don't know, bizillion times removed great grandfather?"

"You know I'm loyal to him, Kat," he assured her. "But millennia ago he was young and impulsive, a far cry from the wise and fearsome leader he is today. When his daughter Aandalena married a human and forfeited her immortality in the bargain, it nearly broke him. He secretly provided her with supernatural objects as a means of protecting her and her descendants."

"He was being a father first, Kassian. You can hardly fault him for that."

"Look, I can understand his desire to take care of his own, but he didn't have the authority at the time to meddle in mortal affairs. He thought with his heart not his head."

"We've all been guilty of that at some point, my love. So, the ring bestowed the power to control demons and the key provided a means to bind them?"

"In a nutshell? Yes. Not that taking Azakriel out of circulation was a bad idea, but after a few centuries, Michael became more and more preoccupied with his responsibilities and managed to lose track of not only his descendants, but of his creations, too."

"So you're saying the ring wasn't a one and done kind of deal?"

"Hardly. He's never actually admitted how many objects might be out there. He's been trying to find them for centuries and every now and then, something turns up. Now that we've returned the ring to him, at least that's safely beyond the reach of the *Fallen,* but if the they get their hands on the key? They'll have the means to release Azakriel. Yeah, baby, it really is that much of a threat."

"But Michael has the ring back now," Kat mused thoughtfully. "Even if the *Fallen* manage to release Azakriel, the ring can be used to regain control of him, right?"

"Theoretically," Kassian agreed. "But the demon could wreak a hell of a lot of mayhem in the interim."

"If only I'd been paying more attention," Kat

groaned into his shirtfront.

"Like you said, you were a little preoccupied at the time."

Kassian pressed his lips to her silvery hair breathing in the scent that was uniquely his wife. His groin swelled in reaction despite the gravity of the situation. Kassian suspected the world could be tumbling down around his ears and he would still be preoccupied with losing himself in his wife's sweet and willing body. His hands cupped her rounded buttocks through the snug denim spanning her backside and hitched her even closer, leaving her in no doubt as to where his mind had wandered.

"There's no way you could have known about it, Kat. Hell, that book disappeared centuries ago. There was even speculation it might've been destroyed. Figures it turning up would have something to do with Rapier. Even dead that bastard still has a hand in making our lives miserable."

Kat wrapped her arms around his neck and pressed herself against him, lifting her face to his. "Well, if you're back to thinking about Rapier, I guess the honeymoon is over," she sighed.

"We do have to head back to Rome, and then probably the States," he confirmed with a growl against her lips. "But, the honeymoon is a long way from over, and I'm definitely not thinking about good ole' Jacques right this minute."

"Really?" she murmured into his mouth. A glint of mischief danced in her thickly fringed silver eyes. "Are you sure we shouldn't get moving? Luca said Calli could be in danger." She tangled her fingers in the long, dark hair at his nape and tugged. "We can't let them get to her, Kassian. Not again."

"We won't," he promised, hoisting her up until she twined her legs around his waist and locked her ankles behind him. "She's safe for now. Luca won't let anything happen to her. My mother is out on the grounds with the landscapers checking out what's left of the vineyard to see if it's worth salvaging. Your brother could have mentioned he'd let this place go to ruin for the last twenty-five years before he gave it to you."

"Don't you dare call my villa a ruin!" Kat protested with a smile. "I absolutely love this place. It's perfect."

"A perfect disaster," Kassian conceded as he nibbled on her full bottom lip. "It's barely habitable. Lucky for you your husband is wealthy. It's going to cost a small fortune to restore this place. On the upside, at least there aren't any grocery stores nearby." When they met, Kat had been appalled to learn Kassian hired people to do his grocery shopping. Since then she'd insisted on dragging him along on a shopping expedition at least once a week. Between the senior citizens, coupon clippers, long lines, and whining kids it was *so* not his cup of tea. He couldn't see the point in torturing himself when it was twice as easy to give one of his assistants a list and pay them to do it, but Kat actually enjoyed the challenge of comparison shopping and saving money even if she no longer needed to. It was a small enough thing that made his wife happy, so he went along with it even though it made him want to jab needles in his eyes.

"Mmm...lucky you. There is the market in town, though," Kat pointed out as she feathered kisses along his jawline. Kassian didn't mind strolling around the market in the small *piazza* hand in hand with her nearly as much as he balked at pushing a shopping cart around a crowded American supermarket. He rocked his hips against the juncture of her thighs where her long legs straddled him, letting her feel the hard evidence of how much he enjoyed her tender attention. She gasped and wove her fingers more deeply into in his hair tugging him closer and flexing her thighs around his torso. "Shouldn't we start packing?"

"The next train doesn't leave for hours," he whispered against her throat as she tipped her head back to allow him better access. "Guess we'll have to find something to do until then. Got any ideas?" He captured her mouth in a searing kiss and felt the rising heat of her right through the fabric where their bodies pressed together.

There was no rush. Luca was with Callista and the *Via Dandolo* house was well protected by *sigils*. They couldn't go anywhere until Michael's men arrived to stay with his mother, anyway. He'd call Dimitri to warn him about Elle later. And if the imposing *Defensori* headed to Kat's place before Kassian had a chance to give him a heads up? Well, Dimitri was a well-seasoned warrior. Surely he could handle one small, slightly ditzy woman. Kassian decided to let the rest of the world take care of itself for a while. He was already busy contemplating some very pleasant and creative ways to fill the next couple of hours. He headed for the stairs with his wife tangled around him. The bedroom renovations had been completed before they even arrived from Rome after the wedding. Kassian had insisted it be the first priority. It was, after all, the most important room in the house.

Chapter Twelve

While Luca discussed strategies on the phone with her brother in the other room, Callista stood in the kitchen doorway looking out over the back garden that had been left to run riot within the walls of the villa. Her mother spent little time keeping up with it since Calli's rescue and their arrival en mass from New York. The few blooms interspersed throughout the verdant greenery were yielding their colors to the approaching darkness while the umbrella pines she glimpsed beyond the wall stood stark and clear against the fading orange and gold of the twilight sky. It was beautiful here and it spoke to her in a way no other place ever had. She understood why her mother had established a residence here and why Luca had always been drawn back. Personally, she wouldn't mind staying here forever.

Michael and Giovanna were long gone, headed back to the *Castel* to reunite Gia and Enrico. She heard footfalls behind her but still jumped as Luca's arms snaked around her waist and pulled her back against him. Every time he entered a room Calli felt as though all of the air had been sucked out. He made her breathless simply by being. Now that they were actually alone in the house, Calli felt incredibly shaky. She was safe with Luca, maybe safer than she'd ever been in her life. So why did she have a flock of butterflies playing tag in her stomach and beads of moisture trickling down her neck beneath her hair? Luca believed she had been the unwilling recipient of Rapier's twisted passions. He would expect her to be experienced in intimacy when in truth she was a bumbling novice without a clue of what to do or what to expect other than what she'd read in books. Earlier, she'd been too caught up in the moment to give it much thought, but now that she'd had time to consider the step she was poised to take, mild panic set in. She was bound to disappoint him, and then he would realize he didn't really love her at all, he loved an illusion she couldn't live up to.

She shivered and Luca turned her fully into his embrace and held her tightly against him. Of course, that position just emphasized the fact that his hard arousal hadn't abated in the least, which sent her into another fit of trembling.

"*Cara*, what is it? Are you cold?" Luca peered worriedly into her eyes and ran his hands briskly up and down her arms, though the temperature in the room was quite comfortable.

"No, I…I'm not cold," she whispered, resting her forehead against his chest. "I'm fine. I…I'm just…" Calli trailed off. She had no idea how to talk to him about this. She'd missed the sexual revolution. In her day, this wasn't a conversation an unattached woman had with a man, even the one to whom she'd completely given her heart. "I guess I'm a little scared."

Luca's arms tightened around her. "Monte will never get near you, *cara*. I swear it. No one will ever threaten you again." He pressed his lips against her hair. "Ignazio Monte will pay for frightening you. He deserves to die for that alone, as far as I'm concerned."

"I'm not afraid of Monte, Luca," she whispered. "I'm not like the other women you've been with, you see. The truth is I'm afraid of…you."

"Me?" He hooked a forefinger under her chin and tilted her face to his. Tears welled in her eyes threatening to overflow and tumble down her cheeks. She looked away, unable to meet his eyes.

"Well, not you, exactly. It's …I'm afraid of disappointing you."

"Baby, look at me. I can't change what happened, but I can promise you whatever you experienced with Rapier, it was not the way it was meant to be."

"Luca, you don't understand. He never…" Calli began. But Luca seemed not to hear.

"He died too easily. If I had it to do over, *dolcezza*, his death would be far more painful. He would suffer endless agonies for every single time he dared to touch you," Luca whispered in a voice vibrating with suppressed fury as he smoothed her hair away from her face. His accent, barely noticeable most of the time, had thickened considerably.

Calli's heart filled with tenderness at the pain and frustration she heard in his voice and she laid a soft hand on Luca's cheek. He held it there with his own larger one and turned his lips into her palm. She melted inside. This was the man she'd longed for and dreamed of. This was the man whose arms she imagined holding her and keeping her safe through the endless nights when she'd been uncertain and afraid. This was the man she'd been sure she would never have. And yet, here he stood, holding her close and trembling with rage on her behalf.

"Callista McAllister, I love you. I know it took me

long enough to say it, but the truth is I fell flat on my face for you over a century ago and I don't think I've ever gotten back up. I want to make love to you maybe more than I can ever make you understand. But it doesn't mean anything if you don't want it, too. It doesn't make the slightest difference to me that I'm not your first. *Carissima*, when I take you to my bed, fear has no place there. If you aren't ready for this, then we wait. However long you need. However long it takes. I'm here. I'm not going anywhere."

Calli reached up with her other hand and cupped his face bringing his lips down to hers. She kissed him, not with passion, but with love. Pure, perfect, and unadulterated love. When she drew back at last, Luca's eyes shimmered with moisture and she knew he understood what she'd been telling him without thoughts or words. She wasn't going anywhere either.

"Can I say something now?"

Luca lost himself in the brilliant sapphire sheen of her large eyes brimming with love and unshed tears. When she looked at him like that she could ask him to walk across St. Peter's square. Naked. In January. At noon on Sunday. In the middle of the Angelus. He would comply without a second thought. In that moment, he understood Kat was right. If fate took Calli away tomorrow, he would gladly bear the pain to have the feeling filling his heart right now, to see that exact look in Calli's eyes, and to experience this precise moment in time. Some things really were worth the risk. Loving Calli, and being loved by her in return, was worth the risk. Yeah, Kat was right. It didn't do his pride any good to admit it, but she usually was.

"Well?" She repeated.

"Oh, sorry. Yeah, sure, *cara*…what did you want to say?"

"He never touched me."

"What?"

"I *said*, Jacques Rapier never touched me. Well, not in the way you mean." Calli flushed. "Inflicting pain was his addiction, Luca, not sex. I've tried to tell you before but do you know, I think you have a real problem with listening? At first, I think he was waiting until he could use my death, or at least the manner of my death, to torture my brother. But then, and don't ask me why or how because I have no idea, he decided he was in love with me. When he felt the madness gaining the upper hand, he made me lock myself in my room and he stayed away."

Luca shook his head in disbelief. "But he must have wanted you Calli. How could he not? Are you telling me he never *acted* on it in all those years?"

"Aside from a few chaste kisses, that's exactly what I'm telling you." She fisted her hands and dropped them to her sides. "You don't believe me. I can hear it in your voice. You've already told me it doesn't matter to you. Why would I lie?"

Luca reached for her and tugged her little fists back against his chest, right over his heart, and covered them with his hands.

"Of course I believe you, *cara.* I'm just…surprised." *And isn't that the understatement of the year,* he thought. Try shocked, confused, elated, relieved, and a laundry list of emotions he couldn't even begin to identify. Surprised didn't seem to cover it at all. "I'm just trying to understand how a madman who had you at his mercy and claimed to love you could have shown such restraint for over a century. I know I promised to wait until you're ready, and I mean it. But a hundred years? I'm not sure even I have that much fortitude."

"Jacques was impotent," Calli said flatly. "The only time the man became aroused was when he inflicted pain. Fear was like…oh, what's the name of that drug in the television advertisements that helps men…well, you know. Fear was that drug for him. In fact, I confess I often wondered how he ever managed to get Mariana pregnant…but maybe he was different then. No, forget I said that. I really don't want to know and it's probably better not to dwell on it too closely. Part of him truly wanted to be different. I really believe that, Luca. I think as long as he could restrain himself where I was concerned, as long as he could continue to exert control over at least one little area, I think he still had hope. But the madness combined with his natural predisposition for evil as a *Fallen* was too strong for him ever to overcome. I think it's terribly sad, really."

Luca blew out a breath he didn't realize he'd been holding in a long, low whistle. He'd seen the aftermath of Jacques' madness up close and personal. He couldn't ascribe any goodness to the monster at all. But if it made Calli feel better to think Rapier had some redeeming qualities, he wouldn't disabuse her of the notion. It made no difference now. Whatever she needed to believe in order to cope, he was totally on board. They'd all noticed a softness in Calli's attitude toward Rapier after her rescue. Kat had even suggested Calli might be suffering from Stockholm Syndrome. Luca thought it more likely her generous heart always managed to find some sliver of goodness in everyone.

Even a murderous psychopath. No wonder that bastard had loved her. His brows drew together.

"What about the witch, *cara*? I thought they were sleeping together?"

Calli looked away and this time she colored to the roots of her hair. "Well, I think Miranda liked things, a little, um…rough. Some sadomasochism, a little Dark Magick and voila! Jacques Rapier at her service. Literally."

"Sadomasochism, Cal? And exactly how do you know about sadomasochism?" Luca schooled his features into a stern expression.

"I told you, I read a lot!" She gasped as Luca suddenly lifted her clear of the floor. He spun her in circles and threw back his head, chuffing out a laugh of pure relief.

"You're making me dizzy!" she squealed. Luca set her on her feet, but kept his arms around her, holding her close, and breathing heavily.

"For someone who claimed it made no difference, you're awfully happy to discover I'm as pure as the driven snow."

Luca buried his fingers in her hair, and stroked his thumbs softly along her jawline until she finally raised her eyes to his.

"I am incredibly happy, *cara*, that you are, as you put it, as pure as the driven snow, but not for the reasons you're obviously thinking. I haven't exactly been a monk, so it would stretch the limits of hypocrisy if I held you to a different standard, don't you think?"

"I know you weren't a monk, Luca. Kassian said you were a man-whore," Calli added quietly. "While I'm not familiar with the term itself, it doesn't take a genius to figure out what it means."

"Your brother has a very big mouth," Luca grimaced. "For years after I believed you were dead, I lay awake nights wondering what horrors you'd had to suffer before you found release from this world. I couldn't share it with anyone. Your family was my family, and they were suffering enough without me adding to it. I was so angry, Calli. *So* angry. I was angry at you for leaving. I was angry at myself because I hadn't been there to save you. Anger was the only thing I allowed myself to feel for a long, long time. Otherwise, I think the grief would have destroyed me. Finally, I managed to find some kind of peace in believing that however bad it had been, at least you were beyond it in death."

"You thought about me? You...missed me?"

"Not all the time," Luca chuckled without mirth. "Only when I was breathing."

Calli blinked rapidly and swallowed hard.

"When my father lost Lilly, he escaped into his anguish until it killed him," he continued in a hoarse voice while staring fixedly at some invisible point on the wall. "Yeah, I know now there were other forces at work, but I sure as hell didn't know it then. All I knew was I hadn't been important enough for him to want to live. And I feared if I allowed myself, I could go down that same road. I made a conscious decision not to...feel. I got to be so good at it, even *I* sometimes had trouble recognizing the real Luca Fiorelli from the fable I'd created. No one ever understood how much I buried inside except maybe Mac and your mother. Alec to a lesser degree. And no one else ever got close, at least until Kat came along. She had my number in no time and wormed her way right into my heart. Heaven knows it's next to impossible to hide much of anything from my sister and her gifts." He took a deep breath. "And then there you were. Alive. That's when it hit me, that for all of those endless years I believed you were beyond pain, you were still living a nightmare and I hadn't done a damn thing to stop it. I'd given up, simply gone on with my life. I should have known you were still out there somewhere. I should have felt it, should have kept looking. It ate at me from the inside out and then, being in your company hurt. It was like looking into a mirror and seeing nothing except how badly I'd failed you. *Dio*, Calli, how I failed you. I am so sorry."

He wrapped his arms around her and buried his face in her hair.

"So you see, my happiness isn't for myself. Having you alive and in my arms is the only happiness I'll ever ask for, and more than I ever expected. My happiness is for you, that you were never subjected to any of the horrible scenes my imagination painted in my head."

"Oh, Luca," Calli choked. She reached up to stroke his hair as though comforting a child. "It wasn't your fault. None of it. Whatever did or didn't happen, it wasn't your fault. It wasn't anyone's fault. You and Kass went hunting for Jacques, you could have done no less. I went to help Mariana. I could have done no less. We all acted in accordance with our natures. It was simply an unfortunate series of events and decisions that culminated in my being in exactly the wrong place at exactly the wrong time. No one could have known I still lived after all these years. *No one*. You have to stop blaming yourself for things beyond your control and let it go." She nudged his head up and offered him a small smile. "If it makes you feel any better, my memories of you were what got me through the worst times. It never occurred to me you would ever think about me once I was gone. I was sure you saw me as nothing but a reckless child. I never believed I would even see you again. Still, keeping you alive in my heart gave me something to hold on to. Even now, it's so hard to believe it's over that sometimes I wonder if I've finally lost my mind and simply imagine that Jacques is dead and you're here. Maybe I'm really still locked in a room waiting for a madman to join me for tea."

Humbled by her confession, he pulled back and looked directly into her eyes. "If you've lost your mind and this is all a dream, *carissima,* I'm right here with you and no one better try to wake me up. Jacques is most definitely dead. I'm most definitely real…and you are most definitely here. We can't change history, so I guess the only thing we can do is try to put it in the past where it belongs. Not anything I've been especially good at, but I'm trying. I probably don't deserve you, Cal," He smiled. "But I'm keeping you anyway."

"Luca," Calli shifted from one foot to the other and looked everywhere but at him. "The women you've been with…"

"Over. In the past. Completely forgotten. None of them were anything but illusions, Calli. They weren't you."

"I'm very happy to hear that, Luca, but you do realize you're doing it again?"

"Doing what?"

"Not listening. I fear it's a habit that will be impossible for you to overcome," she sighed.

"Sorry. What were you saying?"

"Well, those women…they were all…I mean they knew how…well…they were all very…experienced, weren't they?"

She wrung her hands together with such concentration, he was afraid she might snap a bone. He suspected where this was going but she needed to say it. She needed to get over her shyness with him. She needed to know she could talk to him about anything.

"I suppose so," he returned in a thoughtful tone, struggling to keep a straight face.

"I see. Well, I, um…that is, I've read books, of course, dozens of them in fact, but in actual practice, I…" She bit her lip and swallowed hard.

"Just spit it out, *cara*," he encouraged. "It's okay."

"Hell and damnation, Luca. I have no idea what to do. I'm so afraid I won't be any good at it and you'll be disappointed!" She clapped a hand to her mouth and regarded him through eyes as round as silver dollars.

"Calli," he began. He had no clue what would be the right thing to say. He did know if he laughed now she would be mortified and hurt beyond measure. But it did require a good deal of discipline on his part.

"You worry about the most ridiculous things." He said at last, capturing her hands against his chest again to still their nervous motion. "It's not rocket science. It's as natural as breathing, and you could never disappoint me. But really, if you're worried about it, maybe we should just keep practicing until you get the hang of it. Practice makes perfect, *cara*."

He bent his head to capture her shocked gasp in his mouth with a long, searing kiss. She opened readily to his seeking tongue as he stroked and plundered, and when she tentatively stroked back, he hauled her against him tightly. They were so close he could feel the heat from her body, her rapidly accelerating heartbeat, and the force of the breath rushing into her lungs. When she moaned low in her throat, the sexy sound nearly pushed him over the edge.

Luca's lips left hers and traveled across her cheek as softly as the brush of a butterfly's wings.

He swept aside the heavy curtain of her hair and began to work his magic along the smooth column of her throat. He licked and nibbled and Calli automatically tipped her head back to allow him better access. She sagged against him, fisting her hands in the front of his sweater to maintain her balance. Luca hooked one arm around her waist to hitch her even more intimately against him, leaving her in no doubt about the state of his arousal. His other hand snaked beneath her shirt to splay across the soft, warm skin of her lower back, pressing into the sensuous curve of her spine to hold her in place when she began to move restlessly against him. She slowly and daringly bunched his sweater up in her hands until her fingers touched the skin of his stomach. She slid her hands under the sweater and over his chest, and he couldn't control the swift intake of breath when her nails accidentally scraped lightly over the hardened nub of his nipple. He tore his lips from the temptation of her throat and rested his forehead against hers, his breathing ragged. Against her palm, his racing heart beat a rapid tattoo, and he could see by the pulse beating at the base of her throat, hers galloped as well.

"Did I do something wrong?" Calli panted.

Luca could manage nothing beyond a heartfelt

groan. He sucked in great gasping gulps of air in an effort to rein in his raging desire. Slowly. He'd promised himself he would take it slowly. But damn, if she ground her hips against his groin one more time he was going to explode, both literally and figuratively. He could barely think with wanting her. He felt her trembling and saw the uncertainty on her expressive face. Still, he couldn't pull in enough air to speak.

"Remember I told you it was as natural as breathing?" He sent the question into her mind. She nodded.

He peeled his lips back, and she trembled in his arms all over again. *"You've got a great set of lungs, dolcezza."*

"Really?" A slow, satisfied smile spread across her face. "You know, Luca…I had a *lot* of time on my hands. I read an *awful* lot of books. I really can't believe it's physically possible to achieve some of those positions. I learn much better by example. What do they call it these days? A hands-on approach? I hope you're up to it, because I think I'm going to need to practice…*a lot.*"

Luca didn't hesitate. He swung her up into his arms and headed for the stairs. She curled into him like a contented kitten and her soft lips blazed a path along his throat and collar bone as he climbed. He finally reached the top breathing like a horse that'd just run the *Palio di Siena.* Funny, he didn't remember those stairs being so steep. His leg muscles quivered so badly he was simply thankful his knees hadn't buckled and sent them both tumbling to the bottom. Hell, they'd barely done more than kiss and he was already so aroused he felt as if they'd indulged in hours of foreplay. *Merda!* He wasn't some innocent teenager about to get laid for the first time. But Calli made him feel as though he was. And even though it really was *her* first time, she'd read all of those damn books. God only knew what kind of expectations she might be harboring in that virginal little head. He felt like he had a helluva lot to live up to. He set her on her feet next to his bed and took a deep breath that didn't steady him at all. He'd never felt so unsure of his next move. Then again, he'd never been so emotionally invested in taking a woman to his bed. It scared him. That, too, was an unfamiliar feeling. He scraped his moist palms along the sides of his jeans, combed his fingers through his hair, and cleared his throat. Then he risked a glance into Calli's adoring, trusting eyes and found his balance. It would be all right. This wasn't about performance, though he would make damn sure she found pleasure. This was about finding the lost part of his soul. This was about loving Calli.

He tucked her hair behind one ear and allowed the sensitive tip of his forefinger to trace the line of her jaw until he reached her mouth. He rubbed his thumb along her full, lower lip and the tip of her soft, pink tongue flicked out to taste him. He almost lost it. He groaned low in his throat and a shudder moved through him. A sly, secret smile crossed her lips. She seemed to have quickly figured out precisely the effect she had on him and enjoyed it immensely.

"Luca?"

She boldly ran her hands under his sweater and up his chest. The heavy muscles quivered under her touch. She stared at his face. The chiseled jaw, the high cheekbones, and that intriguing cleft in his chin that made her heart flip-flop. The long, smooth expanse of his throat. She licked her lips remembering the feel of it under her mouth, the salty taste, kissing the delicious spot where it joined his shoulder.

"I don't think I'm afraid anymore." She began working the hem of his sweater up his body. She wanted to see him, all of him. At this moment, she wanted it more than she'd ever wanted almost anything in her life. She was tired of feeling like a victim, tired of hiding inside herself, always worried about saying or doing the wrong thing. There was still a lot she didn't know about this strange new century, but she learned quickly. She was bound to make mistakes, but she had a family who loved her and now she had Luca, too. It was time for Callista McAllister to take back her life, starting right now. She reached his chest and gazed up at him with fire in her eyes. "Off. Now."

His eyes widened at her sudden audacity, but he didn't question it. His sweater flew over his head and sailed across the room so fast she never saw him move, baring his glorious body to her eyes and hands from the waist up. She took full advantage as she stroked and traced his naked skin with gentle curiosity, learning him, memorizing the feel of him. The lean muscles of his abdomen twitched in appreciation of her bold exploration. When her hands dropped to his waist and tugged at the button of his jeans, he grasped her hands with his own.

"Slowly, *dolcezza*. We have all night. Now, your turn. Fair is fair." The corners of his mouth curled and he pulled her close for a lingering kiss. While his lips and tongue explored the contours of her ear, his fingers tugged her sweater up and over her head and tossed it in the direction of his. She was glad she'd worn the red lace even though it had seemed positively indecent when she'd first put it on. The bra cupped and lifted her generous breasts as though offering them up for his approval. Suddenly she remembered something and her hands snaked up between them to cover her chest.

"What is it, *amore*?"

"It's…it's so ugly, Luca. I don't want you to see it." She whispered miserably spreading her fingers over the top of her right breast. He'd seen it before, of course, Luca had been the one who pulled Jacques Rapier's dagger from her chest in the first place. But at the time, she'd been more concerned about living than loving. *Earthbound* healed quickly and completely from most wounds, but Jacques had carried a Hell-blade. Fortunately, the blade had passed through Jacques thick, fibrous black wing before imbedding itself in Calli. Otherwise, she would be dead. But because it *had* been a Hell-blade, she would never be perfect like the other women Luca had taken to his bed. She would always carry the scar.

With a tender smile, Luca gently pried her fingers away and held them in his. Then he replaced them with his lips. He feathered kisses along the length of the puckered pink skin, and then ran his tongue up her neck to take her lips once more.

"This scar is part of you, *dolcezza*. It is a badge of courage. Proof that you are a survivor. Never be ashamed of it. Don't you know by now there is nothing that could ever make you less beautiful or less desirable to me?"

Slowly Calli relaxed her fingers and let her arms encircle his waist.

"Really?" she whispered, desperate to be convinced.

"*Dio*, Calli. Every inch of you takes my breath away." His voice fell to a whisper, sounding almost like a prayer as he lowered his head to mouth her straining nipple through the intricate lace.

Calli felt the heat of his moist breath to the very marrow of her bones and she sagged against him under the onslaught of the new and unfamiliar sensations. His nimble fingers worked at the clasp, freeing it in seconds, allowing her breasts to tumble free into his hands. He worshipped first one and then the other with his lips and teeth and tongue. A shiver rolled over her from head to toe. He picked up his head and smiled. It was a smile that told her he hadn't missed her reaction—a smile that teased her with the promise of even more to come.

He unsnapped her jeans with a quick flick of his wrist and tugged them down over her hips to reveal the lacy red panties before she even realized what he intended. As soon as she stepped out of the jeans, Luca moved her slightly until she felt the bed against the backs of her knees. In the next instant, she sprawled upon the satin comforter and Luca's big body stretched out next to her. His jeans were nowhere to be seen and her eyes widened in trepidation at the sight of his erection. It pressed insistently against her hip refusing to be ignored. Her fear returned, but only for a heartbeat. Then Luca opened his mind to her. Her gaze flew to his in alarm at what she read there. Raw desire. But then she saw that wrapped around and through it, bound inseparably to the need, was something more, so much more. The strength of his feelings nearly paralyzed her. Her heart tripped and her breathe caught in her throat. She reached for him and brought his lips to hers. The enormity of his love chased away any lingering vestiges of fear.

As his long fingers stroked the skin along her hip skimming closer and closer to his ultimate destination, she couldn't help wondering what he would feel like under her fingertips, or her lips. Somewhere in the back of her mind she thought such curiosity should shock her, but it didn't, and as Luca's hands and mouth continued to play her body like a well-loved instrument, it simply made her want…something. She squirmed as he hooked his thumbs in the sides of her panties and shimmied them down her hips, following their slow, torturous path with kisses as soft as raindrops along her thighs. He tossed the panties away and stretched out next to her again. As he gently brushed her hair away from her face, and gazed into her eyes, she tentatively reached out and closed her fingers around the hard length of him. He was large. So large she couldn't imagine how they would ever fit together. She swallowed her worry and concentrated on his expression as she tightened her grip. He felt like satin on steel and she ran her fingers up and down his length in exploration. Luca groaned as though in pain and stilled her hand with his own.

"Did I do something wrong?"

"No," Luca whispered in an odd, strangled voice that sounded nothing like him.

"Did I hurt you?"

"*Carissima*, your hands feel so good. If you keep doing that, this will be over before we even get started," he groaned against her neck.

"Oh." She reluctantly pulled her hand away. "I'm sorry."

"*Dolcezza*, never be sorry for touching me. I've waited a lifetime to feel your hands on me. It's only that I want this to be perfect for you, and you're not ready yet." Luca smiled at her tenderly and swooped to reclaim her mouth. She didn't hesitate to open to his sweet invasion. While his tongue plundered her mouth, his hands lavished attention on her breasts, kneading and caressing them before repeatedly grazing her stiff nipples with his heavy thumbs, producing a feeling so exquisite it bordered on pain. Calli felt the sensation to her toes, and a rush of moist heat erupted between her thighs. Luca's fingers teased over her flat belly and slipped into the nest of soft curls guarding her heated core. She tensed, but only for a moment as his clever fingers teased her with a slow, intimate massage that nearly sent her over the edge. He continued to ravage her mouth as a delicious pleasure began to build and spread. She bucked against his hand with a sound that was half whimper half moan as he slid first one long finger, and then another into her slick, wet heat, working them slowly in and out, probing and stretching to ready her while his thumb continued to stroke her sensitive nub.

"Luca," she panted into his mouth. "Please, I want…"

"What do you want, *carissima*? Tell me…"

"I don't know. I…"

"Just let go, baby. It's okay. I'll catch you. I'll always catch you."

Calli looked into his eyes and gave up all caution and uncertainty, abandoning herself to what her heart and body wanted. As the waves of pleasure slammed over her, she clutched Luca's shoulders, breathless with wonder as he rolled to top her and positioned himself at her entrance. Inch by painfully slow inch he eased inside her, beads of sweat peppering his brow as her body stretched to accommodate him, until he was fully seated inside her. He held his weight off her on trembling forearms, keeping perfectly still.

"Are you okay, *cara*?" he panted.

"We fit," she whispered in wide-eyed wonder tilting her hips toward him. Luca closed his eyes and gritted his teeth.

"Slow down, *carissima*," he ground out through stiff lips. "I don't want to hurt you."

"You could never hurt me, Luca," Calli twined her arms around his neck and her legs around his hips pulling him even more deeply into her. She opened her mind and as their thoughts and feelings intertwined, he moved, slowly at first, more forcefully as she relaxed and moved with him. He dug his fingers into her bottom possessively and drove even deeper, guiding her hips until they found a perfect rhythm. As they moved together, their hearts and minds melding as closely and intimately as their bodies, she felt something stir inside yet again, something deep and hot and aching. Calli's eyes filled with tears and she thought her heart might burst as she felt the unmistakably right sensation of invisible ties binding them together heart, mind, and soul. As Luca caught her to him she felt herself falling all over again and he roared his own release as they tumbled over the edge together. Calli didn't doubt he would catch her. He would always catch her. And he did. In Luca's arms, she knew, at last, she had really and truly come home.

When she could finally draw enough breath to form coherent words, she regarded Luca with a frown.

"What is it, *cara*?" Luca murmured, brushing her damp hair back from her forehead. "Is everything okay?"

"I'm not sure," she drawled lazily while tracing a finger down his chest. "I mean, I *think* I've got it, but maybe we should do it again to be sure. I did warn you I would need to practice." It was a suggestion that Luca took completely to heart.

****

Long after Calli had fallen into an exhausted but thoroughly contented sleep, Luca remained more awake than he'd ever been. He'd never been so aware of a woman's body molded to his. He knew how to be alone, he knew how to be empty. He'd perfected it to an art form. He never realized the breadth of the yawning void inside him until Calli filled it so completely. His life had been filled with violence and danger, he'd never really considered how much. But he'd always had control. It was the one thing he'd always felt sure of. He knew that giving up his heart also required giving up control to a certain degree. It was a bit disquieting. It would take some adjustment. He looked down at the sleeping woman in his arms and pulled her closer. Her arms tightened reflexively around him. He tucked the blanket up around her shoulders and closed his eyes. She was worth anything he might have to give up in return. She was the missing part of his soul where love and hope had hidden away for far too long.

Chapter Thirteen

"What was that?" Calli jackknifed up in bed, clutching the sheet to her breasts.

"What was what?" Luca tugged on the sheet to pull Calli back against him.

"I thought I heard something downstairs."

"Probably Maria." Luca began kissing his way up her shoulder to the side of her neck.

"Luca, it's barely five in the morning. Maria never comes in until at least seven."

"You probably dreamed it, *bellissima*. You were pretty worn out when you…" Luca froze suddenly with his lips against Calli's shoulder. He went as still as stone and cocked his head.

Luca sprang from the bed and tossed Calli his robe while poking his legs hastily into his discarded jeans. He quickly drew a dagger from the tattoo on his forearm and moved on silent feet to the door while placing a finger to his lips.

Calli quickly dragged on and belted the enormous robe that covered her from head to toe and moved to the other side of the bed. Luca flattened himself against the wall next to the door and motioned toward the adjoining bathroom indicating Calli should go inside to wait. Calli shook her head.

He motioned again. Calli planted her hands on her hips and stayed exactly where she was. He made a move to step in her direction when the door began to creak open slowly. Luca moved quickly, and in less than a heartbeat, he had the intruder by the shirtfront and the lethal point of his dagger rested against the man's jugular.

Kassian felt the cold prick of the steel against his throat and froze. His gaze passed beyond Luca to the rumpled bed and then came to rest on his sister enveloped in Luca's robe. His eyes narrowed and his face darkened. His initial reaction was derailed by a sharp sting as Kat pinched the sensitive skin beneath his armpit. Hard.

"Back it down, McAllister," Kat whispered in a fierce tone. "We talked about this."

Kassian took a deep breath and blew it out slowly. His wife was right, they had talked about it. In truth, he'd been expecting to find Calli and Luca together. But expecting it and walking in on it were two entirely different things. It was hard to ignore hundreds of years of instinct. Sure, they loved one another, but finding his sister in any man's bedroom, even Luca's, was still a little difficult for Kassian to accept.

Kassian's glance slid to the side and met Luca's unflinching gaze. He wasn't fooled. He knew his friend well enough to read the defensiveness and uncertainty beneath the cool expression. Luca was worried about Kassian's reaction to finding Callista in his bed. But apparently, he would fight for her. It didn't escape Kassian's notice that the deadly blade against his skin hadn't moved.

"You want to put your toy away before you hurt someone?" Kassian drawled.

Luca started as if only now realizing he still held

his weapon at his best friend's throat. He dropped his hand and slapped the dagger against his forearm where it quickly dissolved into his tattoo.

"You shouldn't sneak up on people like that," he growled. "If I didn't have such incredibly good instincts, you'd be dead right now."

"We were hardly sneaking. And if your instincts were so freakin' good you would have heard me coming in the first place," Kassian countered shortly. His jaw tightened as his eyes roved over Callista's wildly tumbled hair and state of undress. "But I guess you were otherwise occupied."

"I was, actually. You have a problem with that?"

Kassian recognized the cool, empty expression contradicted by the tense posture. Luca expected trouble and stood ready for a fight. Kassian was about to oblige him when Kat moved to place her body between her husband and her brother.

"For the love of...stop it! The emotions flying around this room are giving me a headache! Honestly, you're both acting like two children fighting over the last cookie in the jar. Callista, go and get dressed. McAllister, go downstairs and put some coffee on or something. You said yourself that Luca's *sigils* were the most complex you'd ever seen. Obviously, he wasn't relying on his instincts alone. Got it?"

Callista stepped around the bed and came to stand beside Luca, the hem of the overlarge robe trailing behind her, making her appear even smaller than she was. She linked her arm through Luca's and tossed back her hair, eyeing her brother with a defiant expression.

"Go put some damn clothes on, Calli. We'll meet

you and Kat downstairs. Luca and I have a few things to discuss," Kassian scrubbed a hand over his face.

"Are you going to behave?" Calli asked.

"You're sure about this?" Kassian asked his sister using the private mental pathway the two of them shared. Calli answered with a wide, radiant smile that seemed to illuminate the entire room. Kassian conceded defeat. He'd never seen his sister so happy. His wife was right. Luca and Calli were bound, a complete idiot could see it. Kassian knew he was many things, but he liked to think an idiot wasn't one of them.

"I don't answer to you, little sister," Kassian answered in a curt tone that fooled no one. Even Luca relaxed and struggled to keep his lips from curling. Kassian spared a mournful thought for the days when he was actually in charge of his life. Battle, anger, remorse, there was a predictable flow and consistency. He knew precisely what to expect every day. Then Kat entered his life and Callista was found alive, and predictability became a scarce commodity. Kassian regarded three of the people who meant the most to him in the world and his chest ached briefly with the enormity of his good fortune. He wouldn't change a thing. Of course, they didn't need to know that.

"Your badass reputation would take a real hit about now if I wasn't the only empath in the room." His wife's amused voice swirled into his thoughts.

"I am a total badass." He mentally replied with a frown in his wife's direction.

"Save it for the Fallen, McAllister. I know better, but far be it from me to expose you for the big, squishy marshmallow you really are." Katrina stretched up on her toes and planted her lips on her husband's jaw.

"You're pushing, wife." Kassian gave Kat a playful swat on the butt.

"C'mon, Calli," Kat extended a hand to her sister-in-law. "You get dressed and *we'll* make the coffee so the big, bad warrior dudes can talk business."

The women retreated and pulled the heavy wooden door closed behind them leaving a heavy silence in their wake.

"Soooo…you and Calli, huh?" Kassian spoke to Luca's back as the blond warrior strode across the room, yanked a black tee from a drawer, and tugged it over his head.

"Yeah."

"Figures," Kassian chuffed out a laugh. Luca turned to face him from across the room, a puzzled frown creasing his forehead.

"What?"

"You've blown off half the women of the free world then let yourself fall for the one that's been a pain in your ass for as long as you've know her."

"Mac, it's always been Calli." Luca sighed and approached Kassian who hadn't moved from the doorway since entering the room. "She's my soul, brother. No one else ever measured up."

"Yeah, yeah, I know. Don't worry, I'm up to speed. My wife was happy to figure it all out for me," Kassian rolled his eyes and punched Luca in the shoulder.

"Oh, so now your wife is doing all your thinking for you, eh?" Luca grinned with a look of relief, returning the punch.

"You best get used to it, my brother. I have a hunch you'll find yourself paddling along in the same sinking boat soon enough." Kassian burst out laughing at the look of horror that crossed Luca's face.

"My wife will defer to me in all matters," Luca pronounced, but the look on his face told Kassian he was trying to convince himself more than anyone.

"Alrighty then, you go with that. Meantime, we've got problems," Kassian's tone turned from teasing to serious. "Dimitri called. When he got to Kat's, the house was a mess. The boxes shipped from Miranda's were open and the contents were all over the place. Since I never thought to have my people inventory the stuff, there's no way to tell what, if anything, is missing."

"Damn, how could Monte have figured out where to look so fast? We just barely put the pieces together ourselves!" Luca pushed his hair back from his forehead and began pacing restlessly.

"No idea. But that's not all," Kassian continued grimly. Luca stopped pacing and turned to regard him with a worried expression. "We can't locate Elle Gates. She was staying at the house, or at least she was supposed to be. She was there when Kat called to let her know Dimitri would be stopping by and she didn't mention anything about leaving. But there was no sign of her when Dimitri got there and when he checked at her apartment in the city, there was no answer at the door and the newspapers hadn't been taken in. He asked around among some of the neighbors and she hasn't been seen in days. I've tried her cell at least a dozen times with no luck." He rubbed a hand over the back of his neck. "I haven't told Kat yet."

"Well, Kat must know something's up, Mac. She can feel your emotions even if you block your thoughts," Luca pointed out. "But what would Monte want with Elle?"

"Beats the hell out of me. Leverage, maybe?" Kassian thought he pointed out the obvious.

"But if he's got the key already, what would he need leverage for? What's he got to gain?"

"Maybe the key wasn't there, or he's not sure he's actually has it so he took her just in case? Hell, Luca I don't know, but it's one more complication we don't need."

"Maybe," Luca muttered doubtfully. "He knows we'd never let him get near Calli or Kat. Elle would be an easy target, so maybe she was the next best thing."

"Maybe," Kassian agreed, his brows knitting together. "Well, at any rate, I think it's time we paid Monte a visit."

"I don't like it," Luca grimaced.

"I'm right there with you, brother, but Monte isn't stupid enough to try anything in public. He's got too much to lose. Kat and Calli will be safe enough here with the *sigils* up."

Luca nodded and turned toward the en suite.

"Luca, one more thing," Kassian added almost as an afterthought as he slipped out of the door. "You break her heart, I'll break your ass."

Chapter Fourteen

"Admit it," Kat regarded her husband and brother with a smug expression. "You need me. I'm going with you."

Calli and Luca were both showered and dressed, and Kat and Kassian had deposited their bags in their own suite. Now they were all gathered at the kitchen table as though by mutual consent. The room was warm and fragrant with the scent of dark roast coffee and fresh baked goods. Piero's son had already delivered the *cornetti,* and Maria had arrived and filled the coffee pot and left it to simmer on the stove before heading upstairs to begin her daily cleaning.

Kassian glared across the length of the table at his wife, his brow so deeply furrowed he suddenly reminded Callista of Chin-Chin, the Shar-Pei puppy her father had presented to her one year on her birthday. Douglas McAllister had smuggled the creature all the way to London from the Guangdong province of China. How she'd adored that dog. Sadly, the lifespan of a domesticated animal was barely a blip in the long life of an *Earthbound.* As fond as she'd been of Chin, she hadn't given the dog a thought in centuries, but at the moment, she couldn't help but be reminded as the resemblance to her irritated brother was uncanny.

"It's not even a consideration," Kassian growled. "You will stay right here at the villa with Calli where it's safe."

Callista recognized that tone. It was a tone that didn't suggest argument or invite rejoinder. Kat McAllister, however, seemed immune to the implied warning. Callista couldn't decide if her sister-in-law was incredibly brave or just plain crazy as she widened her bright silver eyes in her husband's direction and batted her long lashes.

"I'm so sorry, Darling." She smiled sweetly but her voice dripped with barely concealed annoyance. "Did I forget to preface that with *if it pleases Your Majesty?*"

Callista gasped at her audacity. Luca's dry cough failed to disguise his snort as he rose to refill his coffee, snagging Calli's nearly empty cup on the way. A muscle twitched in Kassian's cheek.

"You're pushing, wife," he ground out through teeth clenched tightly enough to snap.

"I'm being logical, McAllister," Kat replied. "Do you honestly think paying Monte a visit is going to get you any real information? Monte won't admit a thing, even if he does know something about the key or Elle's whereabouts. He'll have his mind battened down tighter than a nuclear submarine. His emotions, however, won't be so closely guarded. Granted, I won't be able to elicit many more details than you will, but I probably *can* determine if he's hiding something or not, and at least we'll know if we're looking in the right place."

"She does have a point, Mac," Luca observed, plunking Calli's steaming mug on the scarred wooden table in front of her and dropping into the chair beside her. He moved his chair so close to hers that they touched from hip to knee. When he dropped his hand onto her thigh and gave a light squeeze, Calli found it very difficult to concentrate on the conversation around her.

"I know she has a point," Kassian snapped, crossing his arms over his massive chest. "That doesn't mean I have to like it.

"I don't expect you to like it," Kat soothed, rising from her chair and coming to stand behind her husband. She wrapped her arms around him from behind and rested her chin on the top of his dark head. "I'm only asking you to see the sense of it. If Monte doesn't know anything about the key or Elle's whereabouts, better we find that out sooner rather than later. Otherwise we're wasting time."

Calli could almost hear Kassian's thoughts tripping over one another. His eyes darkened to black and his lips compressed into a thin, straight line.

"Shit!" He spat, uncrossing his arms to reach around and tug Kat into his lap. "Fine. But hear this, wife...I say go, you go. I say move, you move. I say bark like a dog, you bark like a dog. Got it?"

"If it pleases Your Majesty," Kat quipped with a lopsided grin, wrapping her arms around his neck. "Although you might want to rethink that barking like a dog thing. You know very well I'm a cat person."

"Yeah, and look how well that worked out for you," Kassian goaded. Kat's most recent pet, a tabby cat named Sid, had turned out to be her cousin Miranda's *Familiar.* His sole purpose was to spy on Kat and report back to his mistress who was hoping to locate and claim the Ring of Aandalena for herself.

"It's very ungallant of you to bring that up, Kassian," Calli whispered quietly. Kat's skin crawled every time she thought about exactly how familiar the

Familiar must have been with every private aspect of her life, and they all knew it.

"Thanks for the support, Calli, but it's okay. McAllister thinks that by pointing it out again and again, he can convince me I should never get another animal of the feline persuasion. It won't work though," Kat winked at her sister-in-law. Kassian McAllister had a strong aversion to cats, and they all knew that, too. Calli thought it would be interesting to see who won the battle. Judging by the look in her brother's eyes every time they came to rest on his wife, her money was on Katrina.

"I have four words for you, Mac. *Largo di Torre Argentina*," Luca sniggered referring to the remains of Pompey's Theatre where Julius Caesar was believed to have been assassinated. These days the square was almost more famous for the *Torre Argentina* Cat Sanctuary, a no-kill shelter for the many homeless cats wandering the city streets. "I'll bet Katrina could find a new friend in no time."

"And I have two words for you, Luca. Get. Bent."

"And I have two more," Kat added, untangling herself from her husband's arms and hopping to her feet. "Let's go. The sooner we do this, the sooner we can find out if we're looking in the right place."

"I'll get my jacket," Calli moved to rise from her chair. Luca's hand clamped down on her thigh and held her in place.

"Are you cold?" Luca asked in a soft voice. Kat's sympathetic look spoke volumes as she glanced at Calli and then quickly followed Kassian from the kitchen.

"Well, no," Calli began, covering his hand with her own and nervously stroking his wrist. "But I'm…"

"Staying right here where you're safe," Luca finished for her. He leaned forward to capture her lips before getting to his feet and reaching for the jacket he'd hung behind the door the previous day. He kept his back to her as he threaded his arms into the sleeves and settled the black leather across the width of his shoulders. When he turned back, Calli saw that he'd schooled his features into the cold, dispassionate expression she'd grown to hate. After last night, she'd rather thought they were past that.

"But I'll be here all alone except for Maria and she leaves at noon. Wouldn't I be safer with you? I'll do nothing but worry the entire time you're gone. I'll do exactly what you tell me," Callista hated the pleading tone she heard in her own voice. She hated even more that Luca appeared completely unmoved by it.

"Between my s*igils* and Mac's, no one is getting into this place until we return, *cara*. If we didn't have need of Kat's empathic ability, there's no way we'd be letting her anywhere near Monte, either," Luca replied firmly. "The difference is, she can fade out on her own if things go south. You can't."

"So you're saying I would be a liability?"

"I'm saying I won't put you at risk and it's safer if you stay right here."

Her throat tightened and her chest ached. He might be willing to admit he loved her, but he still saw her as a helpless nitwit. She thought she'd felt a little sizzle when she'd been close to Giovanna, so maybe her sensation of evil was returning, but no one was any closer to figuring out how to break the magic that bound her ability to fade. If something happened at this meeting and her disability endangered any of the people she loved, she would never forgive herself. And if anything happened to Luca because of her...He was right. She was a liability. It was safer for everyone if she stayed behind.

"I understand," she whispered. "Please be careful."

He reached down and tugged her to her feet, wrapping his arms around her. She buried her face in his shirtfront, swallowing the tears that threatened. She blinked them back rapidly as he hooked a finger under her chin and tilted her head back to look into her eyes.

"I'm always careful, *carissima*. And now I have even more reason to stay alive. I have you. Whether you like it or not, there is no way in heaven or hell that I intend to lose you again. Do not leave this house, Calli. This won't take long and we'll go out and do something when I get back. Maybe the *Galleria Borghese*? They have an incredible collection. You'll love it."

"That sounds wonderful," Calli cleared her throat and forced a smile. He headed into possible danger and she would not be cause for distraction. She stretched up on her toes, cupped his face, and pressed her lips to his. "I'll see you later, then."

Luca buried his fingers in her hair and pulled her back for a longer kiss then stepped around her and went into the other room to join Kat and Kassian.

"I love you." Calli sent the thought to Luca as she stepped into the parlor to see him off, only to realize there was no longer anyone there to receive it.

****

"What on earth is going on?" Kat instinctively grabbed at Kassian's arm and Luca's jacket to maintain her balance as she was pushed and elbowed yet again by the oblivious crowd. Kassian and Luca took up positions on either side of her using their enormous size to buffer Kat from the worst of the abuse. The mood was ugly on the unusually congested sidewalks. Luca saw Kat's struggle to hold her shields as the riot of emotions being broadcast by the quarrelsome crowd bombarded her on all sides. Traffic snarled, horns blared, and drivers stopped in the middle of the street, hanging out of their windows screaming streams of rapid fire Italian laced with some of the most originally phrased profanity that even Luca had ever heard. Arguments and shoving matches raged on every side as the *Earthbounds* navigated the jostling crowd.

"Have people lost their minds?" Kat gasped as they finally pushed through a chrome and glass door that clashed incongruously with the ancient façade of the building it fronted. The portal hissed closed behind them, muffling the worst of the chaos outside. Luca hoped it would also provide Kat a respite from the boiling cauldron of negative emotions swirling in the streets. But any relief his sister enjoyed was destined to be short-lived as it was quickly replaced by the creep of evil. They were on Monte's turf, so they'd been expecting it, but Kat already looked exhausted from the battering her empath had taken on the way. He reached to give her shoulder an encouraging squeeze.

"I suspect it's far more likely an outside force is at work," Kassian replied grimly. "Unless I miss my guess, Azakriel has already come out to play."

Luca dropped his hand from Kat's shoulder, nodded a curt agreement, and yanked his cell phone from inside his jacket. He sent Michael a quick and cryptic text, then followed as Kassian reached for Kat's hand and pulled her across the dimly lit but elegantly designed lobby to the reception desk where a sophisticated looking and well-dressed *Fallen* brunette regarded them with a wary, vaguely hostile expression.

"Tell your master that Kassian McAllister is here."

"Mr. Monte is not taking appointments today," the woman responded in a dismissive tone.

Luca arranged his features into his customary steely calm. He planted his hands on the surface of the desk, mere inches from the woman's heaving chest, and leaned in until they were almost nose to nose. She blinked and sucked in a deep breath, but to her credit, she held her ground and barely flinched.

"Irrelevant, *bella*, as we don't have an appointment. So let me explain how this will go down. You will call your boss and give him a heads up, or we will walk in the door and surprise him. Somehow, I don't think he'll appreciate the surprise." Luca's smile was anything but friendly. It could have frozen lava. Fortunately for the woman, she hadn't attained her position of running interference for Ignazio Monte by being stupid. She picked up the phone.

"Third floor, end of the hall," she directed tightly after conveying a rapid, hushed message and replacing the receiver in its cradle.

"*Grazie, bella.* You are as wise as you are lovely. *Ciao, ciao.*" Luca rapped his knuckles on the desk in approval and cocked his head in the direction of the elevator indicating Mac and Kat should precede him. He winked at the brunette as the elevator doors swished closed and grinned as color suffused her face.

"Really, Luca?" Kat rolled her eyes at him. "Now? And under these circumstances? McAllister's right.

You're a man-whore."

"Whatever works, *cara*," he grinned at his sister. "Besides, it's all for effect. I am now a one woman man-whore."

"You'd better be," Mac growled menacingly.

"Never doubt it." In fact, after last night Luca had reached the conclusion that he'd always been a one woman man. He just hadn't known that one woman still lived. "Now, let's get this done. I don't like leaving Callista at the villa alone, *sigils* or no *sigils*."

"I'm on board with that," Mac replied, pushing Kat behind them as the elevator doors slid open. The brunette's directions had been superfluous. Ignazio Monte waited at the end of the hall with an Armani clad shoulder propped against the doorframe. He offered a sardonic lift of his brows as they stepped from the elevator and he spied Kat behind them.

Monte levered himself away from the doorway as the *Earthbound's* boots beat a measured tattoo down the length of the marble tiled hall. He stood aside to allow them entry into his office, and then closed the door with a decisive click. The *Fallen* waved all three toward a comfortably appointed seating area, and then parked a hip against the edge of his desk.

"I would like to say this is a surprise, but frankly, I've been expecting you," Monte began.

"You have?" Kat's brows knit together and she opened her mouth to continue, but at a single look from McAllister, she lapsed into silence.

"*Certo!*" Monte spread his hands before him, palms up. "I knew that, like me, McAllister and Fiorelli will have noticed the, shall we say, aura of discontent swirling about the city this day. However, I am surprised at your presence here, *la mia bella*. I'd heard rumors the *Defensori* were spread a bit thin, but I didn't realize they had become so desperate as to recruit women to join the ranks."

"My wife, Katrina," McAllister offered by way of an introduction. "So you managed to release Azakriel back into circulation, eh, Ignazio? I don't know how you figured it out, or how you got to the key before we did, but enjoy the chaos while it lasts, because it won't. Now if you'll simply tell us what you've done with Elle Gates, we'll be on our way."

"I suppose I should be flattered by your certainty that I beat you at your own game, especially after you managed to take both Giovanna and her uncle right out from under my nose. I would like to help you, McAllister, truly. But I didn't release Azakriel, nor did I ever intend to do so." Monte straightened and made his way to the window. Tugging back the drapery, he gazed out on the mayhem running rampant in the streets below. "Though I will admit the demon certainly hasn't forgotten how to put on an entertaining show."

Luca rose to his feet. He'd already had enough. He wanted to get to the bottom of this whole mess and get back to Calli. She said she understood, but he knew she'd been hurt by the decision to leave her behind. She believed she was a liability. Well maybe she was, but not in the way she thought. True, she still couldn't fade, but any of them could have gotten her away with the slightest touch. The real problem was that Luca found he could concentrate on very little else when she was near and that put not only Calli, but all of them in danger. He needed to stay alert and keep his head on straight until they could rectify the situation. He hadn't explained it very well before he left. He wanted nothing more than to take her in his arms and spend the rest of the day showing her that her only fault was in being too important to him. Quite a revelation for a man who had spent the better part of the last century walking away from any sort of emotional entanglement. He'd wasted so much time avoiding her, afraid that anything Calli felt for him was simply misplaced infatuation for someone safe and familiar in an unfamiliar world. But she continued to believe in him even when he found it impossible to believe in himself. How could someone of his advanced years and experience have been so blind? He'd felt it last night, the invisible ties binding them together heart, mind, and soul. She was meant to be his. And God help her, he was hers. He hoped she was up for the challenge.

"Luca!" Mac's voice cracked into his brain like a well-aimed shot. Luca snapped his attention back to their current situation while acknowledging that apparently Callista didn't even have to be in the room to serve as a distraction. His sister eyed him knowingly. No doubt her empath was having a field day with the emotions she was picking up from him.

"…no intention of releasing Azakriel," Monte was saying. "My sole purpose in seeking the key was to destroy him."

"You'll excuse me if I find that a little hard to believe," Mac responded dryly.

"Believe what you wish, McAllister. It's immaterial to me. But remember, I'm many times your age. One of Aandalena's descendants had bound the demon in that book and hidden it away hundreds of years before you were even a gleam in your father's eye. I have my own history with this demon and I've waited a long time to see him eradicated once and for all. Of course, now it has become a bit more complicated." Monte brushed an imaginary piece of lint from the sleeve of his immaculate suit and regarded them from under his lashes. "But, perhaps if we work together, we can both achieve our goals."

"I've heard about enough, Mac," Luca announced. "Work with you, Monte? When hell freezes over."

"Well, perhaps you should check to see if the temperature is dropping, my friend. Do you know how Azakriel works?" Monte quirked a brow in Luca's direction.

"Of course we do," Mac interjected. "He plays on forbidden desires. Things people want, or think they want, but morally or ethically would never act on. He obliterates the filter between right and wrong…and all hell breaks loose."

"*Esattamente!* You are exactly right. And did you also know that when Azakriel was banished to the book, he became incorporeal?" Monte leaned forward eagerly, jabbing a finger in McAllister's direction.

"Do you have a point, asshole?" Luca asked in a cold, bored voice.

"Indeed." Monte looked down his long, Roman nose as though Luca was an odd specimen under a microscope. "Because his body died centuries ago, in order to escape the book Azakriel must inhabit the body of another. If that body is destroyed while he is in residence, he is destroyed along with it."

"You're sure of this?" Luca growled.

"*Certo!* My plan was to release Azakriel in a contained environment and allow him to inhabit my body. I am ancient, gentlemen...*scusi*, and *signora*." He nodded politely in Kat's direction. "I feel certain I would be able to resist Azakriel's temptations long enough to allow the destruction of us both."

"That's it!" Luca headed for the door. "You may be older, Monte, but we sure as hell weren't born yesterday. Let's go, Mac."

Kassian got to his feet and reached down a hand to pull Kat to hers.

"Wait," Kat said in a surprised tone, her gaze firmly fixed on the *Fallen*.

"I think he means it." She sent her thoughts to both her husband and Luca. *"I'm feeling a lot of things...anger, grief, frustration. What I don't feel is even a whisper of deceit, subterfuge, or fear. Whatever Monte's beef is with this demon, he's not only willing to work with his enemies, he's also willing to die to make sure the demon dies with him."*

"You're sure about this?" McAllister asked.

"Absolutely? No. But if I had to bet on it, I would."

McAllister's phone jangled and he reached into his jacket and checked the display.

"Excuse me," he nodded at Monte.

"What've you got?" Mac listened intently while Luca worked at reigning in his unreasonable need to get back to Callista. She was at the villa surrounded by complicated *sigils*. She was safe. So why did he suddenly feel so uneasy?

"You're absolutely certain?" McAllister's tension showed in his voice and he shot a worried glance in Luca's direction. "Okay. What time do you get in? I have a hunch we might need your big ugly ass."

McAllister shoved the phone back in his pocket

and looked at his wife. Something in his expression, or perhaps the emotions her empath detected swirling around him must have alerted her to trouble.

"What is it, Kassian?"

"Dimitri found something," he said in a tone that Luca recognized as one that didn't bode well. "He went back to Elle's apartment again and this time when he got no answer he uh, let himself in to have a look around. The place was trashed just like yours, but he did find a notepad near the phone. It appears Elle booked a flight to Rome yesterday."

"But..." Kat's face twisted in a confused expression. "If she left yesterday, she should have been here by now. Why wouldn't she have called? Why wouldn't she have come to the villa?"

Kassian's gaze slid away and he didn't immediately answer.

"Allow me to explain, *Signora* McAllister. Your friend did not contact you because it is very likely that your friend is not the entity in control of her body or her actions at this moment," Monte offered silkily. "Am I right, McAllister?"

Luca watched his sister through narrowed eyes and saw the look of horror that crumpled her features as understanding dawned. She jumped to her feet and grabbed her husband by the front of his jacket.

"We have to find her, Kassian," her eyes were huge and her chin quivered. "We have to find her and get that monster out of her."

"And for that, you will need me," Monte interjected smoothly.

"I'm not so sure about that." Monte was not a small man. Still, Luca was larger and as he stepped up to the

Fallen, he had to look down to meet the other man's eyes. He was annoyed to find that his menacing stare had little effect on the evil one.

"Luca, please!" Kat cried. "At least give him a chance to explain."

He turned slowly to his sister with a look that spoke volumes. He knew she could feel the rage building in him.

"You might be willing to trust Lucifer himself to save Elle Gates, Katrina, but I cannot not so easily overlook what Monte's thugs did to Gia, nor the fact that Calli was threatened." Before the sound of his voice had even faded from the air, the look on her face told him he probably should have kept that to himself rather than shouting it at her across the room. And her expression paled in comparison to the one Mac flashed him and as quickly suppressed. Elle Gates was the only person Kat had been able to trust or turn to for years. Losing the woman would devastate her and Kat had lost enough in her life. He tried to remain unmoved as his sister's tears escaped from her eyes and slipped down her cheeks in reaction to Luca's sharp words. He'd never raised his voice or spoken to her in anger, and now he'd made her cry. *Merde!* He supposed for her sake he'd have to try to find a way to reconcile his hatred and distrust of this particular *Fallen* with the fact that Monte might have the answers they needed.

"I admit, the interrogation of the Moscato woman was unfortunate," Monte allowed, intently examining his carefully manicured nails. "While I don't personally condone those particular tactics, I could hardly be overly concerned with the sensibilities of one measly half-breed in the greater scheme of things."

"Why?" Luca asked in a hard voice. "You want us to work with you? Help you? *Trust you*? Then you spill it. Why are you so hell bent on destroying this demon and why are you even willing to die in order to do it?"

"I understand your curiosity Fiorelli, but at the moment I prefer to keep my reasons to myself."

Luca's fingers curled into fists at his sides. It was all that he could do to keep from beating the information out of the bastard. Monte raised his eyes with a vague smile curling his well-defined lips. Luca saw no remorse, no compassion for what had befallen Gia, no apology for the threat to Calli. Well, what had he expected from a *Fallen?* Luca's gut twisted. As far as he was concerned, the son-of-a-bitch deserved no more mercy than he'd ever shown anyone else.

Luca glanced at Mac. His friend's face remained unreadable and his thoughts were equally vague. *Damn!* Mac usually took the lead in these situations but it was clear that he was deferring on this one. Because of Calli. Calli had been threatened. Mac was stepping aside and relinquishing responsibility for Calli to Luca. Luca recognized and appreciated the gesture for what it was, a sign of acceptance and respect. He also realized Mac could simply be preoccupied with plotting ways to kick his ass when this was all over for the way he'd verbally flayed Kat. *Merde!* Was it too much to ask that he give up a freakin' clue?

Luca's gaze then slid to Kat. She clung to her husband's hand and the faint trace of a tear still glistened on her lashes. She met his look and squared her shoulders, letting him know that she wouldn't interfere with anything he needed to do, even if it cost her personally. Today, his sister turned out to be a better soldier than he. Luca, not Kat, had been the one to break a cardinal rule of the *Defensori*: Always present a united front in the presence of an enemy.

"I'm sorry, cara. I didn't mean to jump all over you like that." He used a mental pathway that was specific to him and Kat. He held the aloof expression for Monte's benefit, but hoped his sister's empath would feel his regret for having taken out his frustration on her. She nodded ever so slightly and Luca saw her hand tighten reflexively on Mac's as though to let him know everything was all right.

He returned both his cold stare and his attention to the *Fallen. Diavolo!* Why had he never stopped to appreciate how simple his life had been when he really didn't give a shit about much of anything beyond a good, invigorating battle or a casual roll in the hay?

He sighed inwardly, recognizing the truth. Life had been simpler perhaps, but it had also been empty. He needed to get a grip. Calli was safe at the villa. She wasn't going anywhere. He needed to put her out of his mind and focus on the disaster at hand. They had to find and harness this demon before the situation got any worse. Elle was important to Kat. If this son-of-a-bitch had a way to save her, he owed it to his sister to try. It didn't mean he had to like it. At all.

"You must have loved her very much," Kat unexpectedly addressed Monte in a quiet voice. His head swiveled so sharply in her direction that Luca suspected he might have suffered a whiplash. Monte opened and closed his mouth like a gasping fish. Maybe in shock, maybe in denial, but whatever the reason, no words came out. They didn't have to. Ignazio Monte's face said it all.

Chapter Fifteen

Luca watched the *Fallen* jerk upright from the desk and then fiddle with his jacket lapels as he tried to recapture his former *sang froid*. He failed miserably. Luca kept a tight rein on his reactions, though he couldn't suppress a satisfied smirk when Monte loosened his tie, inserted a finger into his professionally starched shirt, and ran it between the collar and his neck as though he couldn't quite breathe.

Kat had gambled on interpreting the emotions she was sensing and somehow managed to hit the nail right on the head. His sister accomplished what neither Luca nor Mac had been able to do. She'd made the bastard sweat.

"I have no idea what you're talking about," Monte replied stiffly at last.

"I can understand something so personal is difficult to talk about, especially for a man in your position, *signore*. But let's be frank. We don't trust you, you don't trust us. Still, if you are to be believed, we all want the same result. It would seem the best way to achieve that is for us all to cooperate, at least temporarily." Kat said.

"My wife is right, Monte," Mac interjected. "*Our* motives are pretty obvious. We want one less demon in the world. We want to neutralize the threat to humanity and facilitate the safe return of Miss Gates. With us, what you see is what you get. Make no mistake. We'll defeat this demon with or without you, but a temporary truce could expedite it. A *Fallen* looking to take out a demon doesn't make a lot of sense. You're going to have to give us something that does if you expect us to work with you."

Monte moved around his enormous mahogany desk and collapsed into the chair. He leaned forward and tented his fingers in front of him. Then he simply stared at the desk blotter without speaking.

"You've clearly never accepted the loss," Kat continued. "Was she your wife?"

Monte turned slowly in Kat's direction, his eyes widening by the second.

"*Una Strega!*" he hissed. "What are you, some kind of witch? How can you possibly know these things about me?"

His voice quavered. Oh yeah, Kat had him good and rattled. Luca enjoyed watching her focus on unnerving someone other than him for a change.

"My wife is extremely intuitive," Mac answered smoothly before Kat had a chance to respond.

"Again, I say to you, husband, I can speak for myself."

"Of course you can, love. I was simply bragging a little." Mac grinned in her direction.

Kat rolled her eyes and swatted her husband's broad chest.

Luca watched them quietly. He wanted that. He wanted that connection, that capacity to tune out the rest of the world and become lost in one another no matter how dire the circumstances. He'd been happy for his sister and his best friend when they found one another, but he'd also been incredibly envious. He just hadn't recognized the vague discomfort for what it was until now—until now, when he had the opportunity to experience the very same intimacy with Calli.

"Can we get on with this please?" Monte growled. "If your information is correct, Azakriel is already here in Rome. Of course, I would have suspected as much even without your questionable intelligence report. One needs only to look outside and observe the increasing chaos in the streets."

"But I don't understand," Kat frowned. "Why come here? Do you think it could be because he's possessed Elle? Maybe she's trying to get to us for help?" She looked at Monte and then back at her husband with a hopeful expression.

"Doubtful," Monte replied dryly. "She is human, *si*? There is absolutely no possibility she is in control."

Kat's face fell. "Then why? Surely New York would have been ripe with opportunity for a demon who wanted to promote mayhem."

"I believe Azakriel has come to Rome for one of two reasons. One, to destroy the one who created the tools to incapacitate him. Or secondly, to destroy the one responsible for their being used against him successfully. The first, as you know, is Michael. The second is me."

"*You*?" Luca sneered in a voice dripping with disbelief. "Those objects were specifically created to be used by Aandalena and her line, those with Archangel blood. I hardly think you swim in the right gene pool, Monte."

"So skeptical, Fiorelli. But you are correct. I do not possess the right pedigree to manipulate either the ring or the key." An odd smile hovered on the lips of the *Fallen*. He looked in Luca's direction, but his gaze was far away, as though he was seeing something or someone else altogether. "My daughter, however, was another matter."

"Your daughter?"

"Why so surprised, *il mio amico*? *Earthbound* don't hold the monopoly on procreation."

With a visible effort, Monte brought his attention back to his visitors and looked from one to the other. Kat and Kassian were still seated side by side in the gray suede armchairs near the window. Luca remained standing in the center of the office, feet planted, arms crossed impatiently over his chest.

Monte leaned back in his plush leather chair with a fatalistic sigh and waved a hand in the direction of the chairs.

"Please sit down, Luca. While I have no doubt I am now strong enough to prevail over the demon on my own, a joint venture would certainly expedite matters, and as McAllister has pointed out, and the more time we waste, the more devastation he causes."

"Sit down, Luca," Mac added shortly. "Let's hear what he's got to say."

"Why? It's bound to be a load of bull anyway. Let's get out of here, Mac. We're wasting time," Luca grumbled, but moved toward the chair and dropped his ass into it. He stretched his legs out in front of him and crossed one booted ankle over the other as though he had all the time in the world.

He didn't. Not anymore. His work, his mission, his salvation these many centuries now felt like endless minutes ticking away on a tired clock, minutes he would rather be spending with Callista. Still, he had obligations, right? He laced his fingers behind his neck and leaned his head back into them. He looked at Monte from beneath his lashes and quirked a brow. "Well?"

Monte glared at Luca, then turned his attention to Kat. "*Si, Signora* McAllister. The woman was my wife," he began haltingly. "A beautiful, strong, and gifted witch of Aandalena's lineage. But in spite of her power, she was a gentle soul. I never understood my good fortune in winning her love."

"Me neither," Luca mumbled.

"Luca," Mac warned. Luca rolled his eyes in a fair imitation of his sister's favorite response, then simply closed them and wondered how much longer this fiasco was going to continue. Maybe if he didn't actually have to look at the bastard, listening to him would be slightly less irritating.

"My daughter, Daniela, was seventeen and even more beautiful than her mother. Unfortunately, she was also rebellious and headstrong. Perhaps that was her legacy from me, perhaps it was a result of her age. Over centuries, customs and cultures change and evolve until they are sometimes unrecognizable remnants of what came before, yet adolescents seem always to remain adolescents, true?"

Luca assumed either Mac or Kat had offered some sign of agreement when Monte cleared his throat and continued.

"Despite her stubborn nature, she was basically a sweet child, but then her behavior changed and over some weeks became progressively more outrageous. She began sneaking off. She was in love, she said, and would listen to no one. Nor would she bring this man home to meet her parents. There was a terrible argument, and Daniela stormed out after wishing us both dead. My wife was devastated. I was sure Daniela was simply being dramatic, as young girls are, and told my wife this very thing. Then I left her there, determined to discover the identity of this man who was destroying my family. When I returned home later that evening, I did."

"Azakriel," Kat whispered hoarsely.

Luca opened one eye and glanced at his sister. Her face had turned ghostly white, and she bent forward with her arms wrapped tightly around her middle. Mac cupped his hand around her nape and his fingers traced firm, rhythmic circles in the tight muscles at the base of her skull. It was clear to Luca the pain she was feeling from Monte was significant.

He opened the other eye, sat up, and transferred his attention to the *Fallen*. If Kat looked bad, Monte looked worse. Deathly pale and wearing a haunted expression, the dark angel appeared to have aged a century in the last five minutes. *Merde!* The son-of-a-bitch was telling the truth.

"I was too late, of course. Azakriel had taken full advantage of my daughter's childish tantrum and her mother was dead." Monte scrubbed a hand wearily over his face as though trying to erase a memory that would never leave him.

"He stayed only long enough to take his pleasure in Dani's reaction when he freed her mind and she saw what she had done…and to make sure I understood who was responsible, of course. I was much younger then. I had the will but didn't believe I had the strength or the experience to destroy him on my own, and if I died in the attempt, Daniela would be all alone. So I had to find another way, a way to neutralize him until I gained enough power to destroy him. At my request, my wife's sisters and my daughter used their combined power to summon the demon and then used the ring and the key to imprison him. It was Azakriel who orchestrated this tragedy, Daniela was not to blame. I certainly did not blame her. She said she believed me. I promised her that her mother would be avenged. I hoped vengeance would bring her peace. Sadly, peace for her was not to be. She slit her own throat three days later."

When Monte finished, there was complete silence in the room for the space of a heartbeat. He'd shared the story in a calm, matter-of-fact tone that gave away nothing. He waited for a reaction, his face impassive, almost as though he'd been talking about someone else. Then Kat let out a low moan and doubled over completely. Mac reached for her, and Monte's eyes opened wide. He rose awkwardly to his feet.

"She's an empath!"

Kat went limp in Mac's embrace. She took a deep, shuddering breath as Monte apparently slammed a block on his emotions.

"*Mi scusi, signora*. I did not realize. I should have seen that your insight was more than mere intuition as your husband claimed." He favored McAllister with a dark look.

"*Va bene*, it's okay, *Signore* Monte. You couldn't have known." She offered her husband a shaky smile, sat up, and patted his cheek.

Mac's jaw relaxed not one iota, he hauled her back against him and wrapped his arms around her. She snuggled into him, neither of them giving a flying fig who watched.

Luca simply shook his head. He loved Calli with his entire being, but he would never allow a *Fallen* to witness how important she was to him as Mac was doing. He might as well hand Monte a sword and turn his back. What in the hell was he thinking?

"Oh, but I should have," Monte replied. "You see, *signora*, I've known a few empaths in my time. My wife, for instance. The gift is one that is peculiar to the line of Aandalena. It has been centuries since I've encountered it. I had forgotten the signs. I did not intend to cause you pain."

"Yeah, right," Luca shot back. "A compassionate *Fallen*. Who wouldn't buy that?"

"Assuming you're telling the truth," Mac began with a warning look in Luca's direction. "Why? Why tell us this? You could easily have fabricated something that left you less exposed. You'll excuse my hesitation, Monte, but frankly, we're not used to candor from any *Fallen*. Maybe you're trying to play us. Maybe you have a different agenda altogether."

"I can appreciate your qualms, McAllister and if I were any other *Fallen*, they might be valid. But I have walked this earth for a very long time. Longer even than you realize. Just ask your friend, Michael. It's time. Once the demon is destroyed, there is nothing to hold me here. My reasons for living were taken from me long ago. I've endured these many centuries solely to see justice done. Truthfully, I never believed the book would remain lost for this long, and I am beyond weary. No doubt, you find this difficult to believe but I really am ready for this to be over. Working with you increases my chances of ending it once and for all. Who knows? Maybe obliterating Azakriel will even buy me some redemption."

"As if." Luca growled which earned him another cautionary glance from Mac.

"You know redemption isn't something we have the power to offer," Mac said. "So, if that's your motivation for helping us..." Mac trailed off and set Kat on her feet, making a move to rise from the chair.

Monte waved him back into the chair, and Kat resumed her seat beside him.

"I am well aware of that, McAllister. Youth and poor decisions placed reconciliation beyond my reach millennia ago. My remark was simply wishful thinking."

"Considering the things you've been responsible for in your life, Monte, wishful thinking is an understatement," Luca growled.

Monte's attention turned to Luca and a vaguely amused smile hovered around his lips.

"You are quick to judge, my young friend. And yet we are not so very different, you and I. The two of you hunted Rapier for over a century, doing whatever you had to do in order to find him and avenge the supposed death of Callista McAllister isn't that so?"

"Not even remotely the same thing, Monte," Luca retorted. "It's the difference between light and dark. We don't drag innocents into our fight."

"Do you not?" Monte purred. Then his voice hardened. "Perhaps you should tell that to the young woman Jacques left rotting in the dumpster, or the woman at the docks, or maybe the young brother who witnessed his sister's murder and will likely never be the same. Do you think he would agree with your assessment? Oh, yes, I know all about Jacques' little attempts to gain your attention, *Earthbound*. Pray continue to enlighten me on how no innocents were sacrificed in the making of *your* revenge, won't you?"

Mac, a tic visible in his cheek, fixed a stare on Luca and shifted in his chair. Luca knew the deaths of those women weighed heavily on his friend. Hell, they'd both suffered sleepless nights over it. The loss of innocent lives had been unintended and unforeseen on their part, while Monte had involved innocents with deliberate forethought. He saw the same look on Mac's face that he suspected must be apparent on his own. Regret mixed with resignation. They both felt the burden of culpability, yet both knew they would follow the same path again to achieve the extermination of Rapier and exact vengeance for a woman they both loved.

Luca was torn. He couldn't let go of the rage he felt when he considered what had happened to Gia, and he found it difficult to even contemplate what might have happened to Calli if the *Fallen's* thugs had gotten to her.

Yet, knowing Monte's history with this demon, could he really continue to condemn his actions? Would Luca have operated any differently if it were his wife, his child? Would Mac?

Ultimately, whatever the impetus, whether in the name of good or whether in the name of evil, the outcome was the same. Innocent lives had been lost in the quest for justice on both sides. Perhaps Monte had a point. At the heart of it, maybe they weren't so different after all.

Luca forcibly swallowed the bile that rose to choke him at the realization. He looked at Mac whose expression revealed he'd reached the same conclusion. Kat reached for her husband's hand and sent an understanding look in Luca's direction.

"Mac?"

"Your call, brother."

Luca turned to Monte. His stomach churned and his fists were clenched tightly at his sides. He concentrated on his breathing as the minutes ticked by. In. Out. In. Out. 'Atta boy, Fiorelli. You can do this. He hoped he wouldn't live to regret it.

"Okay, Ignazio, what's our next move?" He finally forced out between stiff lips.

Monte rose from behind the desk, loosened his tie and yanked it over his head with the knot still intact. He tossed it on the desk and moved toward a wall of built in cabinets on the far side of the office.

"If you will permit me a few moments to change?" He quirked an enquiring brow in Luca's direction.

Luca nodded stiffly. Monte opened a door and began jerking leathers from their hangers.

"*Signora* McAllister, I suppose it is too much to hope that you have inherited your ancestress' talent for summoning?"

Kat jumped in surprise. "Well, if I have, *signore*, I'm not aware of it."

"Unfortunate, but not unexpected. Then perhaps while I am dressing you can begin to think about your friend, this *Signorina* Gates. The demon will play on her emotions while he toys with us. No doubt, she has confided in you. Try to think of something she wants. Something she would never act on in her right mind. If we can figure that out, we might be able to figure out where to start looking."

Monte disappeared behind another door with his arms loaded. Kat's face twisted in concentration and then her head snapped up as she let out a strangled gasp and a look of dread widened her eyes.

"What is it, baby?" Mac tugged her hand to gain her attention.

"I know where she's going, Kassian. I know what she wants." Kat's horrified gaze swung to Luca.

"*You*, Luca. Elle wants you."

Luca watched the color drain from Mac's face even as he felt the blood leave his own. Mac pulled Kat into his arms.

"We'll get the ring." And they were gone.

Elle Gates wanted him? Kat had no doubt informed her his heart was taken. He was off limits. Now Azakriel possessed her and the forbidden was his specialty. Calli. He had to get to Calli.

"Monte!" Luca roared struggling to contain the total panic threatening to incapacitate him. "Move it, now!"

The *Fallen* threw open the door so forcefully that it nearly tore from its hinges. Dressed in black leather from head to toe, he tossed a thick packet on his desk and then strode directly at Luca without hesitation. Luca reached out and grabbed a fistful of leather. That quickly, they too were gone.

Chapter Sixteen

Callista paced the length of the villa for what felt like the hundredth time that day. The soles of the more comfortable flats she'd adopted after a single day in stiletto boots slapped rhythmically on the marble inlaid floors and terracotta tiles as she wore a path from the front door to the back and then to the front again. They'd said they were only going to talk to Monte. What could be taking so long?

She tugged the cell phone Kassian had given her from the back pocket of her jeans and checked the screen. She hadn't quite figured out to use the device yet, but found when she hit any button, a light came on and the time was displayed. It was nearly three o'clock. Luca had programmed in his number, as well as Kassian's and Kat's, but Calli hadn't yet had any occasion to call anyone. She wasn't even sure she could and it probably wasn't the best time to begin experimenting. She doubted Luca would appreciate her interrupting him while he was working.

She jammed the phone back into her pocket with a sigh. She and Luca had barely had any time alone this morning and no time at all to talk before Kassian burst in. The longer Luca was gone, the more worried Calli became that the distance had given him time to reconsider.

For Calli, last night had been life-changing. Even

now, when she dwelt too long on the things they'd done together her bones melted and her pulse raced. She pressed her fingers to her lips, remembering the tingling heat of Luca's mouth on hers. She imagined she could still taste him. But what if it hadn't been the same for him? She'd believed it had last night, but now the doubts crept in.

What if she was no good at it at all, even after they'd practiced again and again, and he didn't want to hurt her feelings by saying so. Her heart sank. Was Luca already regretting last night and deliberately staying away? He'd said he loved her, but what if it wasn't enough?

Desperate to suppress the worrisome thoughts, she'd spent part of the day practicing Italian with Maria. But that had been hours ago and after putting a large cast iron pot of *pasta fagiole* to simmer on the stove for dinner, Maria had returned home to care for her own family. Now Calli found herself alone with the silence and her uncertainty.

Calli slumped against the window frame in the parlor, absently observing the antics of two younger Ursuline sisters from the convent next door. The white veil over their guimpe and bandeau branded the women as novices who had yet to take their final vows. Ostensibly, the sisters were tasked with watering the rose bushes inside the wall, but away from the watchful eye of the Reverend Mother, the chore had degraded into a water fight. By the time the two ran giggling along the side of the convent toward the back garden, there was more water dousing their habits than nourishing the thirsty plants.

Calli was roused from her contemplation of the

nuns by the arrival of a long black car pulling up to the curb in front of the villa. Her mother told her that the Ursulines rented modest rooms to students and visiting family members of the foreign seminarians studying in Rome, but the car seemed a bit too luxurious for anyone seeking the humble, no frills accommodations offered by the nuns.

Calli watched nervously as a short, stocky man got out of the driver's door, and glanced up and down the street before approaching the villa's front gate. He was dressed in a dark suit with a chauffer's cap pulled low on his forehead throwing his face into shadow. He pressed the button on the intercom, folded his hands in front of him, and waited with his head down.

Calli tiptoed her way to the small box near the front door and bit her lip. Should she answer or simply pretend no one was at home? She'd promised Luca she wouldn't leave the villa, but talking to someone through an intercom was hardly the same thing, was it? Besides, the man was outside the gate and the *sigils* would keep him out, so what harm could there be in seeing what he wanted? At this point, she welcomed almost any distraction. She pressed her eye against the peephole in the massive wooden door. The man *looked* harmless enough. She took a deep breath and pressed the button the way she'd seen Maria do.

"Yes?" she breathed into the small black box in a voice that trembled slightly.

"*Signorina* McAllister? Callista McAllister?"

"Yes. I'm sorry…do I know you, *signore?*"

"Ah! *Buon pomeriggio*, good afternoon. *Signore* Fiorelli sent me."

"He did?"

"*Si, signorina*. I am to take you to meet him."

"Meet him where?"

"It's a surprise, *signorina*."

A surprise? Calli loved surprises, and Luca was well aware of it. Still, she'd promised not to leave the house. Her eyes narrowed as a thought struck her. She'd hoped Luca finally saw her as a mature, responsible woman and not some impulsive, thoughtless half-wit, but what if this was some kind of test? Her lips compressed into a thin line. *Of course, that was it!* No doubt he and her brother were watching in amusement from behind the darkened windows of the car at this very moment, waiting for her to give in to temptation and venture outside.

Katrina would be against it, of course, but Calli could just picture Luca and her brother, heads together, maybe even placing a wager on how long she would last before venturing out of the house despite her promise to remain inside. Calli had lost count of the things that had changed while she existed in her time capsule of captivity, but apparently, men and their need to amuse themselves with silly games was not one of them.

She glued her eye to the peephole and poked the button on the intercom. Luca and Kassian would have done well to remember she had a particular talent for games herself and she had never been a graceful loser.

"I am very sorry, *signore*. I am not free to go with you at the moment. Please convey my deepest regrets to *Signore* Fiorelli."

Calli swallowed a giggle as the man's head snapped up so suddenly that he nearly lost his cap. He recovered quickly however, and tugged it back down over the bridge of his nose.

"Scusi?"

"I said," Calli repeated, being careful to speak loudly and annunciate clearly. "I find I'm unable to leave the house at this time. Please convey my regrets to *Signore* Fiorelli and tell him I look forward to his return."

Calli burst out laughing when she observed the man's reaction to her announcement. He first turned in a complete circle, then looked at the car, looked at the house, looked at the car again. He removed his hat. He scratched his head. Finally, he walked back to the car and knocked on the window.

Well, that would show them! She was so busy congratulating herself on her own cleverness, she almost forgot to be offended that Luca might doubt her even after last night and all that had passed between them. Of course, maybe Luca had complete faith in her and the entire ridiculous production was her charming brother's idea. That seemed more likely. She pressed her eye to the door once again to see if they would give up the game and come into the house now that she had proven them wrong. The car window was open a bit and the driver hunched forward, talking to someone in the back seat. Then the door opened and Calli observed a pair of thigh high leather boots, followed by slim black leggings, a beaded sweater, and a very large pair of sunglasses climb from the car. The entire package was topped by spiked red hair and long, dangling earrings that winked flirtatiously in the late afternoon sun. Stunned, Calli's mouth dropped open in shock. Balanced fashionably on the mile high stilettos stood Kat's friend, Elle Gates.

Calli opened the door and quickly motioned for Elle to stay outside the gate.

"Um, security system," she called. "No one can get in and I don't know how to turn it off. I'm afraid you'll have to wait until the others return. Kat will be so happy to see you, Elle. Everyone has been terribly worried. Where on earth have you been?"

"Oh it's a long story," Elle laughed carelessly. "Come on, I'll tell you on the way."

"On the way? Oh, but I promised Luca I wouldn't leave the house until he comes back." Calli chewed on her lower lip. She felt incredibly rude making Elle wait outside on the walk, but she couldn't undo the *sigils* herself so it really couldn't be helped.

"I know," Elle called back. "But you *can* get out, right? I called Kat from the airport and she asked if I could swing by and pick you up. We're going to meet up with them for a late lunch."

"We are? Have they finished with Monte, then?" Calli asked slowly. Of course, Elle was Kat's friend. If Kat had asked her to stop by and bring Calli along, then it must be all right. So why did her stomach churn with indecision? When in doubt, defer.

"Monte? Ignazio Monte? Well, well, well," Elle's lips curled in a sneer. "What an unexpected boon."

"What?"

"Oh, nothing," Elle waved a hand airily. "I've heard of him, that's all. Yes, I guess they must be finished. Come on, let's go. It'll be fun!"

"I'll need to change my clothes first. I've been, uh…helping Maria in the kitchen. Can I at least bring you something to drink? You must be exhausted after your flight."

"I wouldn't say no to a glass of wine," Elle smiled brightly.

"Wonderful! I'll bring one right out and then I'll get dressed, all right?"

"Sounds like a plan."

Calli smiled and closed the door. She scurried to the kitchen and grabbed a glass from the cabinet, splashing it full of wine from the first bottle that came to hand. Her hands were trembling so badly that it sloshed all over the tiled counter. She barely noticed.

Something wasn't right. In her heart she knew Luca would have come for her himself. At the very least, he would have called to alert her to the change in plans. Wouldn't he? Of course, he would.

She'd become so used to being surrounded by people since her rescue that she'd allowed the temporary solitude to feed her imagination. Luca loved her. He did. And he would never send Elle Gates to fetch her after she'd promised to stay in the house until he returned. He would simply come for her himself.

And something about Elle seemed slightly off. Calli wasn't sure what was going on, but thought the best course of action was simply to stay within the protection of the *sigils* until either she figured it out or the others returned.

Decision made, she picked up the glass and hurried back to the door. She took a deep, fortifying breath and stepped out onto the porch. Elle waited exactly where she'd left her, and the back door of the car remained open, but the driver was nowhere to be seen. Calli assumed he'd gotten back into the car to wait.

She made her way carefully down the porch steps and across the front walk to the stone arch that crouched over the iron gate. Out of the corner of her eye, she noticed two little veil-covered heads peering furtively over the convent wall.

"Here you are," Calli smiled as she half opened the gate and held out the glass. "You know, I'm really not very hungry. Why don't you go along and meet the others? Have a wonderful meal. I think I'll wait here and see you later, all right?"

Being careful to stay within the confines of the arch, Calli reached out a bit further to hand the wine to Elle when she made no move to take it. As soon as Calli's hand passed through the invisible shield of the *sigils*, the other woman's hand shot out without warning and her fingers locked painfully around Calli's exposed wrist. The glass crashed to the ground, shattering on the concrete and spattering red wine everywhere.

"What's the matter with you, Elle? What are you doing? Please let go of me at once!" Calli cried out in alarm while tugging ineffectually against the freakishly strong grip of the other woman.

"Please let go of me at once," Elle mocked in a little girl sing-song voice. Then her voice changed completely. So much so, that it was nearly unrecognizable when she continued in a deep, sneering tone. "Always so polite, Callista. You really are a wishy-washy little thing. Luca may believe he loves you, but what he really needs is a woman who can stand beside him, not one that meekly hides like a frightened rabbit when trouble rears its head. He'll realize that soon enough once you're gone."

As soon as Elle touched her, Calli felt the unmistakable creep of evil along her spine. However, she had no time to contemplate the return of the sensation or the reason Elle triggered it because with one determined pull, Elle jerked her through the gate and clear of the protection of the *sigils*. She spun Calli around and painfully wretched her arm up between her shoulder blades. The driver popped up from behind the car and hurried forward with a piece of cloth bunched in his hand. He quickly clamped it over Calli's nose and mouth. She had scant seconds to glimpse the heads of the two little nuns as they disappeared below the convent wall, and then the world dissolved into nothingness.

****

Calli opened her eyes to darkness so complete that she feared she might actually be dead. When she tried to sit up and only succeeded in rising a few inches before coming into contact with solid rock, the screaming pain in her head convinced her otherwise. The air around her was dry and suffocating, clogging her nostrils with the scent of dust and death.

Gingerly, she reached out and cautiously felt her surroundings hoping for any sort of clue. Positioned on her back, the area beneath her was solid and unforgiving. Thanks to the swollen lump blooming on her forehead, she knew that a few inches above her was a rough wall of solid rock. There was less than a foot of space between the two.

Wherever she was, it was small, it was dirty, and it was dark. When she tried to shimmy down in the direction of her feet, she found she progressed no more than a few inches and then she shifted her weight when her cell phone dug uncomfortably into her right buttock. Her phone!

Calli carefully snaked her arm along her side and lifted her bottom slightly to slide the phone from her pocket and press a button. The light wasn't very bright, but it was better than nothing. Calli turned the device in every direction trying to assess her surroundings. She failed to swallow the scream that rose in her throat when she turned her head to the left and an ancient human skull grinned back at her, mere inches from her face. With her heart hammering and her breath coming in short, painful gasps, she directed the light along the wall on her left and saw what appeared to be a complete skeleton pushed into a tangled heap to the side of where she lay. It took her but a moment to understand the reason the remains were crammed in a pile against the wall. She was currently occupying their former resting place.

Clearly, Elle Gates had gone insane. Panic seized her throat in an iron fist, stealing her breath until she feared she would strangle. Her teeth chattered as she rallied every ounce of determination she possessed to stay conscious and fight against the overwhelming terror that gripped her. Dear God, she was buried alive!

Chapter Seventeen

Luca roared Calli's name before he and Monte had even fully materialized in the parlor of the *Via Dandolo* house. When nothing but silence greeted him, he released Monte's jacket with such force that the *Fallen* stumbled over the coffee table and crashed to the floor. Ignoring him, Luca strode into the kitchen, and the first thing he noticed was the soup bubbling on the stove and the wine spilled on the counter. He ran a finger through the deep red puddle and put it to his lips. Chianti. *Merde!* Calli didn't drink Chianti. He stormed out of the kitchen and headed for the stairs, trying to convince himself she was upstairs in her room, when Monte's voice reached him from the foyer.

The front door stood wide open, as did the gate at the street. Monte was already halfway down the walk when Luca streaked past him, his eyes riveted on the glint of shattered glass and the telltale stain on the pavement outside gate. Somehow, the demon had convinced her to leave the safety of the villa. Somehow, he'd managed to lure her beyond the protection of the *sigils*. Calli would never have willingly left on her own. He understood that now. But, it didn't change the fact that she was gone. Because of him. She'd become the demon's target because Luca loved her. If he'd had the strength to walk away, she would have been safe.

Luca didn't realize he was having an audible

monologue with himself until Monte grabbed him by his jacket and nearly lifted him off his feet despite being the smaller man.

"There will be plenty of time to fall apart later if we fail," the *Fallen* growled. "You are a *Defensori*. Act like one. Pull yourself together, Fiorelli. A babbling idiot is no good to her."

Luca stared at the other man as though he'd never seen him before. Then he took a deep breath and stepped back.

"You're right. I believed she was dead for over a hundred years and she wasn't. I *will* find her no matter how long it takes. This time I won't give up on her. I won't give up on us."

"Good." Monte whacked him on the shoulder and turned to go back into the house. Luca used his boot to kick the glass remnants from the center of the walkway and grabbed the gate to pull it closed behind him. Mac and Kat should be here any minute. They would sit down, put their heads together, and figure it out. And then he would go and bring Calli home. He had to believe it. Otherwise the hole eating through his chest would devour him completely.

"Scusi, signore?"

The words were so softly spoken that for a moment, Luca thought he'd imagined them. He spun on his heel and saw two young sisters, presumably from the convent next door. One hung back as though the very sight of him terrified her and the other reached back and pulled her forward to stand beside her.

"You are looking for the *signorina*? *La bella capelli* ..." her face creased in concentration as she struggled to find the correct word. She put her hands on

209

the top of her head and ran them down the sides until she reached her waist.

"The beautiful long hair?" Luca stepped forward and they both took a step back. He forcibly reigned in his excitement and stopped moving. Dare he hope they'd seen something that could help? "*Si, sorelle*. I am looking for the *signorina con capelli lunghi*. Have you seen her?"

"*Si, signore*. There was a woman in *un automobile. Il grande automobile nero*. She did not want to go. The woman took her."

"A woman in a big black car? She took her?"

"*Si, signore. La bellezza* brought a glass of wine. When she gave it to the woman, the woman grabbed her and pulled her through the gate. And the man, he put a cloth over the *signorina's* face," piped up the second nun.

Chloroform. *Cazzo!* Wherever they'd taken her, she'd likely have been unconscious the entire trip. Even if he could somehow hope to reach her mind, she'd have no way of telling him where she was.

"We wanted to help, *signore*, but we did not know what to do. She did not want to go," the frightened young sister said again.

"No, she did not want to go," Luca agreed. "And it would not have been safe for you to interfere, *sorella*. You did the right thing. *Grazie* for telling me what you saw. *Mille grazie*."

"*Prego, signore*. I hope you find her."

So do I, Luca thought darkly as the two novices scurried back to the safety of the convent and disappeared behind the wall. Luca slammed the gate forcibly enough to knock it from its hinges and stalked back down the walk to the villa, taking the steps two at a time. Monte paced the length of the porch restlessly waiting.

"Anything helpful?"

Luca scrubbed a hand over his face.

"Not really. She was taken in a black car, probably a limo. They chloroformed her." How in the name of all that was holy could he find her with nothing more to go on than that? Luca knew he was in danger of letting his fear for Callista control him. Monte was right, and if that didn't beat all. Luca Fiorelli taking advice from a *Fallen*. He could fall apart later. Right now, he needed to find his center, his dispassion. Right now, he needed to be a warrior. Right now, Calli needed him. This time, he would not fail her.

"Mac, where in the hell are you?"

"Right here." Kassian and Kat appeared in the parlor the moment Luca sent the thought. They took one look at his face and went completely still. "She's gone?"

Luca turned away from the pain in his friend's eyes. He knew it was a pale reflection of his own. He concentrated on breathing. Until Calli was in his arms. Until the demon was destroyed. He just had to keep breathing.

"She left the house?" Mac roared loudly enough to rattle the glass in the windows. "I'll kill her! First I'll find her, and then I'll kill her!"

Luca turned back to him.

"She didn't leave willingly," he sighed in a tired voice. "Apparently she took Elle a glass of wine. When she handed it through the gate, they grabbed her and dragged her out. Then they chloroformed her and drove away in a limo."

"How the hell do you know all that?" Mac demanded hotly.

Luca jerked his head in the direction of the convent. "A couple of the nuns saw it all."

"And that helps us, how?" Mac snapped.

"Well," Kat laid her palms on her husband's chest and stroked him soothingly. "We know she was alive. The demon could have simply induced Elle to kill her outright, but he didn't. Maybe Elle is stronger than we're giving her credit for. Maybe she's fighting to do the right thing."

"I very much doubt that," Monte said. "A human doesn't have the ability to block him from the mind as we do. Still, your wife is right. We know she was alive when they took her. That means there is a chance she is still alive."

"But for how long?" Luca muttered miserably. He'd been sending out thought after thought in an attempt to reach her since they'd arrived at the villa. Either she was too far away, still unconscious, or...No. He couldn't go there. Could. Not. Go there. He had no idea how they would find her, but he had to believe they would. Hell, he had to believe it, or he would disintegrate into a hot mess right here in the parlor.

"May I make a suggestion?" Monte asked.

"Well, any idea is one more than we've got now," Mac retorted glumly.

Monte cocked a brow. "Does Callista have a cell phone?"

"Yes, she does," Kat spoke up. "But I don't think she's ever used it. She finds it complicated and frustrating. She rarely even remembers to carry it."

"I'm not sure how that would help anyway." Mac rubbed the back of his neck and shook his head. "I mean sure, we could try calling her, but do you honestly think Azakriel would let her answer and tell us where she is?"

"I was thinking of GPS," Monte said. "Is her phone equipped with any tracking applications?"

"Damn! I never even thought to activate it," Luca exploded. Why would he? Until recently, Calli hardly left the house.

"Perhaps we can find her, anyway," Monte replied. "There are websites that provide the service for such things for a fee."

"You know how to do this?" Mac asked.

"Not exactly, but I am willing to try. I need her phone number and a computer."

Mac waved Monte toward a small table near the window where a laptop sat among a pile of papers. He hung over the *Fallen's* shoulder as Monte powered up the machine and began typing.

"I'm going to text her," Luca announced suddenly. He yanked his phone from his pocket.

"Luca," Kat stepped over to her brother and laid a comforting hand on his arm. "Calli has no idea how to text."

"I know that." Luca's fingers shook and he had to backspace and re-enter time after time. "But she can read, can't she? If there's any possibility she will see this, I want her to know I'm coming for her. I want her to know I won't give up this time…I want…"

Luca raised his eyes to his sister's and saw the pain and compassion. She believed it was futile. He glanced around at the others. Monte's attention was glued to the computer screen. Mac's face could have been carved in stone. Luca recognized that look. Mac was already grieving. None of them believed there was any chance of finding Calli alive. Well screw them all. Anyone who wanted him to believe Calli was lost to him would have to prove it.

Diavolo! He would not accept that he'd found his soul and regained his heart to lose it after one night of incredible passion. She was a part of him now. He would feel it if her soul had moved on. But the minutes were ticking by, and they were no closer to knowing where to look. He blew out a long, shaky breath. He tapped the screen to send the message and shoved the phone back in his pocket. "Well, it can't hurt, right?"

"No," Kat replied softly. She stretched up and pressed her lips to Luca's cheek. "No, it can't hurt."

****

Calli concentrated on counting breaths until she tamed her initial panic. Hysteria did not lend itself to logic and if she had any hope of surviving this, she had to think. Wasn't Luca always telling her she had to use her head? She listened carefully, but beyond the confines of her dusty tomb, she detected nothing but complete and utter silence. During her years with Jacques Rapier, she'd read anything and everything, including dozens of archeological texts and had come to the conclusion that she'd been sealed in a loculus, a recess in a catacomb where the ancients buried their dead. Given the number of catacombs in Rome, it was the only thing that made sense. Though why Elle would do this to her escaped Calli's understanding completely. She did know that unless she could find her way out, she was doomed. There were hundreds of kilometers of dark and narrow underground tunnels and tombs running beneath the city of Rome and its surroundings, some well-known, but others scarcely explored. Even if she managed to escape the confines of the tomb, she realized she was likely to find herself in what amounted to a dark and confusing maze. But doing something had to be better than doing nothing. She'd survived over a century in the clutches of Jack the Ripper. Surely she could outwit a lunatic redhead with designs on Luca.

She turned on her side as far as possible, holding her phone up to the wall that ran the length of the compartment opposite the dusty remains of her companion. It looked as though it had been cobbled together from brick, dirt, and loose tufa, a porous, volcanic rock found beneath the city. She didn't know how long she'd been unconscious, but deduced it couldn't possibly have been long enough for the moist earth packed among the rubble to harden. She felt along between the stones and her fingers came away damp. She began to claw methodically at the moist edges with her nails but it wasn't long before they were ragged and bloody. She sucked her first two fingers into her mouth and laved them with her tongue to soothe the sting, grimacing at the dusty, metallic taste.

"Well, so much for my first manicure," Calli sighed in the direction of her sightless and still grinning companion. She shone her light in his direction and regarded him critically.

"Since we find ourselves in such intimate quarters, I feel as though you should have a name. I'm sure you were once called something lovely and noble like Atticus or Horatio, but honestly you look like a George to me." Not surprisingly, her fellow cellmate offered no objection. "All right then, George it is. What's that you say, George? You're feeling a bit cramped? Yes, I understand completely and I promise to give you room to stretch just as soon as possible. I must say, this is a sticky wicket, George. If only I had a tool of some sort, I'm sure I could loosen this mess."

Mother of God, Calli thought semi-hysterically. I've been reduced to conversing with bones.

Bones? Calli carefully avoided looking directly at her new found friend as she grimaced in distaste and tentatively plunged her hand into the tangled nest of his remains.

"Do forgive me, George," Calli apologized as her fingers curled triumphantly around a humerus that had been broken to a point near the epiphysis. "But at the moment, your arm is of far more use to me than it is to you."

She shifted again and laid her phone on the ground, freeing both hands. Using the pointed end of the bone, she laboriously began to scour a groove along the edges and between the stones of the makeshift wall. Up and down, back and forth, as far as she could reach, over and over, until her arms shook and her upper back burned. It might have been minutes, it might have been hours, but finally the grooves felt as though they were relatively deep. She set the bone carefully at her side and angled her body diagonally. Then she began to push. Every muscle in her body protested as she braced her shoulders and strained her legs against the stones. She paused to rest and dragged the back of her wrist across her eyes. It came away wet. She hadn't even realized she was crying.

"It's no use, George," she sniffed. "All the desire

and determination in the world can't take the place of sheer physical strength." She would die here in this airless tomb with a silent pile of bones the solitary witness. She would never again feel Luca's arms around her or feel his body moving against hers. She would never again see the light in his bright silver eyes or the smile that was hers alone. She had gained Luca's heart only to lose him after such a brief time. Her chest ached with it, a dark, empty pit of nothingness. And weighing on top of it all was the knowledge that he would believe she'd left the house willingly and the fault had been hers. Again.

"Damn, damn, damn!" She raged, pummeling her feet against the stone in impotent despair. And then she felt the rocks shift. She froze, breathing heavily. She flattened her feet upon the wall and gave another tentative push. The earth around her groaned and creaked, and the entire conglomeration crashed down into the tunnel outside with a roar and a choking cloud of dust.

"Bloody hell!" Calli croaked right before fit of coughing overtook her.

"I suppose that's what I get for swearing, George," Calli gasped. As the dust began to settle, she wiped her eyes on the sleeve of her sweater and leaned cautiously toward the gaping hole. She aimed the light from her phone down and peered over the edge. Relief swamped her when her inspection revealed she lay less than three or four feet up from the floor of the tunnel. She felt around until she found the fractured humerus. She stretched behind her and gently replaced it in the pitiful heap of bones.

"Thanks for your help, George. I couldn't have

done it without you," she whispered softly. A slave, a merchant, a politician, or a pope. Calli would never know the identity of her temporary cellmate, but in her heart, he would always be plain old George. She replaced her phone in her back pocket to ensure she wouldn't drop it. She took a deep breath, swung her legs over the side, and dropped to the floor. She failed to accomplish the graceful landing she'd been hoping for. Her feet struck the uneven pile of rubble where it had come to rest. Thrown off balance, she tumbled head first into the tunnel wincing at the coarse scrape of stone and debris further abrading her already raw hands when she instinctively threw them forward to catch herself. She paused to regain her breath, and then climbed painfully to her feet.

She shook out her sweater and started to dust off her backside when her phone vibrated against her buttock. She fished it out of her pocket and looked at the screen, startled to see Luca's face. Tears blurred his image as she reached to stroke his cheek with a grubby finger as though she could actually touch him. To her further amazement, when she ran her finger along the screen, the image disappeared and a message took its place. Texting. Kat had called it texting.

"Hold on. I'm coming. I will find u. I will always find u. I love u."

Calli used the back of her wrist to dash away the tears, leaving her eyes gritty and burning. She didn't know how to text. In fact, using the phone for a light was the first time she'd found the device even remotely useful. How would Luca and the others ever find her if she couldn't even tell them where she was? She squinted down at the little screen. REPLY? Well, yes of course she wanted to reply. She touched the screen. There was an empty space and below that, rows of letters and the word SEND. Obviously, she wanted to *send* a reply, otherwise what was the point? Really! Sometimes these modern contraptions were just plain silly. She poked her finger at the screen to confirm she wanted to send a message and then stared, dumbfounded, as the keyboard disappeared and the display returned to the home screen.

Calli growled in frustration. Apparently, she was supposed to use the little keyboard to spell out a message *before* confirming she wanted to send it. She swiped her finger along the screen and poked angrily at the icons but failed to bring up Luca's message again. She slumped against the wall and sighed wondering if she would ever get the hang of technology. She blew a tendril of hair out of her eyes and then decided if she didn't find a way out of the catacombs, it would be a moot point. She stuck the phone in her pocket and combed her fingers through her tangled hair. She pulled it over her shoulder and quickly began to plait it into her signature braid to keep it out of her way, thankful she hadn't given in to the stylist's suggestion to cut even more of the length than she had. She wrapped a strand of hair around the end to hold it in place. It wasn't perfect but it would have to do. The phone vibrated again. Calli quickly yanked it free and touched the screen.

"Touch REPLY. Type a message with the letters. Then touch SEND. R U ok? Can U tell us where U R?"

Calli groaned in relief. She took her time and carefully followed Luca's directions hoping she could send an actual message this time. After tapping reply, she began touching each letter in turn, delighted to see the message appearing in the space above. She frowned when she couldn't see a way to keep the letters from all running together, but hoped Luca would be able to decipher her meaning.

Calli thought the message looked like unintelligible gibberish but she'd done what she could. She touched send and hoped for the best. Calli closed her eyes, held her breath, and concentrated intently. She faintly discerned a hint of active thought coming from somewhere to her left. She couldn't make out the specific thoughts, but someone was definitely out there. The light on her phone started to dim and she realized the battery could give out completely before too long leaving her completely alone in the endless darkness. She started moving carefully in a direction where she sensed life, praying whoever was waiting was friend and not foe.

Chapter Eighteen

Kat moved away from Luca to return to her husband's side. She'd barely taken a step when she spun on her heels like a top and regarded her brother with an incredulous expression.

"Was that your *phone*?" she gasped.

Luca's eyes opened impossibly wide. He fumbled in his pocket, feeling like he was all thumbs, hardly daring to believe it. He stared at the display. The message frame was blank but the reply had come from Calli. It brought them no closer to finding her, but at least he had proof she had gotten his message and was still alive. At the moment, he'd take whatever he could get.

"What does she say?" Mac strode across the room holding out his hand for the phone. A look of tentative relief had replaced the stony grief he'd been sporting since returning to find Calli gone.

"It's blank," Luca answered. "But the fact that she responded at all means she's alive, right?"

"She doesn't understand how to text," Kat deduced quickly. "She probably just hit whatever the screen prompted. Give it to me."

Luca barely resisted as his sister snatched the phone from his nerveless fingers and began to type away. She sent the message, took a deep breath, and handed it back.

"Let's see if that helps," she said.

Luca gripped the phone and stared at the screen as though he could will something to appear, afraid if he looked away for even a second he would lose this tenuous connection. The minutes ticked by, and Luca's gut clenched. He swore he could hear the Jeopardy theme playing in the background. And then, miraculously, there was a response.

"amokburiedintombdugoutwithbonethinkiamincata combitwaselleiloveutoo"

"What in the hell is that?" Luca exploded in frustration. He held the phone out to Kat. The message looked like alphabet soup. How was he supposed to find her before the demon decided to finish his work if this was all they had to go on? Luca blamed himself. He should have taken the time to make sure Calli knew how to use the phone, how to text. Just because it was second nature to anyone who'd lived through the birth of the internet and digital communication did not mean it came naturally to someone to whom light bulbs bordered on miraculous.

"Let me see it," Kat coaxed patiently while prying his reluctant fingers away. She looked at the screen for a minute and smiled. "No spacing and no punctuation. It all runs together, but if you take a deep breath and go slowly, it makes perfect sense."

"It does?" He twisted his body to look over her shoulder at the screen.

"Well, yeah. Look." Kat ran her finger across the line a few letters at a time. "She says she's okay, was buried in a tomb, used a bone to dig her way out, and is in a catacomb. Says, it was Elle. Oh, and she also says she loves you, too." Kat handed the phone back with a smirk.

"Well, okay so we know she's alive and the demon seems to have taken a powder, at least for now," Mac said with a frown. "But there must be at least forty known catacombs in and around the city. She could be in any one of them. How in the hell do we figure out which one?"

"If I may?" Monte pushed back from the table and approached them. "You say she used a bone? There is only one catacomb I am aware of that is open to the public and known to still contain bones." He squinted at the computer as a beep sounded and turned back to them with a smile. "The Catacombs of Domitilla."

"*Merde!* They're the most extensive in the city. Four levels of burial chambers alone and the tunnels go on for miles. It's like looking for a needle in a haystack," Luca groaned.

"That's where you're wrong, brother. Forty catacombs are like looking for a needle in haystack. Monte has narrowed it down to maybe a needle in a shoebox. Totally do-able." Mac whacked Luca on the shoulder. "Now let's go get my sister. That sickly look on your face is starting to get on my nerves."

"You aren't looking all that healthy yourself." Luca grumbled in return.

"Perhaps we should split up," Monte injected. "After all, we still need to locate Azakriel, do we not?"

Luca shook his head. "No, we stay together. If we find Azakriel, we need Kat and the ring to control him and we need you and your body to destroy him."

"Ah, *certo*," Monte nodded in agreement. "I was not thinking."

Luca narrowed his eyes in Monte's direction. He

still wasn't completely convinced that the *Fallen* was on the up and up and didn't have some ulterior motive. It simply went against everything he believed to put any trust in a dark one. Whatever. His concern for Calli overrode any devotion to duty at the moment. If the *Fallen* was playing them, Luca would deal with both him and the demon later, once Calli was safe.

"Okay, then," Luca glanced at his wrist. "The catacombs will be closed to the public by now, but there could still be stragglers milling around. Best if we fade inside the wall using the trees as cover. Agreed?" Luca asked.

The others nodded.

"The entrance to the tombs is through the basilica. Once we're sure the coast is clear, we'll get inside and head down into the tunnels."

In a heartbeat, all four peered out from a stand of olive trees within the wall of the complex. After making sure they were unobserved, they sprinted across the courtyard with its well-tended shrubs and stone benches, to the sunken fourth century church that served as the entrance to the vast network of underground tombs. They clambered down the relatively modern staircase until it combined with the more ancient one to reach the floor of the basilica.

The entrance to the tunnels was at the far end, beyond the nave and to the right, and Luca wasted no time in heading straight for it. The others followed closely behind. It didn't escape Luca's notice that Mac carefully kept Kat between the two of them and let Monte bring up the rear. Maybe his old friend wasn't quite as trusting of the *Fallen* as he initially appeared.

As they reached the first stone column, a woman

stepped out from behind the forth, effectively blocking the entrance to the tunnels.

"Elle!" Kat gasped on a sob, starting forward.

Luca's hand shot out and grasped her upper arm.

"Get back, Katrina. That isn't Elle," Luca growled.

"She's in there, Luca. I can feel her," Kat replied in a strained voice. "She's fighting. She's fighting so hard. And she's scared."

"Yeah, well until she's alone in there, there's nothing you can do for her, so get behind us and be ready to use that ring," Luca ordered. As Kat stepped back with obvious reluctance, he drew a dagger from the intricate tattoo on his forearm and knew by the hiss of steel behind him that Mac had drawn his Claymore from the ink on his back.

Monte and Kassian stepped around Kat to Luca's side, forming a wall between her and her possessed friend.

"Ignazio!" squealed the demon in Elle's voice. "A trio of *Earthbound*. What a lovely gift you bring. And here I thought you would still be angry with me after that unfortunate business with Daniela. It's good to know you still remember what side you fight for."

Monte stepped forward, fists clenched at his sides. Mac's free hand closed around the back of the *Fallen's* neck and he leaned into him until his lips nearly touched the other man's ear.

"If you've betrayed us, Monte, there is no place in Heaven or Hell you'll be able to hide," he hissed.

"Don't be a fool, McAllister," Monte growled back. "Discord is how this demon operates. He's trying to divide in the hopes of being able to conquer."

"I hoped you'd see it that way, Azakriel," Monte

called out across the basilica stepping forward and away from Kassian's grip. "I have a proposition for you. Leave the woman. She is weak and it's only a matter of time before your presence kills the body. Join me. Combined, our strength will be tremendous."

"What in the hell are you doing, Monte?" Luca hissed quietly. "This wasn't part of the plan."

"One final effort to avoid a dagger to your friend," Monte muttered. Elle cocked her head at an impossible angle and regarded the *Fallen* with a puzzled look. Then her features twisted into a demonic sneer.

"Tempting, my dark friend, but I see your intent. You reek with despair, old man. By all means, join your dead ones if you wish, but you won't take me with you. True, this body weakens, but an *Earthbound* would give me strength equal to yours. I've already taken your woman, Fiorelli, perhaps McAllister's should be next?"

"Aim well, Fiorelli. Azakriel won't leave the body unless he fears the woman is dying," Monte said in a low, tense voice. "As soon as he emerges your sister must snare him with the ring, direct him into me, and hold him there while McAllister runs me through."

Luca heard Kat's audible gasp behind him. His jaw clenched painfully. He and Mac may have conveniently forgotten to mention the part about possibly killing Elle to force the demon to release her.

He slammed his shields into place. He couldn't afford to let himself dwell on how difficult this would be for his sister. It would affect his ability to do what had to be done and the additional emotion swirling about the confined space would only be more of a distraction for Kat. Luca hoped his skills were up to inflicting a wound that appeared mortal enough to fool a demon while actually being benign enough to save Elle when it was all over.

Otherwise, he wasn't sure his sister would ever be able to forgive him. In fact, he'd be struggling to forgive himself. Sometimes he thought there was nothing in Elle's head but squirrels playing with knives, but she was an innocent and Kat loved her.

"Can you do this, cara?" Luca sent the thought to his sister on the common pathway which allowed Mac to hear.

"Yes," came the faint, pained reply.

"As soon as Elle goes down, the demon will rise and head straight for you, Kat," Mac directed his wife. His fear for her was apparent in the strained tone of his thoughts. *You need to gain control of him before he can reach you. Are you ready?"*

"Hell no, but I will be. Let's do it."

Out of the corner of his eye, Luca saw his sister twist the Ring of Aandalena into place with the stones facing her palm. She tightened her fist around it.

He flexed his own fingers nervously and then balanced the dagger in his hand. His vision focused on Elle Gate's chest and the pinpoint area that would seat his dagger a hair's breadth from taking her life, but close enough to convince the demon her body was doomed. There was no room for error. He had one chance to get this right, and he hoped to hell his sister could keep it together long enough to control the demon.

Then he would find Calli. He took a deep breath and blew it out slowly. His world contracted to a spot less than the size of a dime. With a lightning quick flick of his wrist, he released the dagger. Kat brought her hand up simultaneously as though they were participants in some well-rehearsed dance instead of two desperate people flying by the seat of their pants.

Elle's mouth dropped open, and her eyes widened in pain as the dagger pierced her flesh. She dropped heavily to her knees on the cold, stone floor.

A writhing black shadow rose from the top of her head as the demon left her, and she slumped to the ground. Her face wore a mask of agony as she reached out and gasped Kat's name. Then her eyes closed, and she went motionless except for the still quivering dagger buried in her chest.

The dark form hovered over her as if undecided, then swirled in a circle and launched itself directly at Kat. Mac pulled her against him, and Monte stepped in front of her as she brought her hand up over his shoulder and directed her palm toward the demon.

Tears streamed down her face, and her breath came in great gulping sobs, but her hand remained steady and her voice strong as she chanted the Latin incantation Michael had given her.

The temperature in the church dropped noticeably as the demon approached. Despite the frosty puffs of breath emanating from Kat's nose and mouth, Luca could see the shiny beads of sweat forming on her smooth brow and dripping into her wide, gray eyes as she concentrated on her task. Midway down the aisle the shadow hesitated, thrashing wildly as it fought to resist Kat's power. She had him!

Luca swiveled his head toward the entrance of the catacombs as an unexpected movement entered his peripheral vision.

"Luca!" Calli's face lit up at the sight of him, and

he felt the steel fist squeezing his heart loosen for the first time since he returned to the villa to find her gone. He realized he wasn't the only one distracted as Calli began to run toward him.

Kat stumbled over the incantation. It was a momentary lapse, but it was enough to allow the demon to break her hold on him. With a roar that shook the stone pillars and caused dust to trickle from the ceiling, Azakriel changed direction and headed straight for Luca.

"Calli, no!" Luca yelled as he understood the demon's intent. Calli picked up her pace, screaming his name.

Luca barely had time to register the terror on her dust streaked face before something hit him with the force of a freight train, driving him back. The ancient stone offered no cushion whatsoever as his head slammed into the wall and everything went black.

Chapter Nineteen

Calli cradled Luca's head in her lap, trying to remain as inconspicuous as possible as she watched Kat struggle to regain control of the shadow. She felt as though she had been wandering the maze of tight, dark corridors, roughly carved in the tufa and lined with tomb niches, for hours. She'd lost count of the times she'd stumbled on the uneven floors and banged her head on low ceilings or hanging oil lamps. Finally, she'd fortuitously wandered into an area usually open to tourists and followed the dim lights to a stairway that led back up to the basilica. She emerged from the tunnels and nearly collapsed in relief to find Luca waiting. She hadn't given a moment's consideration to what he was doing there, she simply honed in on him like a heat seeking missile.

It was only when he called out her name that she became aware of the others and saw the dark shape streaking toward Luca at top speed.

Terrified, she faded in the middle of her sprint and hit Luca with the determination of a linebacker, or maybe it was called a quarterback? She still didn't understand the finer points of the game that kept her brother and Luca glued to the television on Monday evenings. She had no idea how she'd done it, but she wasn't about to question it as it had gotten Luca out of the way just in time.

She hoped she hadn't driven his head into the wall hard enough to cause amnesia. If he woke up and didn't remember that he loved her, it would simply be too ironic! Of course, she had no problem devoting the next several hundred years to reminding him.

A faint smile hovered around her lips. She could think of a few interesting ways right off the top of her head.

"Now!"

Calli tore her gaze away from Luca's still face and returned her attention to the battle unfolding to her left. Kat had regained control of the demon and directed it into the body of the *Fallen,* Ignazio Monte. Her sister-in-law trembled from head to toe with the strain of holding him there as Monte threw out his arms, exposing himself to Kassian's sword.

"You must hold him until I am dead," Monte gritted out, staring intently at Kat. She nodded her understanding, and Calli saw her jaw tighten until the cords in her neck stood out.

"Are you sure, Monte?"

Monte threw his head back and screamed at the ceiling. His body undulated wildly as he struggled to dominate the demon possessing him.

"Do it, McAllister," Monte gasped. "It's the only way and your wife weakens."

Kassian gripped the Claymore in both hands and brought it back to strike.

"Nooooo," the *Fallen* roared loudly enough to shake the church and dislodge several of the stone inscriptions displayed on the walls.

Kassian hesitated for a heartbeat and Monte lunged at Kat through the settling dust.

Kassian impaled the *Fallen* in one smooth motion before the demon could touch his wife.

Kat's arm trembled violently and she dropped to her knees, using her other hand to hold steady the one wearing the ring, as the demon fought to escape the *Fallen's* dying body.

Kassian stood over the man, his feet spread on either side of Monte, and rested his weight on the hilt of his sword, pinning the *Fallen* to the stone floor with his blade as a widening pool of crimson spread beneath him. Monte's body continued to twitch and convulse as the demon refused to give up.

At last, he stilled. Monte opened his eyes one last time, unmoving except for his chest heaving with his labored breathing. His eyes rolled unfocused in his head until he managed to fix them on Kassian. Then he smiled through the blood trickling from his lips.

"*Bravo*, McAllister," he gasped. "*Grazie.*" His body arched against the sword once, and then he was gone.

"It's over." Kassian pronounced solemnly. After reaching down a hand to help Kat climb to her feet, his head swung in the direction of his sister where she leaned against the wall still cradling Luca's slowly stirring form.

"*You okay?*" Calli heard her brother's quiet voice in her head.

"*Fine. You?*"

He nodded stiffly before withdrawing his sword, wiping it clean on Monte's jacket, and sliding it into the neck of his shirt where Calli knew it would dissolve back into the intricate tattoo decorating his back. He rubbed his palms together briskly until they began to glow with a blinding blue light.

Calli saw him swallow hard. Then he turned his palms toward the body and bathed it in the supernatural light until all traces of blood, death, and demon were gone.

"I will speak on his behalf." His tone challenged anyone to disagree.

Kat moved behind her husband and wrapped her arms around his waist, laying her cheek against his back. Her eyes met Calli's and a look of understanding passed between them. Kassian would advocate the *Fallen's* pardon with Michael and they would all support him in the attempt. Monte may have had his own reasons, but in the end, he'd sacrificed himself for them and for the greater good, exactly as any *Earthbound* would have done. One couldn't help but admire that, even if he had been a *Fallen*.

Luca groaned and opened one eye, fixing it on Calli's worried face as he reached to cup her cheek with one hand and used the other to rub the back of his head. His eyes darted wildly around the basilica until he saw Kassian, with Kat tucked under his arm, striding toward the spot where Elle lay.

Elle's arms moved weakly and her muffled sobs echoed off the high ceiling. He swallowed hard, thankful his aim had been true. He hadn't killed her. He grinned and blew out a pent up breath. His relieved smile quickly changed to a grimace as he probed his injury and attempted to sit up.

"Shhh," Callie soothed, stroking his hair away from his forehead. "Give it a minute."

With little choice at the moment, he did as he was told and relaxed back into her lap. He used his thumb to wipe a smudge of dirt away from her cheek then traced a single finger from her earlobe down the length of her neck, pausing briefly on her racing pulse before stopping at her collarbone.

Calli failed to suppress the delightful shiver that moved through her entire body. He felt it and his smile grew wider. He bit the inside of his mouth hoping the pain would distract him from the inappropriate thoughts that had popped up without warning as soon as his fingers touched her bare skin.

"I was so afraid I'd lost you again," Luca whispered quietly.

"You'll never lose me, Luca. Not even if you try. My heart is yours. It always has been."

He narrowed his eyes and blinked rapidly. "Well, at the moment, not only have I found you, but if I'm not careful about the way I move my head, I get two of you for the price of one. Not that I'm complaining. That demon must have hit me like a charging bull. How did Kat get him out of me?"

"Um, she didn't." Calli bit her lip and shifted beneath him. "What I mean is, he was never in you. It wasn't the demon who hit you. It was me. I'm so sorry," she went on in a rush. "But he was heading right for you and I was so afraid and I was running and... well, I faded I guess, and slammed right into you when I materialized. I didn't know I would hit you that hard."

"You faded? But how?" His brows knit together. "Hell, Calli. I was supposed to be saving you, not the other way around."

"You saved me last time," Calli pressed her lips to his forehead. "It was my turn. Now we're even."

Luca opened his mouth to reply but was interrupted

by the sound of heavy footfalls on the outside stairs. Dimitri, in all his massive, wild glory, stood in the entry with his hands planted on his hips. A look of utter disappointment etched his intimidating features.

Luca dragged himself to his feet. Then he reached down a hand to pull Calli up into his arms. After dropping a kiss on the top of her head, he tucked her into his side and led her over to the others.

"Well, damn!" Dimitri exclaimed. "I guess I missed all the fun."

"I'm not sure fun is the term I'd use," Kassian returned dryly, settling Elle's unconscious form into the larger man's arms and tugging the weapon from her chest. He handed Luca his dagger as he and Calli drew level with the group and rubbed his palms together briskly, directing the healing light toward Elle. The blood flow from the chest wound ceased immediately. Then he turned to wrap his arms around his wilting wife. "But fortunately, you showed up right on cue to play doctor."

Elle moaned and relaxed into the leather clad giant's chest as if she belonged there. Luca grinned and Calli giggled at the look of revolted astonishment on Dimitri's face.

"Now wait one freakin' minute, Mac," Dimitri protested, staring at the woman in his arms with the same horrified fascination he might afford a basket of rattlesnakes. "I don't even like redheads."

"Not a problem," Kat said softly. She stepped away from her husband and tugged at Elle's carroty pixie cut. It came away easily in her hand. Then she pulled a flesh colored skullcap free and a mass of dark waves spilled over Dimitri's arm. "The wig started as a joke, but she's become so well known, you see. The red hair has become her trademark and now she never makes a public appearance without it. That way, when she doesn't wear it, she can maintain some degree of anonymity."

"Well, I'll be damned," Kassian muttered, tugging his wife back into his arms. "Don't worry, brother. I'll make sure you have everything you need. You're just going to take care of her and make sure no one gets close enough to ask questions while she recovers. It's not as if we can explain this at any hospital. Seeing as how you have an actual medical degree, you're the best person for the job, don't you think?"

Dimitri looked only slightly mollified, but he shifted Elle's weight in his arms and nodded shortly.

"Are you all right?" Luca dropped a hand on his sister's shoulder and gave it a gentle squeeze.

"Fine," she replied with a sigh. "Exhausted, but fine." She shot a grateful look in Dimitri's direction. "And now Elle will be fine. Thanks for not killing my best friend, Luca."

Luca shrugged. "Thanks for not letting the demon get me."

"Oh, don't thank me," Kat smiled. "Calli is the one who plowed into you like the entire defensive line of the Pittsburgh Steelers."

"How?" Luca persisted, picking up the thread of their conversation before they were interrupted by Dimitri's arrival. He pulled Calli around to stand in front of him. "What about the binding spell? Wanting to escape Rapier didn't break it. Being lost alone in the city didn't break it. Even being buried alive didn't break it. I don't get it."

Calli shrugged. When she looked up at him, Luca caught his breath. Calli apparently had figured it out and her love shone in her eyes. She didn't even try to hide it. She didn't have to. Not anymore.

"Maybe love is its own kind of magic, Luca. I think my love for you is a magic too powerful to be bound."

Dimitri rolled his eyes, Kat snuggled into her husband's chest with a contented sigh, and Luca dipped his head to capture Calli's lips to show her he agreed. In fact, he agreed for a very long time.

Epilogue

Michael needn't have worried how they were going to explain Monte's disappearance. The *Fallen* obviously had been planning ahead. When Luca and Mac returned to Monte's office to ensure no evidence of their visit remained, Luca discovered the suicide note among the papers in the packet Monte had tossed on his desk before they'd left. Perhaps in a last ditch attempt to make amends, he'd left Giovanna more than enough money to realize her dreams for expanding the bakery, and the remainder of his vast holdings were earmarked for various charities. After hearing their story, Michael had agreed to enter into negotiations to revoke the damnation from Monte's soul, and though there were lingering questions among the Italian authorities regarding the whereabouts of Monte's body, there was no evidence to link his disappearance to anyone other than the man himself.

According to Dimitri's regular updates, Elle was healing well physically. Psychologically was another matter. Surprisingly, he'd offered to continue as her personal keeper until she was fully recovered. Knowing he hadn't caused Elle any permanent damage made Luca feel remarkably better. But no matter what he or Mac said, and despite the letter Elle had written apologizing for peeking through Miranda's things and inadvertently unleashing a demon, Kat was determined to blame herself. She remained convinced it was her fault Elle had been exposed to the danger in the first place. It didn't help that Elle refused to take her calls.

He and Calli sent Giovanna off to London with Enrico in tow to spend some time with Mariana's family soon after Calli had arranged the introductions. Gia had initially met their easy and complete acceptance of her existence with suspicion. But, Helen Ducati was a force of nature and her unwavering persistence at last convinced the doubtful girl that the family was sincere and was simply ecstatic to have found Marianna's child. Exactly as Calli had predicted, Gia's paternity made absolutely no difference to them.

Michael remained holed up in his solitary sanctuary in the *Castel*, offering no explanation for his declination of the wedding invitation. Both Luca and Mac suspected he was busy cataloging the other angelically infused items he'd bestowed on Aandalena and her descendants millennia ago. How many more were out there? That was the sixty-four thousand dollar question, and only Michael had the answer. At the moment, he wasn't sharing.

The afternoon of the wedding had finally arrived. Luca had wanted an intimate gathering and, thankfully, the crowd did turn out to be relatively small. But despite the humble size, his sweet, biddable Callista had turned into a rabid bridezilla when it came to the details. Hell, who was he kidding? Sure she was sweet, but she'd never been biddable. That was simply wishful thinking on his part.

On some level he understood that never having expected to escape her captivity, let alone contemplate marriage, Calli was determined to have the wedding of not only this century, but of every one in which she'd lived. And if it made her happy, Luca decided to swallow his discomfort and go with the flow. Given the Victorian theme, and the fact that the entire McAllister family had decided to stay at the villa, Calli had also decided to become a born-again virgin and spend the long, dark nights leading up to the wedding in her own bed. Alone. He hadn't been nearly as on board with that decision. Luca ruefully recalled boasting to Mac that his wife would defer to him in all matters. Now he understood Mac's skepticism. When Callista gazed up at him with those big blue eyes, being in charge seemed a whole lot less important that making her smile.

Luca ran his finger between his neck and the uncomfortably stiff collar for at least the tenth time. It came away damp, and he knew the fact that it hovered around sixty-eight degrees in the cold stone chapel meant that it wasn't the temperature making him sweat. He spared a fond thought for his legendary dispassion. It seemed to have deserted him completely since Calli came back into his life. He closed his eyes and counted to ten when his cell phone vibrated in the inside breast pocket of his tuxedo jacket. Again.

Following her ordeal in the catacombs, Luca sat Calli down and spent hours and hours teaching her how to use every feature on her phone until he felt confident she'd mastered it. She'd been obsessed with texting him ever since. She texted him in the shower. She texted him from the kitchen. She even texted him in the middle of the night from her room down the hall when he tossed in bed nursing his body's painful response to the memory of her soft, warm skin pressed against his.

At first, he'd found her delight in the new

technology charming, but she'd continued to text him all morning and was already ten minutes late. The wedding guests were beginning to whisper behind his back. At his side, Mac glanced over his shoulder and then back to the front with a barely suppressed smirk. Luca resolutely faced the altar and tuned out the crowd behind him, working hard to convince himself that Calli actually would show up.

His phone continued to buzz insistently. Luca continued to ignore it.

"She changed her mind, didn't she?" he asked Mac out of the corner of his mouth. "I rushed her into this. I knew I should have given her more time."

"Grow a set, will you?" His best friend retorted quietly. "A bride is always fashionably late. Kat said so. I liked you better when you didn't give a shit. You were a damn sight more tolerable."

"Get bent, brother."

Someone cleared his throat. Loudly. Both men looked up in surprise at the priest who hadn't missed a word of their exchange. He regarded them now with brows knit so tightly together it was impossible to tell where one left off and the other began.

"Uh, sorry, Padre," Mac offered. "Forgot where I was for a minute."

Luca's phone vibrated again.

"You gonna check that?"

With a frustrated grunt, Luca pulled the phone from his pocket under the disapproving gaze of the priest and glanced at the display.

I luv u.

When he began to tuck the phone back in his jacket, it vibrated again. Seriously?

Well?

With a resigned sigh, his fingers flew over the keys.

I luv u 2 now get ur butt out here and marry me.

Luca dropped his phone into the outside pocket of his jacket. He suddenly became aware of the hushed silence in the chapel. Not that he was complaining. Frankly, he thought if he never heard Pachelbel's Canon in D for the remainder of his unnaturally long life it would be too soon. Again, his phone buzzed insistently. It sounded incredibly loud now that there were no other sounds to drown it out. Kat moved up on his left and arched a brow in the direction of his pocket. Okay, what was she doing here? She was supposed to be walking down the aisle ahead of Calli. Luca dropped his head back on his shoulders, looked at the ceiling, and prayed for patience. Then he dug in his pocket and looked at the phone. The screen was blank. What the hell?

"Turn around."

The directive echoed inside his head in Calli's soft, sweet voice. Wanting nothing more than to get this over and start the honeymoon, he did as he was told. And then he promptly forgot how to breathe.

She looked like a fashion plate from Godey's Ladies' Book. The white silk bodice detailed with hand embroidered lace clung to Calli's every curve. Sharp knife pleats peeked below the heavy swag of the draped overskirt that drew back on both sides to form a bustle that then flowed into a short train. Forgoing the traditional veil, her beautiful, dark hair was pulled to the side and arranged in an intricate design of curls and twists woven with orange blossoms that started at the crown of her head and tumbled down over her shoulder. A vision from his past, standing in his present, promising him the future. Luca hoped he would be able to force words over the tightness in his throat when it came time to speak his vows.

With a radiant smile and a wink, Calli pointedly held up her phone and then tucked it in her brother Alec's jacket pocket and laid her hand on his arm. The musicians started up again, but it wasn't the traditional Wedding March Luca had been expecting. Deviating slightly from her eighteen-eighties' theme, Calli had gone all nineteen-eighties and walked down the aisle to the movie theme from *After All.*

Luca's heart swelled as he concentrated on the lyrics and realized how utterly appropriate the song was for them. They really were two angels who'd been rescued. Luca may have been instrumental in gaining Calli's physical freedom from her captor, but she'd turned right around and rescued him in an even more profound way. Not that he'd be sharing any of this aberrant emotional crap with anyone over a *Moretti* any time soon. It was enough that he understood it. He heard a subdued sniffle beside him. Okay, so maybe Kat understood it, too. Sometimes it was a real bitch having an empath for a sister.

Alec and Calli reached him just as the final strains of the music faded. Her heart shone from her eyes, and Luca saw more than he'd ever expected, and far more than he thought he deserved. His. Forever. Alec kissed his sister's cheek and placed her hand in Luca's then stepped back to take a seat next to Madge as the priest stepped forward and the ceremony began.

Luca looked down into Calli's eyes and saw the

life ahead of them unspool like a roll of shiny ribbon. It might tangle sometimes, or tie itself in knots. It might even fray around the edges. But the fibers of that ribbon were woven together as strongly and intricately as Luca's soul was intertwined with Calli's and whatever awaited them, they would navigate it together.

For so many years, he'd embraced denial as a close friend, existing in an emotional state of beige requiring little attention and less response. Well, if beige was a comfortable neutral, loving Calli was like being hit in the head with a kaleidoscope—painful, blinding. He'd been afraid to trust in those rainbow colors, but taking the chance had rewarded him with his own personal pot of gold staring up at him with the most incredible blue eyes in a shade that no rainbow could ever duplicate. Eyes that trusted him completely. Eyes shining with an adoration he hoped he could live up to. Eyes that were suddenly narrowed and topped by finely arched brows that slammed together in a frown.

"Luca!" Calli hissed in a peeved undertone. The hem of her gown jumped up and down in rhythm to her tapping toe. It was the only sound to be heard as the congregation held their collective breath.

"What?" he whispered back in confusion.

"Father said you may kiss the bride. In fact, he's said it three times. We really must work on your problem with listening."

Calli reached up and grabbed both his ears, pulling his head, and his lips, to hers as the guests chuckled warmly in the background. Luca Fiorelli, The Ice Warrior, the *Earthbound* hunter who personified calculated control, found himself completely lost in the kiss. His arms came around her slender waist, and he pulled her hard against him. He felt her smile against his mouth when his body reacted instantly, and he realized he needed to get a grip. There was no sense stoking a fire he had no opportunity to extinguish, at least not for the next few hours. But damn, she felt good.

He pulled away slightly, then unable to resist, cupped the back of her neck and went back in for seconds. His fingers traced the row of tiny satin covered buttons that started right below her hairline and continued down the length of her spine for as far as he could decently run his hands in their present surroundings. Suddenly he remembered all of the things he hated about nineteenth century clothes. Well, okay, maybe just the one thing, the long and torturous process of removing them. Judging by the style, he'd be willing to bet she was wearing layers and layers of petticoats under the damn thing, too. *Merde,* it was going to be a long night.

Mac cleared his throat. Luca lifted his head and turned to face the thunderous applause of the congregation echoing off the ceiling and ancient stone walls. Kat handed Calli her bouquet and Luca pulled her arm through his as they stepped down from the altar and processed down the aisle.

Calli paused to hug her mother. Magdalena's thousand megawatt smile shone through her tears.

"You've always been my son, Luca," she stretched up to kiss him on both cheeks. "This makes it official."

Luca didn't know what to say to that. In fact, he was pretty sure speech was beyond him. He had no words eloquent enough to express what filled his heart. He swallowed hard, and Calli squeezed his arm. Madge thumbed a tear from the corner of his eye and Luca realized no response was necessary. Magdalena understood him, she always had. She'd never had any difficulty seeing the man beneath the façade.

"Buck up, *bello*," Madge whispered in a teasing voice. "Your reputation is going to be shot to hell if you start blubbering with joy."

"You look beautiful, Madge," Luca smiled crookedly. If Calli was the picture of Victorian innocence, Madge was the epitome of modern Milan. Svelte and elegant in a body hugging one-shouldered silver designer gown crisscrossed with Grecian draping, she could never be mistaken for a frumpy mother of the bride. Madge had always been a beautiful woman and never more so than when her face glowed with happiness for her family.

"*Certo!*" She grinned. "Now move. If we don't get to the reception on time, 'Tonio will never let me hear the end of it."

"See you later, Mother," Calli winked, tugging on Luca's hand as they moved down the aisle with Mac and Kat following close behind.

"Exactly how attached are you to that dress?" Luca leaned down and whispered in Calli's ear while keeping a cordial smile plastered on his face.

"It's my wedding dress, Luca. It will become one of my most treasured possessions. Don't you like it?" She whispered back worriedly.

"You look like a dream, *carissima*," Luca sighed dramatically. "But I like you much better out of it. There must be close to a hundred buttons. And a bustle? Really? Couldn't you have picked something a little more *modern* and a lot less complicated and time consuming to *remove?*"

Calli flashed him a decidedly saucy grin. As the first of the guests approached, she stretched up on her toes and brought her lips close to his ear. The moist heat of her breath on his neck caused his mouth to go dry. He couldn't help it. The reception was scheduled to last four hours. Four *long* hours. He was a man in pain.

"Actually, I've become quite a forward thinker, open to new ideas, embracing modern inventions," she breathed in a husky voice. "And to prove it, I have one word for you to ponder for the next four hours."

"What's that, *carissima?*" Luca whispered back.

She offered him a small, secretive smile and grasped his hand. She guided it around to her back, and her nimble fingers tugged at the Velcro securing the placket to which the buttons were attached with faux fabric loops.

"Zipper."

A word about the author...

Sharon Saracino was born and raised in the beautiful anthracite coal region of Northeastern Pennsylvania. A lifelong love of writing took a back seat to real life while she got married, raised a family, went back to college, and finally decided what she wanted to be when she grew up!

The oldest of three siblings, she was raised in a small town rich in history and filled with characters galore. She began writing seriously again in 2006 in the non-fiction arena. Her work has appeared in *Rehabilitation Nursing* and *The Pennsylvania Patient Safety Advisory*. Sharon is a member of Pennwriters, Romance Writers of America, and the Maryland Romance Writers. When she is not reading, writing, or dabbling in photography and genealogy, she works full time as a Certified Registered Rehabilitation Nurse.

She plans to win the lottery just as soon as she remembers to purchase a ticket, fantasizes about moving to Italy, brews limoncello, and spends time with her incredible husband, funny and talented son, and two crazy dogs.

Visit her at:

http://sharonsaracino.com